Books by Tom Hoffman

The Eleventh Ring

The Thirteenth Monk

The Seventh Medallion

Orville Mouse and the Puzzle
of the Clockwork Glowbirds

Orville Mouse and the Puzzle
of the Shattered Abacus

Orville Mouse and the Puzzle
of the Capricious Shadows

Orville Mouse and the Puzzle
of the Last Metaphonium

Orville Mouse and the Puzzle
of the Sagacious Sapling

Available online at Amazon and Barnes & Noble

An Orville Wellington Mouse Adventure

ORVILLE MOUSE

and the Puzzle of the
Last Metaphonium

by Tom Hoffman

Tom Hoffman
Visit my website at thoffmanak.wordpress.com
Email: BartholomewtheAdventurer@gmail.com

Printed in the United States of America

First Printing: 2017
ISBN 978-0-9994634-0-6

With lots of love for
Molly, Alex, Sophie, and Oliver

A very special thanks to my
wonderful editors
Beth, Sophie, Oliver,
Alex and Amanda
for their invaluable assistance
and excellent advice.

Table of Contents

Chapter 1 The Beautiful Mouse 3

Chapter 2 The Ghost 12

Chapter 3 Okeanos 17

Chapter 4 The Sound Piano 26

Chapter 5 A Knock on the Door 34

Chapter 6 Mirus' Surprise 38

Chapter 7 Elevator Music 46

Chapter 8 The Invoice 54

Chapter 9 Cathne 69

Chapter 10 Puella the Wise One 75

Chapter 11 Project Haven 85

Chapter 12 Revelation 92

Chapter 13 Proto's Discovery 100

Chapter 14 Brother Solus 105

Chapter 15 Caterpillars 116

Chapter 16 The Note 127

Chapter 17 The Elysian Inn 133

Chapter 18 Old Captain Tobias 141

Chapter 19 Over the Bounding Main 147

Chapter 20 The Blue Pirates 152

Chapter 21 Orville's New Watch 159

Chapter 22 Isle of the Silver Ship 164

Chapter 23 Orville's Bed and Breakfast 174

Chapter 24 Madam Beasley 179

Chapter 25 Reach for the Stairs 183

Chapter 26 The Crater's Secret 189

Chapter 27 Squeaky 195

Chapter 28 Time for Launch 202

Chapter 29 Downtown Bellumia 213

Chapter 30 Fear 218

Chapter 31 Charon the Ferrymouse 225

Chapter 32 Lost and Found 232

Chapter 33 Laurus 243

Chapter 34 Orville the Ghost 251

Chapter 35 By Chance 261

Chapter 36 The Thirteenth Monk 267

Chapter 37 The Swamp of Despair 273

Chapter 38 Okeanos Revisited 281

Chapter 39 A Knock on the Door 288

Chapter 40 Papa's Old Trunk 293

Chapter 41 The Secret 302

Chapter 42 Gnuj's Infinite Wonder 309

Chapter 43 The Visitors 313

Chapter 44 Aislin's Gift 318

Chapter 45 Treasure 322

"Mind is the Master power that moulds and makes,

And Man is Mind, and evermore he takes

The tool of Thought, and, shaping what he wills,

Brings forth a thousand joys, a thousand ills: —

He thinks in secret, and it comes to pass:

Environment is but his looking-glass."

- James Allen, 1903

"Man's task is to become conscious of the contents that press upward from the unconcious."

–Carl Jung

An Orville Wellington Mouse Adventure

ORVILLE MOUSE

and the Puzzle of the
Last Metaphonium

Chapter 1

The Beautiful Mouse

Twilight was painting a soft orange glow across the horizon, its dim spectral light illuminating the quaint thatched roofs of a nameless village. Orville listened intently as he stepped through the gossamer shadows cast by rows of long neglected cottages, his eyes alert for movement. There were no distant voices drifting across the still evening air, no boisterous laughter reverberating from a bustling inn, no gentle bedtime stories floating out of half opened windows. The village was deserted, the only sounds being the scuffling of Orville's heavy boots on the hard packed ground and a curious but ultimately unidentifiable scratching noise.

Orville felt a certain pride in experiencing this shadowy realm on his own, although truth be told, part of him wished his best friend Sophia was there by his side.

"The sun has gone down, I have no idea where I am, no idea why I'm here, but I'm not scared. Even that weird scratching sound doesn't bother me. It's probably a tree branch brushing against one of the houses."

Orville stopped to listen, his ears turning slowly. The air was silent and still, the leaves in the surrounding trees motionless.

"It is a bit weird that there's no wind but I can still hear that scratching sound. I bet Sophia could figure out where it's coming from."

Orville followed the winding village lane to its abrupt end in front of a thirty foot tall cylindrical wooden building topped with an artfully thatched roof.

"It must be an old barn or something."

He approached the weathered gray structure, squinting in the dim evening light at a crudely painted sign resting on a wooden easel.

OKEANOS BOOK FAIR
TODAY ONLY
ALL VISITORS WELCOME

"This is great, I love book fairs. I hope they're still open." Orville hesitated, furrowing his brow. He had a vague memory of Ebenezer Mouse asking him to find a book, but he couldn't remember the title. He raised the heavy iron latch on the front door, pushing it open.

"Whoa, this is amazing!"

Orville stood facing a twenty foot wide circular table piled high with books of every imaginable size, shape, and color. The room was illuminated by an enormous wrought iron chandelier holding dozens of flickering orange candles. He rubbed his paws together in eager anticipation.

"This is perfect, they're sure to have the book Ebenezer wants, and I can probably find a nice one for Sophia. I bet they have a lot of science books, she loves those. It's a little odd that I'm the only one here. I'll just poke around for a bit and see what they have."

Orville stepped over to the massive table, perusing the vast array of books. Some looked almost new, but most were old and worn, many in languages Orville was unfamiliar with, obscure scientific tomes filled with charts and diagrams and all manner of incomprehensible mathematical equations.

"This is the kind of stuff Sophia likes. I'm sure to find something here. I hope they're not too expensive."

Orville's thoughts were interrupted by a soft rustling sound coming from behind him. It was mildly disconcerting, but not especially scary. He turned around to see a beautiful mouse in a flowing white robe staring at him with unblinking eyes. When he studied her face with his intuitive mind he sensed a surprisingly complex assortment of emotions. She had an aura of kindness and gentleness about her, but also great sadness, a deep longing, and a profound weariness. She was tired beyond measure. Perhaps some bright chatty conversation would cheer her up.

"Hi, I'm Orville Mouse. I'm from Muridaan Falls, but I don't imagine you've ever heard of it. It's a little fishing village in Symoca. This is a marvelous book fair, I've never seen one with so many wonderful books to choose from. I work at a book store called Master

Marloh's Book Emporium. We carry a lot of books, but nothing like this. They're amazing. Sophia would love them. She's my best friend in the world and a brilliant scientist. She'd probably understand all the science stuff in these books. She's from Quintari, but she's going to school at the Symocan Institute of Mechanistic Studies. We're both Metaphysical Adventurers and we're going to marry, I don't know exactly when, probably when she finishes her schooling. We're going to have two mouselings."

Orville had no idea why he was telling the beautiful mouse so much about himself, but he couldn't seem to stop.

"I'm looking for a book that our neighbor wanted me to find. He's kind of old and crabby but I like him, even though he yelled at me when I was screeching like a Gnorli bird in Proto's vegetable garden. You have to give a big screech to make the red snackles fall off the vine. Proto is a Rabbiton, a ten foot tall robotic rabbit built by the Elders over fourteen hundred years ago. He's an old friend and really funny, but some of his jokes are a bit confusing."

The beautiful mouse stared at Orville with unblinking eyes.

Orville pressed on.

"So anyway, I'm not exactly sure about the title of the book old Ebenezer wants, but I'll probably recognize it when I see it. I think it's big and sort of square. I'm also looking for a science book, something with lots of numbers and diagrams and technical stuff in it.

It's for Sophia, that's the kind of book she really likes."

The beautiful mouse glanced at the far wall, then motioned for Orville to follow her. She stepped slowly but purposefully around the table, giving Orville time to examine the mounds of scientific volumes.

"I like the cover on that one, it's a lovely shade of green. It reminds me of the color of new leaves in the springtime. I think that's my favorite time of year. It's really pretty out, but I still have the whole summer to look forward to. What's your favorite season?"

The beautiful mouse stared at Orville with unblinking eyes.

On their second turn around the enormous circular table Orville noticed the green book which reminded him of budding leaves in the springtime was gone, replaced by a tattered square yellow book.

"That's weird, what happened to the green book?"

He watched closely, realizing the books he had already seen were transforming into new ones as he stepped around the table.

"Oh, I get it, each time I walk around the table the books change. Clever. That way you can fit a lot more books on one table. Master Marloh would love a table like this for his shop. You don't know who makes them, do you?"

The beautiful mouse did not reply, motioning for Orville to follow her.

On the fourth turn around the table Orville picked up a small red book which had caught his eye.

"This one looks interesting, it's just the right size

and color. Reminds me of fresh red snapberries." He flipped it open. "It's in a weird language but it does have a lot of mathematical symbols and diagrams and stuff. I have a good feeling about this one, I think Sophia will like it. It's small and really old so it shouldn't cost too much."

Orville tucked the red book under his arm, following the beautiful mouse in the flowing white robe.

On the eighth turn around the table Orville noticed the number of books was decreasing, retreating from the outer edge of the table like snow melting in the springtime.

"I hope I can find that book Ebenezer wanted. I wish I could remember the title, I'm not even sure if it was a science book."

On the tenth turn around the table there was only a six foot wide pile of books remaining.

On the eleventh turn around the table there was only one book left, a huge one with a gleaming silver cover.

"That's it! That's the one, I'm sure of it. That's definitely the book Ebenezer wanted me to find. It's big though, three feet across, I'm not sure how I'll get it back to Muridaan Falls. It looks really expensive with that silver cover."

Orville hopped up onto the table and stepped over to the silver book.

"Whoa, this is going to cost a lot, it has gold embossed lettering and little inlaid gemstones." He turned to the beautiful mouse. "I want this one, but I'm not sure I can afford it. How much is it?"

Orville gave a sudden yelp, covering his ears.

"Why is that scratching sound so loud?"

The beautiful mouse's face had transformed to a mask of fear. She turned, pointing to the shimmering, undulating far wall, the dreadful scratching sound now roaring and pounding in Orville's ears. When the great black smoldering stick creature scuttled through the ghostly wall Orville let out an involuntary scream. The beast stood over fifteen feet tall, constructed of long black irregular sticks of smoking glowing charcoal, a cloud of sparking orange embers trailing behind it. Orville couldn't tell how many legs the creature had, but it moved faster than it should be able to, like some nightmarish jumping spider.

The beautiful mouse pointed to the silver book, gesturing wildly for Orville to open it.

"You want me to open the book? Will it stop that thing?"

The horrific glowing charcoal stick creature sprang across the room, grabbing the beautiful mouse with something that vaguely resembled claws, her mouth opening in a silent scream. She pointed again to the great silver book.

Waves of overwhelming formless fear thundered through Orville. This was the most terrifying monstrosity he had ever set eyes on. For a moment he thought his legs would collapse, but managed to regain his focus, scrunching down and flipping the silver book open. The book contained no pages, but opening the front cover had revealed a square shaft leading down into inky blackness.

Orville looked up at the beautiful mouse. "What's down there?"

The captive wriggling mouse motioned desperately for Orville to jump into the silver book.

Orville was peering into the eerie shaft when the smoldering charcoal stick creature sprang onto the table, scrabbling madly toward him, its horrible sharp legs scratching and scraping against the wooden surface. One of its burning black arms lashed out, clawing at the red book in Orville's paws, trying to rip it from his grasp. Orville yanked the book away, but in the process lost his balance, tumbling backwards into the silver book, into the infinite nothingness below. He shrieked as he plummeted through the heavy darkness, shrieked until he remembered he wasn't really falling, he was only dream falling.

"This isn't so bad. Sophia always says you can't get hurt in a dream. I guess I'll wait and see what happens. I'll probably wake up in a few minutes."

His eyes were just getting accustomed to the dark when the black glowing stick arm shot out from the shadows, grabbing at the red book. With a shriek Orville wrenched it back from the hideous abomination, pushing its arm away, sending a shower of sparking embers into the air. Two things happened in rapid succession. First, the stick creature vanished, and second, Orville noticed he was drifting down toward a small white rectangle far below him.

"So tired, this dream was exhausting, that burning

charcoal creature was so much worse than Mendacium the Dark Wizard. I wonder who that beautiful mouse was? She looked really sad and really tired."

Orville gazed down at the approaching white rectangle, recognizing it for what it was, his own snuggly bed.

"So sleepy."

He rolled over onto his back, landing gently on his comfy feather mattress.

"Mmmm... so soft."

A moment later Orville Wellington Mouse was lost in the world of dreams.

Chapter 2

The Ghost

Orville peered through half closed eyes at the morning light filtering in through his faded blue curtains.

"Too early. So tired."

He groaned and rolled over, yelping when an unknown object jabbed him sharply in the ribs.

"Ow! What is that?"

He grabbed the offending object, pulling it out from under the covers. It was a small red book. A rush of images flashed through his mind; a book fair, a beautiful mouse, a horrifying smoldering stick creature, the strange deserted village, the great silver book.

"Did I bring this back from the book fair? I know I was holding it when I fell into the silver book, and I remember that crazy creature trying to grab it. I couldn't have, Sophia says you can't bring physical objects back from a dream. I must have shaped it in my sleep, just like when I shaped the orange and the coiled brass serpent. In my dream the book was for Sophia, that's probably important. I'll show it to her at lunch."

Orville opened the small red book, flipping through

a few pages.

"It's in a weird language, not one I recognize. I've never seen glyphs like this before. Maybe Sophia will know what it is, she's pretty good with weird languages."

Orville hopped out of bed and grabbed his clothes. "Whenever I shape something in my sleep it's always important, and usually leads to some crazy adventure. Last time it was that creepy Mendacium the Dark Wizard. This is way worse though." Orville shivered, his thoughts churning with dark visions of the terrifying smoldering black charcoal stick figure.

"What was that thing? So scary. It didn't even have a face."

He threw his clothes on, grabbed the red book and ran downstairs. Proto was humming softly in the kitchen.

"Morning, Proto. What's for breakfast?"

"And a lovely good morning to you. We're having warm oatmeal with brown sugar, cinnamon, and crunchy roasted beezle nuts. Mum thinks you need more protein in your diet."

"You're putting beezle nuts in my oatmeal? Wait, they're not from your garden, are they? From those weird old seed packets you found in the Cube?"

"No need to worry about deadly poisonous beezle nuts. Mum bought them at the market yesterday and assured me they are quite fresh and crunchy. Very healthy, filled with protein."

"I guess that's okay. I'm not too crazy about having

beezle nuts in my oatmeal though. Hey, do you recognize this language?"

Proto took the red book from Orville, flipping it open and scanning a few pages.

"I am unfamiliar with these glyphs. They do have a faint resemblance to certain ancient Mintarian scripts, but I'm afraid that's all I can tell you. Wherever did you find it? It looks extremely old."

"Umm... I found it at a book fair. I thought Sophia might like it so I got it, I think it's about science stuff."

"I don't recall you mentioning anything about attending a book fair. I quite enjoy them, I wish you had mentioned it to me."

"Oh, I...it was just one I happened to be at."

Proto's eyes narrowed. "That's a rather vague answer. Exactly where and when did this book fair take place?"

"Um... it was... um..."

Proto let out a screechy laugh. "I knew it, you're hiding something! We're off on another terrifying adventure filled with all manner of horrifying beasts scuttling about in the darkness, waiting to pounce, snaring us with their razor sharp claws and venomous fangs."

"I'm not sure what's happening, I haven't shown the book to Sophia yet. It might be nothing, just an old science book."

"I'll start packing tonight. Perhaps I should bring a heavy particle beam vaporization projector?"

"That sounds kind of dangerous. I don't think we'll

need whatever that is. Besides, we're not going anywhere until I find someone who can translate this book. I'm meeting Sophia at lunch. I'll let you know what I find out when I get home."

With breakfast over, Orville threw on his adventurers hat and headed out the front door, slamming it behind him.

It was a lovely fall day, the green summer leaves having magically transformed over the last week to brilliant oranges, reds, and yellows, the air crisp and cool, the early morning sun filtering down through the gently swaying branches.

"Another beautiful fall day. I can't wait to show this book to Sophia. I hope she can read it. If she can't, maybe Amanda Mouse will know what it is. She knows all about history stuff. I wonder why I'd dream about a beautiful tired mouse and some creepy burning charcoal stick monster?"

Orville shivered at the thought of the hideous creature, trying to erase it from his mind.

"Enough of that. The trees are lovely this time of year, but I think springtime is still my favorite–"

Orville's train of thought was abruptly derailed by a strange and overpowering feeling that someone was watching him. He whipped around to see if he was being followed, but found himself to be quite alone. He studied the woods on both sides of the road, searching the shadows for movement, rewarded only with the gentle fluttering of orange and yellow leaves.

"This is weird. I've never felt anything like this before."

He continued down the meandering country lane, unable to shake the feeling that he was not alone.

"Maybe that dream scared me more than I thought it did. I hope I'm not going loopy. Sophia says I scare myself by imagining things that aren't really there, that my imagination is sometimes my worst enemy."

He stopped again, the peculiar feeling stronger than ever. He turned slowly toward the deep woods, afraid of what he might see. There was a soft sparkling light glimmering in the dappled shadows. He rubbed his eyes, trying to focus on the phantasmal floating lights. The sparkling grew brighter, becoming a swirling cloud of translucent light, then denser, transforming into a wavering blue apparition. Orville's knees grew weak. He knew exactly what he was looking at.

"It's the beautiful mouse, but she's a ghost!" Orville was terrified. He turned to run but was stopped by the soft whispery voice in his head.

"Help me. Please, Orville, please help me."

"Help you? How do you know my name? Who are you?"

Before the beautiful ghost mouse could answer she glowed brightly with an eerie purple light and vanished. Orville stood motionless, stunned by the unexpected appearance of the beautiful mouse.

"Creekers, I just saw a ghost. She wants me to help her, but how am I supposed to help a ghost?"

Chapter 3

Okeanos

Orville swung open the front door of the Book Emporium, stepping into the familiar musty smell of old books, the shop feeling almost like a second home to him now. Master Marloh was at the front counter peering through his small gold glasses, which meant he was sorting through the previous day's sales receipts. He glanced up at Orville when he heard the little bell above the door jingle.

"A fine good morning to you. A lovely fall day out, perfect for an exhilarating walk to work, good for the constitution."

Orville grinned. Master Marloh was a bit old fashioned, but he liked that, it was like having a wise old grandpapa. He remembered how surprised he had been when Master Marloh first told him he was a gifted shaper and invited him to join the Metaphysical Adventurers. He also remembered the first time Master Marloh unlocked the mysterious blue door in the back of the shop and took him down to the vast secret complex hidden beneath the building, the Symocan Metaphysical Adventurers headquarters, filled with a myriad of strange and marvelous technological devices brought back from other worlds by the members.

"It is nice out. The leaves are beautiful but they'll be gone in two or three weeks."

Master Marloh nodded. "Time and tide wait for no mouse, of that there is no doubt. We'd best enjoy these glorious days while we are able."

"Say, I found this book yesterday, but it's written in a strange language. Do you recognize it?" Orville passed the red book to Master Marloh.

"Curious, I'm afraid the glyphs on the front cover are unfamiliar to me, a rather inauspicious start." He flipped the book open, studying it through his small round glasses.

"You've stumped me again, Orville. Something about it makes me think it's Mintarian, but it's written in an obscure form I've never seen before. Where did you find it? It looks extremely old."

Orville was remembering his breakfast conversation with Proto, and decided to be completely forthright with Master Marloh, a highly esteemed Metaphysical Adventurer and head of the Muridaan Falls Shapers Guild.

"I think I shaped it in my sleep. I was having a really weird dream about a book fair in an old abandoned village. In my dream I picked up this book because I thought Sophia would like it. When I woke up the book was in my bed."

"Much like when you shaped the orange and the coiled snake figurine. It must hold some deeper significance. What else happened in the dream? Remember, even the smallest details in dreams are very important."

"Um... there was a beautiful mouse in a white robe and a weird scary smoldering black stick creature who was trying to take the book away from me. It all took place in a dusky deserted village. I think the name of the village was Okeanos."

Master Marloh peered over his glasses at Orville, a curious light in his eyes.

"Okeanos? You're certain that was the name?"

"There was a sign on an easel saying it was the Okeanos Book Fair. What's Okeanos?"

"I believe it to be a name taken from the ancient mythologies. Unfortunately my memory isn't what it used to be, so I'll need to do a little research, perhaps have a chat with Amanda Mouse. She's a fount of knowledge when it comes to historical and mythological matters. It is possible you read about Okeanos a long time ago and it just now popped into a dream. That happens more often than you might think."

"You could be right, maybe I read about it in a history class or something. It was really a weird dream though, and I didn't recognize the beautiful mouse or the crazy burning stick creature."

"Time will tell. I suspect we will soon discover where this particular chain of events is taking you."

"I'm going to ask Sophia about it at lunch, she's

pretty good with old languages." Orville was hoping this chain of events would not include a face to face confrontation with a certain smoldering black charcoal stick creature. He managed a small grin when he realized that would never happen because the stick creature did not have a face to confront.

"I'll start unpacking the crates of books that arrived yesterday."

The morning passed quickly. Orville was busily marking prices on the new books when he heard a soft rustling sound behind him. He gave a shriek and whipped around, banging his knee on the cart of books. Instead of the vaporous blue ghost mouse he was expecting, he saw Sophia, a rustling lunch sack in her paw.

"Sorry, I didn't mean to scare you. You look like you just saw a ghost. Are you all right?"

"What? Why did you say ghost? You shouldn't blink up behind someone like that, it's kind of surprising. I wasn't scared, just surprised."

"Sorry, Orville the Brave, I didn't mean to surprise you so badly. Let's have lunch behind the old barn. The leaves are spectacular and it's warm and sunny. It will be lovely there."

"You may have scared me just a little bit, but after I tell you about the dream I had last night you'll know why."

Master Marloh waved to the pair of best friends as they strolled past the front desk.

"Have a lovely lunch, watch out for ghosts!"

Sophia raised her eyebrows. "I think you'd better tell me about this mysterious dream. This is starting to get interesting."

As they basked in the toasty noonday sun behind the weathered old barn, Orville recounted in great detail his dream of the previous night. He also told Sophia about the mysterious ghostly mouse he'd seen on the way to work.

"She asked you to help her? And she knew your name?"

"Yes, it was really scary, she called me Orville. She was definitely a ghost, a real ghost."

"You said she was beautiful? Really beautiful?"

"Yes, extremely beautiful."

Sophia had a curious expression on her face, one Orville did not immediately recognize.

"Why would an extremely beautiful mouse know your name and be asking you for help?"

"I don't know, that's the weird part."

"You're sure you've never seen her before, never met her?" Sophia's eyes had a sharp and piercing look about them.

A light of realization blinked on in Orville's mind.

"Are you jealous? Jealous of a ghost?"

"Don't be ridiculous, I'm not jealous in the least, I'm simply curious why a beautiful mouse would be asking you for help, and why this particular extremely beautiful mouse would know your name if you have never met her?"

Orville gave a cackling laugh. "You're jealous.

You're jealous of a beautiful ghost mouse!"

"I'm not jealous, Orville. But just to be clear, to avoid any possible future misunderstandings, if I ever see you strolling through Muridaan Falls holding paws with a beautiful ghost mouse I will pound you into the ground like a big wooden stake."

Orville burst out laughing. He took Sophia's paw in his.

"I can promise you that is something you will never see. You're the only mouse I will ever hold paws with."

Sophia kissed him on the cheek. "Good. Now show me this book you shaped in your sleep."

Orville pulled the book from his coat pocket, giving it to Sophia.

"Master Marloh and Proto were right, it does have a resemblance to ancient Mintarian script, but that's all I can tell you. It must be a lesser known form I'm not familiar with. There are quite a number of mathematical symbols and equations in it, but taken out of context I have no idea what they mean. We need to find someone who can translate this. That weird burning stick figure sounds frightening. I've never heard of anything even remotely like that, but it feels more like a dream creature than a real one. What's even more interesting is how you could shape a book in a language you don't know."

"I never thought about that. That's kind of spooky. Master Marloh said he was going to talk to Amanda Mouse about the book. He said even if she can't translate it she might know someone who can."

"I'm getting a strange feeling about this. I think your dream is important, and I think it's going to take us on an extraordinary adventure, a really scary one."

Orville attempted a brave smile.

After lunch Sophia blinked back to the Symocan Institute of Mechanistic Studies and Orville walked back to the Book Emporium, where he found Master Marloh and Amanda Mouse in deep conversation.

Amanda looked up, waving to him.

"Hello, Orville. Master Marloh said you have an old book you need translated? Why did you buy a book you can't read? That seems like a very odd thing to do."

"Um... I didn't exactly get it for myself, I got it for Sophia. I thought she might understand it because it had some mathematical stuff in it."

"May I see it?"

"Sure."

Amanda took the book, studying the dark red cover, her eyes fixed on the gold symbols. She pulled a large magnifying glass from her coat pocket, slowly turning the book as she examined it.

"Interesting. Quite authentic." She set the book gingerly on the counter and opened it.

"Why did you think Sophia would be able to read this?"

"She's really smart."

"I see, she's really smart so she should be able to read a book like this." Amanda closed the book, slipping the magnifying glass back into her pocket. "Where did you find it?"

23

Orville hesitated, then said, "I had a dream I was at a book fair, found this book, and when I woke up the book was in my bed. I think I shaped it."

"Is there anything else you can tell me?"

"The book fair was in a town called Okeanos."

Amanda's eyebrows shot up. "What?"

"It was in a town called Okeanos?"

"You're certain that was the name of the town?"

"It was on a sign in front of the book fair."

Amanda rubbed her chin, her eyes on Orville.

"What is it? What's Okeanos?"

"Have you ever shaped a book before? Shaped a book in a language you're unfamiliar with?"

"This is the first time I've ever shaped a book. I'm not really sure how I did it."

"Okeanos is a name found in the ancient mythologies. It exists in the Borderlands."

"What does that mean?"

"The Borderlands, the reality that lies between the waking world and the world of dreams. If you truly were in Okeanos, there's a very good chance you did not shape this book in your sleep. There's a very good chance you may have brought it back with you from Okeanos. From Okeanos. You brought a book back from Okeanos."

"I don't really know what that means."

Orville had the strangest feeling Amanda wanted to examine his brain with her big magnifying glass.

"It means you traveled to a reality that exists between wakefulness and sleep, which is why you were able to return with a physical object."

"Um… can you translate it?"

"I just said the book is from Okeanos. Why would you think I could translate it?"

Orville stared blankly at Amanda, uncertain how to respond.

Amanda continued, "Of course I can't translate it, but I may know someone who can. I need to talk to Captain Patcher about this. This is a far, far more complex issue than you might imagine." She raised one eyebrow. "Than anyone might imagine. Anyone. Far more complex."

Orville gave his best impression of a mouse who clearly understood what Amanda was trying to tell him, his best impression of a mouse who clearly knew the deeper significance of her raised eyebrow.

"That would be wonderful, thanks so much."

"This is beyond exciting, a book from Okeanos. I never thought I would live to see this day. You're an amazing mouse, Orville. I should have more information for you in a few days. I hope you're not afraid of bloodthirsty bandits."

Chapter 4

The Sound Piano

"Have you ever painted a house before?"

"I helped Papa paint our house when I was a mouseling, but I got more paint on me than on the house. I remember Mum laughing about it."

Proto nodded. "We'll need a canvas drop cloth, two large brushes, two narrow brushes for the trim, plus two wire brushes and scrapers to remove the old paint. And two painter hats."

"What are painter hats?"

"White hats with wide brims on the front, kind of square. Painters always wear them, although I'm not precisely certain why."

"This is sounding like a lot of work. Can't I just use a low power vaporizing beam to take off the old paint?"

"I look forward to seeing the expression on Ebenezer Mouse's face when the orange vaporizing light shoots out from your paw."

"Good point, he doesn't know about shapers. I'll

shape all the stuff we need and we can head over. I told him we'd start first thing in the morning. He has the paint and a ladder. He actually seemed kind of friendly, not crabby at all."

"Perhaps he doesn't have many friends. I will confess that my days in the Cube with only the glowbirds for company were often lonely ones. Your friendship and the friendship of Sophia changed my life."

"You're right, it can't be much fun for him, living all alone in that house. I'll go over more often, take him some tasty little cakes." Orville flicked his paw and a box of painting supplies blinked into existence.

Fifteen minutes later Orville and Proto were industriously scraping the cracked and peeling paint from Ebenezer Mouse's house.

"You're so tall we don't even need the ladder. I'll scrape the bottom half and you scrape the top half."

Orville's arms were aching when he sat down on the old garden bench.

"Whew, that's hard work, and it's hot out today." He was about to shape a glass of cold water when Ebenezer Mouse stepped around the side of the house with a pitcher of lemonade and a tray of oatmeal cookies.

"Thought you might like something cold. It's warm for a fall day. Made the cookies myself. I used Aislin's old recipe." Ebenezer sat on the bench next to Orville, setting the tray between them.

"Thanks. You're right, it's hot today, feels almost like summer. Who's Aislin?"

"My wife. I lost her twelve years ago. Nothing's

been the same since. She's the one who kept the gardens so lovely, reminded me to paint the house."

"Oh, I'm sorry, I didn't know. I remember when I was a mouseling you found me wandering around town and brought me home." Orville studied the glass tray holding the cookies. "I think I remember that tray. I think maybe Aislin gave me some cookies."

"Good memory. Your parents were out looking for you so I left you with Aislin while I went to get them. Aislin said she gave you a plate of oatmeal cookies. Said you really liked them." Ebenezer stood up. "Come see me when you're done painting. There's something I want to show you."

Three hours later Orville was scraping the third side of the house. "This is going a lot faster than I thought it would. It would have taken me a week to do it by myself."

"I couldn't help but overhear your conversation with Ebenezer Mouse. What do you think he wants to show you?"

"I don't know, probably old stuff. You know, pictures of when he was young, maybe pictures of Aislin. She must have died soon after he found me. I don't remember anything about it though, I barely even remember her. I guess Mama thought I was too young to hear about stuff like that. Maybe that's why he's so unhappy, because he misses her."

The sun was dipping toward the horizon when Orville and Proto finished scraping off the last of the old paint.

Proto gave a start. "Oh dear, I have to dash home and prepare dinner before Mum and Papa get back. Visit as long as you want with Ebenezer. I'll keep your dinner warm."

"Thanks for all your help, Proto." Orville waited until Proto was gone, then walked around to the front door. He knocked gently, filled with the sudden and powerful realization that his meeting with Ebenezer would be far more significant than looking at dusty old photographs and taking a stroll down memory lane.

The door swung open and Ebenezer motioned him in. "Have a seat on the couch." Ebenezer peered outside, looking in both directions, then swung the door shut.

Orville's eyes scanned the interior of the house. The day after Ebenezer had hollered at him for screeching like a Gnorli bird, Orville had brought him a tin of tasty little cakes as an apology. His knock went unanswered, but the door was ajar and he had entered, afraid something was wrong. Resting against the far wall was a curious contraption, a device with some slight resemblance to a piano, but with far more keys, six brass dials, rows of glass tubing, and a row of small yellow lights. When he pressed a key, instead of a musical note he had heard the sound of distant drums, then the sound of wind whistling across a vast desert. The strange device was now carefully concealed beneath a large white sheet.

"Aislin and I called it our Sound Piano."

"Oh, I was wondering what that thing was. I figured

it was some kind of musical instrument. Pretty fancy piano." Orville smiled politely, still uncertain why Ebenezer had invited him in.

"I might be old, but I'm not blind."

"What?"

"Saw your silver ring this morning. I know what you are."

Orville shifted nervously in his seat. This was not what he had been expecting. Ebenezer knew he was a Metaphysical Adventurer?

"No need for games, shapers are okay with me. I spent a few years in Lapinor when I was young. Saw plenty of shapers, plenty of Shapers Guild rings. Heard a few stories about the Metaphysical Adventurers, only ever saw one ring though. I need your help."

Ebenezer now had Orville's undivided attention.

"What kind of help?"

"I know you saw the snow I tracked into the house this summer when you brought me that tin of little cakes."

Orville nodded. It had been a scorching summer day and Ebenezer had tracked snow across his living room floor.

Ebenezer stepped over to the Sound Piano and pulled the sheet off, revealing the curious contraption. Orville was filled with a sudden feeling of dread.

Ebenezer pulled up a chair in front of Orville. He took a deep breath, slowly letting it out.

"I have a story to tell you. It's the story of how I lost my dear Aislin."

Orville's insides tightened. This was not good, this was too personal, too painful. He didn't want to hear how Aislin had died, but he had no idea what to say.

"Um... I'm sorry she died. She seemed really nice, you know, when she gave me the oatmeal cookies."

"I didn't say she died, I said I'd lost her. I'm telling you the story of how I lost her."

Orville was desperately wishing he was somewhere else.

"When we moved into this house it was already old. They said it had been here before the founding of Muridaan Falls. It had long been abandoned and was in a state of decay and disrepair when we found it, so we got it for a song. Needed a lot of work. We moved in and spent over a year fixing it up, making it new again, making it our home. It was hard work, but those were the happiest days of my life." Ebenezer stopped, clearing his throat. Orville looked away, realizing Ebenezer was trying not to cry.

"It was Aislin who found the Sound Piano. She was repairing an old wall. Had a hole in it and she looked inside, saw a little yellow light. We tore out a panel and found the Sound Piano in a hidden alcove. Had no idea why someone would hide such a treasure. Thought it was our lucky day. Aislin loved music but we didn't have much money, couldn't afford a piano. She was like a mouseling on her birthday."

"How long do you think it had been there?"

"At least two hundred years, probably much longer."

"The little yellow lights were still on after all that

time?"

"They were. Never seen anything like it. Aislin was the first to try it. Took only one note to realize it wasn't any ordinary piano. She pressed the key and we heard the sound of a thousand birds flying overhead, saw a quick flash of a dark forest."

"When I touched the key I heard distant drums and saw a desert. What is it? What does it do?"

"Aislin loved it. We called it our Sound Piano. We tried to figure out what it was for, thought maybe they used it to make sounds for stage plays, make them seem more real. She used to play it when she got up in the morning. She loved the sounds, especially the birds flying. She would close her eyes and just listen to them, said she could see them in her mind. There was one of a roaring river that she played all the time. Nature sounds were her favorite. I was half asleep the morning she disappeared. Heard her playing the Sound Piano, different sounds, ones I hadn't heard before. Hard to describe, I didn't recognize a lot of them. She called out, said she was making breakfast, called me a sleepy bones, said we were out of flour, she was going to run to the general store. She'd be right back. I heard the door open, heard her say, 'Good heavens'. Heard the door shut. Never saw her again."

Waves of overwhelming grief rolled through Orville. It was almost too much to bear. Ebenezer was hunched over, his paws covering his eyes. He rose up from his chair.

"I'm tired. Come back in a couple of days, I'll tell

you the rest." He turned and walked into his bedroom, closing the door behind him.

Orville sat in the echoing silence, his eyes on the Sound Piano, his thoughts a jumble. What had happened to Aislin, and why did Ebenezer need his help?

Chapter 5

A Knock on the Door

"Orville, could you get that? It might be Madam Beasley with my violets."

Orville jumped up from the sofa, thoughts of Ebenezer Mouse and the Sound Piano swirling through his mind. When he swung the front door open, rather than a smiling Madam Beasley with a tray of lovely purple flowers, he stood facing a clearly distraught Amanda Mouse, the red book clutched tightly in her paws. She glanced anxiously behind her, then turned back to Orville.

"May I come in?"

"Sure, sorry, I was just surprised to see you, I was expecting Madam Beasley and–"

"I think someone is following me. I think they're watching me."

Orville closed the door. "Have a seat. Who's following you?" He did not ask her if it was a beautiful ghost mouse.

"I don't know, I haven't actually seen them, but ever since you gave me this book I've had the strangest feeling I'm being watched."

"Maybe you should give me the book."

"Yes, please, thank you so much." Amanda breathed a sigh of relief. "That's better. I don't know how you Metaphysical Adventurers live with all these peculiar feelings and spooky happenings. I enjoy reading about them, but I don't want to actually... you know..." Her voice trailed off into silence.

"I understand. I was really scared when I first joined the Metaphysical Adventurers. I guess I'm kind of getting used to the spooky stuff though. It's fun figuring out what's making it happen. Sophia says it's all just science, there's nothing to be afraid of."

"I know who can translate the book. Captain Patcher told me about her last year, but I had to check with him, to make sure she was still there."

"She lives in Muridaan Falls?"

"Muridaan Falls? No, of course not, that's why I had to talk to Captain Patcher. She lives in Cathne, in western Opar, a thousand miles west of Symoca. I'd better go, it's getting late. I don't want to walk home in the dark."

"Wait, what's the translator's name? How do we find her?"

"Oh, sorry, her name is Puella the Wise One. Captain Patcher said she lives in the last standing cloud-scraper in Cathne. Up near the top, I think. She lives with a gang of bloodthirsty bandits. Captain Patcher said be sure to tell them he sent you, otherwise they'll probably kill you. You will tell me what the book is about, won't you? I do wish I could read it. It's quite thrilling, a book from Okeanos."

"Amanda, thanks so much for finding a translator, and I promise to tell you everything we find out about the book."

Amanda stopped, tilting her head as if she was listening for something. "That strange feeling is gone. They're not watching me anymore." She stepped through the door with a quick wave and a smile.

* * * *

Orville leaned back against the old barn, relaxing in the warmth of the noonday sun. "Nice and toasty. Feels good."

"Ebenezer didn't say how Aislin disappeared? Just that she walked out the front door and never came back?"

"That's all he told me. He said there was more, but he was too tired to talk about it. He wasn't tired, he didn't want me to see him cry. I feel really bad for calling him a crabby old mouse. He really misses Aislin."

"You couldn't have known. Mice like Ebenezer keep those things private. They don't like to talk about them because it's so painful and they don't want to be a burden on other mice."

"I sort of understand that. I never talked much about it when I thought Papa's fishing boat had gone down in the Vesarak. I was afraid I might start crying."

"And I didn't tell you my papa had been murdered by Draken Mouse."

"I'm glad we're best friends and we can talk about those things now."

"Me too. Tell me what Amanda said about Puella the Wise One. She lives in a cloudscraper?"

"She said Puella the Wise One could translate the book and that she lives in western Opar, in the city of Cathne, at the top of the last standing cloudscraper. She also happened to mention that Puella lives with a bunch of bloodthirsty bandits who will try to kill us if we don't tell them Captain Patcher sent us."

"Good to know."

"We have a couple of days till I see Ebenezer again. I guess we should pay a visit to Puella the Wise One. I'll talk to Master Marloh about requisitioning a Dragonfly from Mirus Mouse. It's going to be a long flight, at least ten hours to Cathne."

"It will be fun, think of all the beautiful fall scenery we'll get to see. We can take Proto with us."

"Good thinking, he always brings lots of tasty little cakes, and he can protect us from the bloodthirsty bandits when they try to kill us."

Chapter 6

Mirus' Surprise

With Master Marloh's blessing, Orville, Sophia, and Proto set off for Mirus Mouse's sprawling complex. Mirus was the most brilliant and innovative inventor in all of Symoca, fondly referred to by the Metaphysical Adventurers as the Mad Mouse of Muridaan. He was also widely considered to be the most eccentric mouse in Symoca.

At the request of Sophia, Mirus Mouse had built *The Glowbird*, the flying machine they used to reach Pavorak Gorge and the Cube where Proto had lived with the clockwork glowbirds for over fourteen hundred years. Their current vehicle of choice was the Dragonfly, a thirty foot long gleaming iridescent green flying machine with four sparkling transparent wings. The ship was powered by duplonium motors and capable of vertical take off and landing, with a top speed of one hundred and ninety miles per hour.

"Proto, what in the world do you have in that giant

backpack? You didn't bring one of those particle beam vaporizing things did you?"

"If I remember correctly, you were quite insistent that I not bring one, although the logic behind your decision seemed a little spurious and untenable."

Orville had no idea what spurious or untenable meant, but he wasn't going to let Proto know that. He made a note to himself to look the words up in the dictionary when he got home.

"You mean the very logical part about me not wanting the Dragonfly to explode a mile up in the sky, turning us into glowing specks of space dust?"

"As I previously mentioned, your fear is driven by emotion, not logic, not facts. Such a cataclysmic event is highly improbable, I assure you. Although I am programmed with the L7 Sincere Friendship Simulation Package, I also possess several advanced particle engineering programs, and I have spent many years studying the–"

Sophia groaned. "Good heavens, will you two please stop? I'm trying to enjoy the lovely fall foliage."

"Sorry, it just seemed like a very logical conclusion that bringing one of those particle beam things was completely dangerous, especially since we have no idea–"

"Enough, we're here. Mirus said to meet him in the yellow building at the far end of the complex."

"We usually meet him at the red building, did he say why we're meeting him in the yellow one?"

"He said he had a surprise for us."

Orville frowned. "I'm not sure I like the idea of Mirus Mouse having a surprise for us. He's a little unpredictable."

"I like Mirus. He's funny."

"I like him too, but suppose he forgets to tell us something really important?"

"We're Metaphysical Adventurers. We'll sort it out."

"I guess. Did I tell you I wasn't scared at all in the dream about Okeanos? Except for the part when the smoking charcoal stick creature came through the wall, and even then I didn't faint, I jumped into the silver book when the beautiful mouse told me to."

"Yes, you've mentioned that three times."

Proto snickered. "Fourth time for me."

Orville gave Proto a dark look. "I was simply making the point that we are brave and resourceful Metaphysical Adventurers."

"There's the yellow hangar. Mirus said to use the side door."

The trio of adventurers stepped over to the entrance and pushed the door open. Orville stepped into the hangar.

"There's nothing here, no Dragonfly."

"That's odd, I'm certain Mirus said to meet him here. He was quite specific about it. He said he'd have the ship ready for us."

"I guess we should wait for him. I hope he didn't forget about us."

Ten minutes later Mirus had still not appeared.

"He must have forgotten. Maybe we should go look for him."

Proto scanned the interior of the building, his eyes glowing with a pale green light.

"Most curious, I'm seeing an oddly shaped energy field in the center of the hangar."

A raucous voice rang out. "Took you long enough! You call yourselves Metaphysical Adventurers and you can't even find your own Dragonfly?"

Orville and Sophia jumped. "Mirus? Is that you?"

"Of course it's me, I told you I'd meet you here, didn't I? What's wrong with you? Let's get this bug in the air!"

"We'd really love to, but we're having a bit of a problem finding the ship. Where are you?"

Mirus gave a great screechy bird laugh, the thirty foot iridescent Dragonfly blinking into view in front of the startled adventurers. He scrambled down from the ship, his raucous jungle bird laugh echoing through the hangar.

"That's my surprise, mouse! I scavenged a cloaking device off the old Mintarian scout ship you found on Varmoran and reverse engineered it. Bingo! All the new Dragonflies have cloaks, you can fly anywhere you want and no one can see you! What do you think of that, mouse?"

Orville gaped at Mirus. "We'll be invisible?"

"What did I just say? Push the red button and the ship vanishes, push it again and the cloak is off. It's as easy as that."

"Wait, if the ship is invisible, how do we find the red button to shut it off?"

Mirus' eyes bulged out. "Are you trying to be funny? More wing flapping and less jaw flapping! Time to hit the clouds!"

Sophia nudged Orville, whispering, "The ship is invisible to mice outside the cloak, but not to the mice flying the ship."

"Oh, that makes more sense, it would be scary trying to fly an invisible Dragonfly."

Mirus strode over to the hangar doors and rolled them open.

Sophia grinned as she climbed into the ship. "This is going to be fun, we can fly right over Muridaan Falls and no one will see us. I wish I'd brought a camera."

Proto stuffed his enormous backpack into the rear storage compartment. "The cloaking device will also come in handy when we confront the hordes of Anarkkian attack spiders in Cathne."

"The what?" Orville whipped around in his seat.

"The hordes of Anarkkian attack spiders who still prowl the streets of Cathne. Many have become nonfunctional over the centuries, but a great number still roam the area, attacking anything that moves, pulverizing it with their deadly force beams."

"Orville, don't you remember the historical records Proto showed us in the Cube? The Anarkkian Battle Cruiser dropping all the spiders on Cathne during the war?"

"I thought they'd be gone by now. Creekers. Amanda never said anything about attack spiders roaming the streets."

"Relax, we'll be fine. We'll turn on the cloak when we reach Cathne, land on top of the cloudscraper, visit Puella the Wise One, then fly home. No problem at all."

"Right, no problem at all. That's what you said about our trip to Tectar." Orville was well aware that the boundlessly optimistic Sophia had a way of drastically underestimating the obstacles and dangers they would be facing on their adventures.

Sophia thwacked Orville's arm. "Hold on to your adventuring hat, Orville the Brave!" She pushed the left stick forward and the Dragonfly's glimmering wings became a blur, the ship lifting ten feet above the floor, a low hum filling the hangar.

"Duplonium motors sound good, all wings functional."

"Whoo hoo!"

Sophia slammed the stick forward and the hum became a roar, the Dragonfly's powerful motors sending them through the open doors at over ninety miles an hour, pressing Orville back against his seat, his eyes wide, his paws gripping the arm rests.

The Dragonfly flashed across the grass runway and blasted almost straight up into the sky. Orville let out a screech. "What are you doing? Slow down! Are you trying to kill us?"

Sophia gave a cackling laugh. "I switched on the cloaking device. We're invisible now, we can fly over Muridaan Falls and no one will see us."

Orville's eyes lit up. "Fly over my house, I want to see what it looks like from up here. And fly over the Book Emporium, maybe we can see Master Marloh."

"Whoo hoo!" Sophia pulled back on the left stick and the ship went into a steep dive, screaming down toward Muridaan Falls. An involuntary smile appeared on Orville's face.

"This is kind of fun. I can see the Book Emporium!"

Sophia slowed the ship to a hover several hundred feet above the shop.

"This is amazing! The mice on the street aren't even looking up. There's the old barn where we have lunch. Fly down the road to my house."

Sophia did a slow banking turn, flying two hundred feet above the familiar winding lane that led to Orville's home.

"Look how beautiful the leaves are from up here! The whole town is orange and red and yellow. I'd like to see it in the winter when it's covered with a big snowy blanket."

Orville nodded, looking toward the snowcapped mountains. His insides turned to ice when he saw the beautiful translucent blue ghost mouse flying alongside the ship, her unblinking eyes staring at him.

"Uh… uhh… it's the…"

"What?"

Orville pointed mutely, but the ghost mouse was gone. "Nothing, just… the leaves are really nice."

"Should I slow down? Are you getting airsick?"

"I'm fine, I don't get airsick. Just that one time when

it was really stormy. Fly over Ebenezer's house, I want to see what it looks like with all the paint scraped off." Orville glanced behind them, but the beautiful ghost mouse was nowhere to be seen.

"There's your house!"

Proto leaned out of the cockpit. "Oh drat, I forgot to water my vegetable garden this morning."

"Mum said she'd water it for you. Ebenezer's house looks really different with no paint. Hey, the front door is opening. I can see Ebenezer! Maybe he's going to paint the–"

Orville never finished his sentence. He never finished it because the moment Ebenezer Mouse stepped out through his front door he vanished. He was there, and then he was not there.

"Whoa, did you see that?"

"I saw it. It didn't look like blinking, it was something else."

"Do you think he can make himself invisible? He never said anything about that, all he said was there was more to the story."

"We need to get the red book translated. Maybe then we'll understand what's happening here. I'm more certain than ever the book has something to do with the story Ebenezer is going to tell you."

Sophia made a sharp swooping turn, sending the Dragonfly across a brilliant fall sky toward the distant city of Cathne.

Chapter 7

Elevator Music

"What happened to the vegetation? It's all black, like there was a big fire or something."

"The Anarkkians peppered Opar with thousands of cloud bombs during the war, killing or mutating all life forms, poisoning the earth for millennia. Creatures still living in those areas are to be avoided at all cost."

Orville glanced back at Proto. "What kind of creatures?"

"Bad ones, creatures even I don't want to meet."

"Um, maybe we should fly around those areas instead of flying over them? Just to be safe."

Sophia nodded, angling the ship to the northwest.

"Why are you slowing down?"

"I'm not slowing down."

Orville looked over the side of the Dragonfly. The ship was still directly above the stark wasteland left by the Anarkkian cloud bombs.

"We're not moving, we might even be going back-

46

wards."

"That's not possible, the speedometer says were cruising at one hundred and ten miles an hour. It's probably just an optical illusion."

Proto's head popped out from between the seats. "I would have to concur with Orville's observation. My Interworld Positioning System indicates we are moving backwards at precisely three miles per hour. We are also losing altitude at the rate of twenty feet per second."

Sophia jammed the stick forward, the duplonium motors roaring, the gleaming translucent wings barely visible, their ferocious wind forcing Orville to hold on to his adventurers hat.

"It's not working! We're still going backwards!"

"The motors are running at full capacity, I'm giving her all she's got! The speedometer says we're flying at one hundred and ninety-five miles an hour."

"We're descending! Something is pulling us down!"

"There's no wind, it can't be a downdraft. What's doing this? I can't go any faster!"

Orville froze. Far below them on the desolate tortured ground two gigantic rusty metal doors were sliding open, revealing an enormous black rectangular shaft beneath them.

"What is that? Proto, look! Big doors are sliding open down there!"

"This confirms my suspicion that we have been ensnared by a powerful gravitator beam, most likely Anarkkian. It is pointless to fight it, such beams are fully capable of capturing a medium sized attack scout ship. I'm afraid our little Dragonfly has no chance of escape."

"Who's doing it? What do they want?"

Proto shook his head. "I have magnified my vision by a factor of twenty, but am unable to see what lies beneath the open doors. In all probability the shaft is the entrance to an old Anarkkian military outpost lying several hundred feet below the surface. It would appear the outpost is currently occupied by unknown inhabitants."

Sophia pulled back on the stick. "I'll burn out the motors if I keep this up, I'm reducing our speed to a hover. I've lost all control of the ship."

Orville watched the scorched and blighted landscape moving up toward them as the ship rapidly descended.

"How could anyone still be there? The Anarkkians left at the end of the war."

"It very well could be an autonomous defense system."

The Dragonfly was now only a hundred feet above the ground, Orville anxiously scanning the ravaged land, the crusted black remains of ancient trees and plants barely recognizable.

"Something is moving out there! What is that?"

Sophia saw them, long writhing blue and white striped wormlike creatures undulating and pulsating through the charred earth.

"It looks like they're swimming in the ground, like it's water. I've never seen anything like it."

"I think I'm going to throw up. We need to get out of here."

Orville let out a shriek when the Dragonfly was drawn into the dark shaft. The ship shot downward, the opening above them shrinking until it had become a small blue rectangle.

"We are currently two miles below the surface, far deeper than I had anticipated. Such great depth would have provided the outpost with an impenetrable defense against even the most powerful pulsar beam weapons possessed by the Elders."

Orville flicked his wrist, a brilliant orb of light shooting out.

"The sides of the shaft are all rusty and corroded. It looks really old. Maybe we can just shut off that gravitator beam thing and then fly out again. That won't be so bad. We'll just shut it off and leave."

Ten minutes later the Dragonfly touched down on a heavily scarred metallic floor. Orville's light orb flashed across the room. They had come to rest in a cavernous hangar filled with innumerable flying machines in varying states of disrepair and decay, some barely recognizable hulks of rusted twisting metal.

"Creekers, what is this place?"

Proto scanned the jungle of derelict ships. "These are old, some flown by the Elders, some by the Anarkkians, but there are many which I do not recognize."

"Do you think they were caught by that gravitator thing?"

"Impossible to tell. Clearly the beam is still functioning, but when the last ship was captured I cannot say."

Sophia sent out a second orb of light, brightly illuminating the interior of the hangar.

"I like Orville's plan to shut off the gravitator beam. We need to find the outpost's command center. Orville, blink up a sphere of defense, there's no telling what we might run into. You saw those blue striped worm things swimming in the ground. There could be other mutations living down here."

Orville blinked up a shimmering sphere of defense, his eyes darting around the hangar.

Sophia hopped out of the Dragonfly.

"Let's take those doors on the other side of the hangar."

The three adventurers cautiously wove their way through the dismal graveyard of long abandoned flying machines.

"Did you hear that? I think I heard something moving."

"That was me stepping across this wing. I have scanned the hangar and found no evidence of life forms."

"That's a relief. Some of these flying machines are really weird looking. I can't even tell how they fly. There's a blinker ship over there but half the hull is missing. We should bring Mirus Mouse back here sometime to look around. He'd like all these weird machines."

Proto approached the two massive doors at the far

end of the hangar. He slapped a glowing violet disc on the wall and the doors slid open with a dreadful screeching and rending of metal.

"Whoa, that could use a bit of oil."

Sophia laughed. Sometimes Orville could be so funny.

"This corridor is really long, lots of doors. Do you think there's anything in the rooms?"

"Probably filled to the brim with giant squirmy blue striped worms."

"That's not even funny. We have no idea what might be living down here."

"Proto said nothing is living down here."

"I'm going to peek inside one of the rooms. Maybe the Anarkkians stored all their gold down here."

Orville gingerly raised the rusted lever, inching the door open, sending in an orb of light.

"No squirmy blue worms. It looks like racks of weapons, sort of like those vape guns we found on Periculum."

"Don't touch anything, it's all really old, probably unstable. The last thing we need to do is accidentally set off a gigantic explosion."

Orville eased the door shut. "Now we know for sure it was a military outpost. Next step is finding the control center and shutting off the gravitator beam. Proto, any idea where it might be?"

"The beam originates from beneath the shaft, so I would surmise that the control center is located on a lower level, most likely the one below us. Although there are currently no living creatures in evidence, we must remain vigilant. Outposts such as this often had deadly security systems in place. One wrong move and we could be instantly vaporized."

"That doesn't sound especially appealing. What are we looking for?"

"Impossible to tell, many are quite undetectable until it is too late."

"I wish you hadn't told me that."

Proto pushed through a set of battered swinging doors at the end of the corridor.

"Excellent, an elevator, and it appears to be functional."

He tapped a glowing violet disc on the wall and the two corroded metal doors squealed open.

Orville peered inside. "Look at all the buttons, how do we know which one to push?"

Sophia stepped into the elevator. "It's easy, the top one is lit, so it must be our floor. We just press the button below it, one floor down. Nothing to it. I like this soft music, it's kind of relaxing."

Orville stepped hesitantly into the ancient elevator. "It feels kind of wobbly."

The elevator made a painful groaning sound when Proto stepped in, the floor sagging slightly.

Orville looked anxiously at Sophia. "That doesn't sound good, we should look for stairs."

"You're being a nervous ninny." Sophia slapped the elevator button.

Two things happened when she hit the button. First,

the doors squealed shut, and second, the elevator shuddered violently, dropping like a stone. The three adventurers were in free fall, plummeting toward the ground sixteen stories below at over fifty miles an hour.

Chapter 8

The Invoice

The ancient rusty elevator brakes gave an ear splitting shriek, clawing wildly at the fraying steel cables, sending the trio of adventurers tumbling to the hard metal floor. Moments later the car groaned to a stop, the soft music still playing.

Orville staggered to his feet. "Creekers."

Proto grinned. "Quite a thrilling descent."

Sophia stood up, dusting herself off. "That was unexpected. Next time we should take the stairs."

The doors creaked open.

"I guess we go through the doors at the end of this corridor."

The adventurers strolled down the long hallway, Orville eyeing the old photographs of uniformed Anarkkians hanging on the wall.

"Definitely a military base."

Proto swung the two large brass doors open. Orville's jaw dropped. He stood facing an enormous brightly lit, luxuriously appointed room.

"Whoa, this looks like a really fancy hotel, something you'd find in a big city."

The floor of the magnificently opulent room was covered with deep plush maroon carpeting, almost a dozen beautifully embroidered couches artfully placed next to ornate gleaming bronze tables.

Sophia grinned. "This is amazing, it rivals anything I ever saw on Quintari. Look at the murals, jungle scenes with those yellow and orange birds, only a master artist could have painted that."

"What's a place like this doing in a creepy old military outpost? It seems kind of weird, doesn't it?"

"It must have been for the highest ranking members of the Anarkkian military. It is odd to find such a luxurious setting in a military outpost, most of them were stark and utilitarian."

"Like Norrich Bunker on Periculum."

"Exactly."

Sophia strolled across the brilliantly lit room, running her paw across the gleaming marble table tops. "There's no dust on the tables. These books are definitely Anarkkian. They look like travel books, but the skies are pale green."

"Look at the front counter where the guests checked in. Fancy. It must have cost a fortune to stay here, there's no way I could have–"

Orville stopped in mid sentence when he saw the gleaming golden door behind the registration desk opening. A twelve foot tall gaunt rubbery looking speckled blue creature with no nose stepped into view. Fastidiously dressed in a smart gray pinstriped suit and red bow tie, the creature was humming softly to itself, holding a sheath of papers. It turned around, carefully locking the door behind it.

Orville whispered, "What is that thing?"

Proto studied it closely. "It is most likely an Anarkkian automaton possessing some high degree of engineered intelligence. It looks vaguely familiar, something I may have seen in the storage records back at the Cube. I am uncertain as to why it is wearing a suit."

The creature looked up at the sound of Proto's voice.

"Ah, we have guests. A wonderful good afternoon to all of you, and welcome to the magnificent Imperial Inn of Anarkkia. Might I inquire if you have existing reservations?"

Sophia stepped forward, smiling brightly. "I'm afraid we don't have reservations, we stumbled upon your marvelous inn by accident. It was quite a surprise to find it here."

"I do hope the gravitator beam was not too jarring, and I apologize for that dreadful elevator. I have called numerous times for a repair technician, but the service department has been painfully lax in their response."

"You know about the gravitator beam?"

"Of course, it is just one of the many conveniences offered by the Imperial Inn of Anarkkia, bringing your ship safely into our complimentary and secure parking area."

"Um, we didn't have a lot of choice, it just grabbed us out of the sky and pulled us down that big shaft."

The blue creature nodded sympathetically.

"And how many days will you be staying with us?"

Orville was about to tell the blue creature what he thought of their convenient gravitator beam service when he was interrupted by Sophia.

"Just one night I think. Do you have a restaurant? Or maybe room service?"

"Of course, madam, there are four marvelous restaurants offering a wide variety of exquisite gourmet cuisine, or if you prefer, you may dine at leisure in your room. It is your choice."

"That sounds perfect, we'd like to stay for one night and have meals brought to our room."

Orville pursed his lips, his eyes on Sophia. He turned to the strange rubbery blue creature behind the counter.

"How much does all this cost?"

The creature gave a disarming and empathetic smile. "Nothing to worry about, good sir, I assure you, our rates are most reasonable. You will be pleasantly surprised, no need for concern. I will add that all meals, including room service, are included in the cost of the room."

"Oh, that's not so bad, I guess."

After checking in, the adventurers followed the blue creature down a long softly lit corridor. Orville eyed the curious blue creature.

"How long have you worked here?"

"Do forgive me, I have neglected to introduce myself. I am Master Grymm, sole owner and chief executive officer of the magnificent Imperial Inn of Anarkkia."

"It's a remarkable hotel, when was it built?"

"I began construction of the inn at the end of the great war, our grand opening taking place precisely one hundred and seventy-four years later, to the day."

Orville stopped in his tracks. "One hundred and seventy-four years? How old are you?"

"Orville, don't be rude, it's not polite to ask someone their age."

Orville glared at Sophia.

"Do you get many guests here? It's a little out of the way."

"Quite a few over the years, our complimentary parking service draws in many of our guests."

"You mean the gravitator beam."

"Quite so, one of our most popular services. Ahh, we have arrived at your room. I am placing you in the sumptuously appointed Princess of Amtori Royal Deluxe Five Bedroom Palatial Suite. Feel free to relax in the warmth of your heated eucalyptus scented soaking pool while pampering yourself with a complimentary box of our luscious gourmet chocolates."

Master Grymm swung the heavy gold inlaid doors open, motioning for them to enter.

Sophia let out a gasp. "This is stunning, I've never seen a more beautiful room." She ran over to the exquisitely embroidered sofa, sinking down into the soft cushions.

"Mmm, so comfy."

"Excellent. You'll find menus from all four of our gourmet restaurants on the table, just circle what you would like, slip the menu under the door, and your meal will be delivered in less than one hour."

Master Grymm gave a gracious sweeping bow and backed out of the room, closing the door softly behind him.

Sophia couldn't stop grinning. "This is amazing, I've never stayed in a hotel like this before. We even get room service. I've never had room service. I'm going to go soak in that big warm tub and have some of those gourmet chocolates. Why don't you pick out something yummy from the menu? Get whatever you want. We can leave in the morning for Cathne."

Orville and Proto sat on the enormous stuffed couch.

"This place is amazing, but something is off about it. Why would there be a fancy deluxe hotel at the bottom of a corroded old military complex? It doesn't feel right. It's also weird that they use the gravitator beam service to attract most of their customers. Wait, they *attract* customers with a gravitator beam? Get it? *Attract* customers?"

Proto stared blankly at Orville.

"Never mind." Something else was nagging Orville, something he couldn't put his paw on.

Sophia emerged an hour later wrapped in a huge fluffy white robe. "This robe is so soft and luxurious, it's amazing. I wonder if they sell them here? Maybe we get to keep them, maybe it's included in the price of the room."

"He never did tell us how much the room was, which is a little concerning. I only have nine silvers."

"I have at least twenty, that should cover it. Even the best rooms in Muridaan Falls are only six or seven silvers a night."

After a spectacularly delicious dinner the weary adventurers retired to what Orville would later say was the most comfortable bed he had ever slept in. Unfortunately, he didn't sleep in it for very long, his eyes popping open in the middle of the night.

"All those derelict ships, where did they come from? There's a hundred decaying old ships, and now ours is one of them."

Orville jumped out of bed, running to Sophia's room. "Sophia, get up, this hotel is a trap, that's why there are so many abandoned ships here. Master Grymm traps ships in his gravitator beam and no one ever leaves!"

Sophia's mind was racing. "You're right, I was so excited about staying in a fancy hotel that I didn't even think about that. Master Grymm is up to something, and it's not good. We have to find the gravitator beam, shut it off, and get back to the Dragonfly. If the elevator was damaged in the fall we'll have to find another way back up to the hangar."

"We know the gravitator beam is under the big shaft that goes up to the surface, but the controls could be anywhere. Wait, think about it, Master Grymm is the one who operates the gravitator beam, and he's trapped a lot of ships, so he must use it fairly often. It has to be somewhere nearby."

Sophia grabbed Orville's arm. "His office, the controls are in his office! Did you notice how he locked the door behind him?"

"That has to be it. The good news is he doesn't know we're shapers, a locked door isn't going to stop us."

Proto was listening intently to Orville and Sophia's conversation. He snapped his fingers. "Great heavens, I just remembered where I have seen automatons like Master Grymm before. I didn't recognize him at first because of the suit he's wearing."

"Where did you see them?"

Proto hesitated. "I'm afraid it's not entirely good news."

Orville groaned. "What is it?"

"Master Grymm is a B-17 Warrior Android, also known to the Elders as Blue Nightmares, the Anarkkian version of the Elders' A6 Warrior Rabbiton. He is armed with similar weaponry and is indestructible, short of dropping a pulsar fusion bomb on him."

"What kind of weapons does he have?"

"Thermal energy beams, more powerful than those found on medium sized Anarkkian attack ships. I'm afraid your sphere of defense will provide no protection against such force. One blast of his energy beam would be the end of you."

Sophia's expression did not change. "We'll have to

use stealth, we'll have to sneak out, and what better time than now, in the middle of the night?"

"Proto, would his beam damage you?"

"I would be instantly converted into a puddle of glowing molten plasma."

Sophia gripped the knob on the room's golden inlaid doors.

"It won't open, we're locked in!"

A purple beam shot out from Orville's paw, a hole appearing where the knob had been.

"Now we're not."

The three adventures crept silently out of their luxurious Princess of Amtori Royal Deluxe Five Bedroom Palatial Suite.

Sophia whispered, "No talking, use thought clouds or paw signals. No light orbs."

Step by step they padded softly down the long corridor, reaching the doors that opened to the hotel lobby. Sophia's ears turned slowly, listening for the slightest sound. She tapped the violet button and the doors slid silently open. A thought cloud shot out to Orville.

"We'll go into his office, shut off the gravitator beam, and make certain the doors at the top of the shaft are open. Grymm may have closed them."

"Once the beam is off I'll disable the controls so he can't turn it on again."

"Good idea."

They stepped into the dimly lit lobby, soft ceiling lights glinting off the bronze and marble surfaces of the grand room.

Orville crept toward the front desk, stopping every few yards to listen.

"I don't hear anything. Maybe he's on another level doing maintenance or something."

"Maybe. We should hurry."

Orville padded across the plush carpet, stepping behind the front desk. He studied the heavily inlaid gold office door, noting the precise location of the locking mechanism.

He was about to vaporize it when Proto grabbed his arm, shaking his head, whispering, "Internal alarm system."

He stepped in front of Orville, touching the knob for ten long seconds. A small spark shot out from his finger and the lock clicked. Proto pushed the door open, the interior overhead lights blinking on. They darted into the office, closing the door behind them.

"Do you see it?"

Proto pointed to a curved silver console at the far end of the room.

Orville darted over to the control panel.

"It's all marked in some weird language."

"It's Anarkkian, I can read it. The gold toggle switch is for the gravitator beam, the gold dial is for the surface doors. The outer doors are still open, but the gravitator beam is on. He probably never shuts it off." Sophia flicked the gold toggle switch. "The beam is off."

"That was easy." A blast of purple light shot out from Orville's paw, a wide hole appearing in the control panel. "He won't be using that for a while."

"Let's get out of here. No talking, if he hears us it's all over. Don't forget, he's a B-17 Blue Nightmare."

Proto eased the door open, peering out into the lobby. He stepped out, motioning for the others to follow.

Sophia closed the door silently, pointing toward the exit.

Orville was creeping across the room when he caught a sudden movement in the shadows.

"Checking out so soon?"

Orville's blood turned cold.

Master Grymm stepped out from a darkened alcove, his eyes glowing with a dreadful crimson light.

"I do hope you enjoyed your stay at the Imperial Inn of Anarkkia. If you wouldn't mind stepping over to the front desk I shall tally up your invoice. We serve a lovely complimentary breakfast for our guests, but not for another four hours, I'm afraid. Most of our guests wait until morning to check out."

A thought cloud shot out from Sophia to Orville.

"Don't panic, he doesn't know we shut off the gravitator beam. We'll just pay our bill and leave."

Master Grymm stepped behind the registration desk. "Unfortunately I must charge you for one full night even though you're checking out early. Rules are rules, I'm afraid."

He picked up a long gold pen, scribbling quickly on a sheet a pale yellow parchment paper deeply embossed with the name of the inn.

"There you are, all set. As I previously mentioned, meals are included in the daily room rate. I trust the beds were comfortable? No complaints? Meals were fine?"

"It was lovely, thank you so much, the meals were scrumptious. We'd love to stay longer, but Orville remembered an unavoidable prior engagement."

"Quite understandable. Here is your bill. We accept cash only, I'm afraid, no credit." He slid the invoice across the smooth marble counter to Sophia.

Sophia scanned it, her eyebrows raising. "This can't be right."

Master Grymm gave a frozen smile. "Can't be right?"

"It says we owe three hundred and seventy-five thousand golds. That's insane."

Master Grymm hissed, "What's insane is three guests trying to sneak out in the middle of the night without paying their bill. You have precisely three minutes to pay, or suffer the most dire of consequences."

Sophia gave a pleasant smile. "I was just surprised, that's all. We should have enough gold in our ship. We'll run get it and be right back."

Master Grymm gave a sarcastic snort. "Your ship must be far more powerful than it appears. Three hundred and seventy-five thousand gold weighs precisely twenty-three thousand, four hundred and thirty-seven pounds. Your quaint little flying insect ship has a maximum payload capacity of two thousand pounds at best."

"We could fly back to Muridaan Falls and bring the

gold back in a larger ship. A blinker ship will carry that much."

"I'm afraid that is not going to be possible."

"You can't keep us here, that's against the law."

Master Grymm's crimson eyes flared with a fearsome light.

"You will do as I say or become a pile of smoking charcoal. From this moment on you are employees of the magnificent Imperial Inn of Anarkkia. You'll start first thing in the morning. I'm adding a spectacular shopping plaza with dozens of upscale stores and restaurants, stunningly elegant, exquisitely appointed, first class all the way. My previous employees are no longer with us due to an unfortunate incident involving some hideous blue and white striped worm creatures, but you appear to be quite resourceful. I'm certain you'll do just fine."

"How long do we have to work for you?"

"Until the balance of your bill is paid, of course. It shouldn't take long, my wages are most generous, one silver a week for each of you."

Orville's insides were twisting. Master Grymm was clearly loopier than a three eyed flatbird. A thought cloud flashed out of his ear to Sophia.

"Get ready to run."

A red beam flashed out from Orville's paw, the plush maroon carpet across the room bursting into flames.

Master Grymm let out a howl of unparalleled fury, his eyes bulging out.

"WHAT HAVE YOU DONE?"

Orville and Sophia dashed toward the exit. Proto tore past them, smashing through the doors, knocking them off their hinges.

"MY PRECIOUS DOORS! YOU WILL PAY WITH YOUR LIVES!"

"Run! Hurry!"

The three adventurers sprinted down the long hallway, Proto blasting through the doors into the elevator room. They could hear Master Grymm pounding down the corridor after them.

Proto jammed his fingers between the elevator doors and pried them open.

Sophia shrieked, "The lights are out, it's not working!"

"Put your arms around me, hold on tight, don't let go!"

Orville and Sophia wrapped their arms around Proto as he leaped up, grabbing the massive steel elevator cables, climbing hand over hand up the elevator shaft. Orville was careful not to look down.

Halfway up they heard screams from the bottom of the elevator shaft. Master Grymm was coming after them, shrieking barely intelligible threats, something about the blue worms. Grymm was only thirty feet below them when Proto reached the top of the shaft and forced open the elevator doors. He scrambled out, Orville and Sophia still clinging to him. The adventurers raced wildly down the corridor and into the hangar, weaving through the maze of ships, sprinting over the rusted remains of decrepit flying machines.

"There's the Dragonfly!" Orville dashed toward it, leaping into the cockpit, joined seconds later by Sophia and Proto. He flipped on the duplonium motors. "Hold on!"

Master Grymm's demented shrieks reverberated through the hangar.

"YOU CAN'T ESCAPE MY GRAVITATOR BEAM! I WILL FEED YOU TO THE BLUE WORMS! WORM FOOD! WORM FOOD!"

A blinding blast of red light shot across the hangar, the ship next to them exploding in a ball of radiant molten fire.

The Dragonfly's wings were a blur, the deep roar of the motors filling the hangar. Orville slammed the control stick forward and the ship shot straight up at over one hundred and twenty miles an hour, pushing them down into their seats. He could still hear the deranged screams of Master Grymm as they flashed up toward the surface. Seconds later they rocketed into a clear blue sky, squinting in the bright sunlight.

"Creekers, that was close. That is one extremely crazy automaton."

Sophia leaned back in her seat with a long sigh. "I wonder where he got those gourmet chocolates? Do you think he made them himself? They were so delicious, and those beds were so comfy. That's the first time I've ever had room service."

Chapter 9

Cathne

"Keep heading east-northeast, we should reach Cathne in about an hour. Did Amanda say anything else about Puella the Wise One?"

"Only that she could translate the book and to watch out for the bloodthirsty bandits. She thought someone was watching her, she wasn't very talkative."

"A beautiful ghost mouse?"

"She didn't see who it was, but it must have been her."

"Doesn't it seem odd that someone who can translate obscure ancient languages would choose to live with a gang of bloodthirsty bandits?"

"Copo lived with bandits and he was nice." Orville grinned, remembering their visit to the Temporal Displacement Museum on Tectar.

"I liked Copo. I hope he made it up to the surface of the planet. Maybe he found another gang of ruthless bandits to live with, and he's tapping his foot to one of those lively bolaphone tunes he was always talking about."

An hour later Sophia nudged a sleepy Orville.

"Wake up, it's Cathne."

"Creekers, is that all one city? How could it be so big? It goes on as far as I can see."

Proto answered, "Cathne was one of the largest cities on the planet before the war, home to over twenty million mice."

Orville snorted. "That's not possible, there couldn't be that many mice in one city. Where would they get their food and water? I don't see any farms or lakes."

"Back then the skies were filled with enormous flying ships carrying food and supplies from farms and factories across the continent. Water was piped in from distant reservoirs."

"Like those aqueducts on Tectar?"

"The same principle, but it was a far more advanced and complex system utilizing enormous duplonium powered generators and water pumps."

"I wouldn't want to live in a big city like that, I'd probably get lost. I like Muridaan Falls and I like buying our food from the market or picking it from Proto's garden. Not the red snackles though."

"It looks a little like the city where I grew up on Quintari. It was exciting, but I've come to love Muridaan Falls. I like the trees and the mountains and the fresh air. And my best friend happens to live there."

Orville grinned. "What a strange coincidence, so does mine. Speaking of cities, Amanda said Puella the

Wise One lives in the last standing cloudscraper. That's a really tall building, right?"

"Yes, it shouldn't be hard to spot. Keep your eyes open."

"I'm turning on the cloaking device in case we run into any Anarkkian attack spiders in Cathne."

"A wise move, our Dragonfly would not survive a direct hit from one of their force beams."

Sophia blinked up a sphere of defense around the Dragonfly. "That might help a little."

"Over there!" Orville pointed to a towering silver spire in the distance. He twisted the dial on his flying goggles, one of Mirus' marvelous inventions, magnifying his vision.

"Whoa, I can't believe how tall it is! It's way taller than the buildings on Varmoran."

Sophia adjusted their flight path, heading them toward the cloudscraper.

"I'm going to shut off the cloak before we land on the building. I'm guessing bloodthirsty bandits are not fond of surprises, especially cloaked ships landing on their roof."

"Good idea. Wait till we're a bit closer, in case we run into spiders."

Proto was studying the cityscape below them. "The Anarkkians did a thorough job of destroying Cathne, there's nothing but rubble down there. I can just make out where the streets were. Orville, look ahead, to the left!"

Orville looked across the mounds of devastation.

"Spiders! There's a whole bunch of them just standing there. What are they doing?"

"Waiting for something to move so they can destroy it."

"I'm taking us up. Their force beams are powerful, but I think they have limited range."

"You are quite correct, they were designed for close quarter battles, not for taking down high flying ships. Two thousand feet should do it."

Sophia watched the city shrink as they rose up into the sky.

"That's it, two thousand feet. I'm turning off the cloak. We're almost there, I'll circle around the building a few times to let them know we mean no harm. Hopefully they'll recognize the Dragonfly, maybe even think it's Captain Patcher."

Sophia made a long lazy turn around the top of the cloudscraper.

"Creekers, the roof is huge, it must be half a mile across, maybe more. At least we have lots of room to land. Look, a mouse just came out of that shack! He has one of those glass vape gun things, like the one we found on Periculum."

"Look behind us, we have an escort."

Orville whipped around. "Whoa! They're riding giant birds! Not as big as Gnorli birds, but close. They don't look very friendly, they both have vape guns."

The mouse on the building waved one arm, pointing to a large yellow circle painted on the rooftop.

"I guess we land on the yellow circle. They haven't

fired their vape guns, that's a good sign."

Orville blinked up a second sphere of defense around the ship.

"It's windy up here, hard to keep it steady." Sophia brought the Dragonfly to a hover, slowly descending until they landed on the rooftop with a small thump.

A rough looking mouse carrying a long cylindrical vape gun strolled casually toward the ship. He stopped when he saw Sophia, his vape gun suddenly aimed directly at them.

"Where's Patcher? Who are you?"

"Captain Patcher sent us. We're here to see Puella the Wise One."

"What for?" The bandit's vape gun was pointed directly at Sophia.

"We need to get a book translated. It's in a language we don't understand. He said Puella the Wise One could translate it for us."

"Is that an A6 Warrior Rabbiton?"

"I'm nothing at all like that. I'm a prototype Rabbiton with the L7 Sincere Friendship Simulation Package."

The mouse slowly lowered his weapon, waving off the two mice circling the building on the gigantic birds.

"You two follow me. The Rabbiton stays up here. No exceptions."

Orville studied the long scar on the bandit's scowling face, then turned to Proto. "I guess you stay here and keep an eye on the ship. I have no idea how long this will take."

Sophia and Orville climbed down, following the bandit to a squat rectangular structure at the west end of the roof. The bandit grunted as he forced open a stout metal door.

"Down to level 142, use the rope, in the yellow door. Don't go anywhere else. Clear? Nowhere else."

"Okay, clear. Will Puella the Wise One be waiting for us?"

"Go."

Orville and Sophia stepped through the doorway into the mysterious cloudscraper, one step closer to their meeting with the mysterious Puella the Wise One.

Chapter 10

Puella the Wise One

Sophia descended the dusty gray stairs into the depths of the cloudscraper. She pointed to a large faded yellow number on the wall. "We're on level 163."

"We have to walk down twenty sets of stairs?"

"It will be good exercise."

"It's not as dark as I thought it would be, the windows let in a lot of light. I can't believe how tall this building is. Why doesn't it fall over?"

Sophia was more than happy to display the depth of her engineering acumen.

"I learned about cloudscrapers in my structural engineering classes back on Quintari. A cloudscraper isn't like a big stack of blocks that will topple over in a strong wind, it has a strong internal framework, like a mouse's skeleton, and the building can bend and sway in a strong wind without breaking, the same way a tall tree does. Its framework extends far below the surface, like a giant fence post buried in the ground."

"That's amazing. I can't imagine how they could build it though. It would be scary to live up in the sky.

What do you think Puella the Wise One will look like? I bet she's like Madam Molly, all mysterious and spooky, probably really eccentric like Mirus Mouse."

"Madam Molly isn't spooky at all. She's really nice once you get to know her. She just comes from a world where the mice read each other's minds."

"She has those weird green eyes with gold flecks that swirl around. That's very spooky. It's not normal."

"If we all had eyes like that it wouldn't be spooky, it would be normal, just like it is in her world. This is level 145, we're almost there."

"What do you think the bandit meant about using the rope? Do you think we pull a rope to open the door?"

"Maybe."

"My legs are burning. Walking back to the roof is going to be rough."

"If you ask nicely maybe Puella the Wise One will carry you back up the stairs."

"Very funny. I hope she's not all creepy and weird. Hey, only one more floor. Last one there is a purple monkey butt!" Orville gave a shrieking laugh and dashed down the stairs, his echoing footsteps coming to an abrupt halt.

"Sophia, come look at this!"

Sophia found Orville standing on the bottom step, overlooking a deep chasm cutting across the building's interior.

"What do you think happened here? I can see down at least ten levels. It looks like something ripped through the side of the building."

"It must have been damaged during the Anarkkian wars, maybe a force beam from an attack ship."

"Is that the yellow door we're supposed to use? How do we get across the chasm?"

Sophia pointed to a long rope dangling from a twisted metal beam high above them. "I think you're supposed to swing across on that rope. You go first, in case the rope breaks."

"Ha ha. There's no way I'm swinging across on that rope. Look how far I'd fall if I lost my grip, I'd never even–"

Sophia vanished in a flash of blue light, appearing a split second later on the other side of the divide.

Orville had a silly grin on his face. "Oh, right, I forgot about blinking." An instant later he was standing next to Sophia.

Sophia eyed the corroded yellow door. "We should probably knock." She rapped gently.

"I hear footsteps. I hope she doesn't have tentacles and claws and stuff."

The door opened, revealing the oldest mouse the two adventurers had ever seen, a pale white mouse wearing a lime green robe adorned with several dozen colorful beaded necklaces. Perched atop her head was an old adventurers hat festooned with five feathers, each one a different color.

Orville nudged Sophia. Puella the Wise One definitely rivaled Mirus Mouse in eccentricity.

The ancient mouse gazed at them silently, her deep set eyes moving slowly back and forth between them, her expression unreadable.

Sophia bowed her head respectfully.

"Puella the Wise One, we have traveled far to see you, and we thank you for graciously taking the time to speak with us. Captain Patcher of the Metaphysical Adventurers Dragonfly Squadron has told us you might be able to translate a book for us, a book written in an ancient and long forgotten form of Mintarian. It is our fervent hope that you will grant us this favor."

Sophia removed the red book from her coat pocket, holding it up for Puella to see.

The old mouse studied the book, then turned, motioning for them to follow her. Orville and Sophia stepped into an enormous room, the outer wall consisting of floor to ceiling windows.

"Creekers, you can see the whole city from up here! This is amazing. It's not as scary as I thought it would be."

Puella's room was furnished in a decidedly eclectic fashion, containing a wide assortment of mismatched chairs, sofas, rugs, tables, lamps, and dozens of cryptic wooden sculptures. Orville thought one of them looked a lot like a pile of spiders. The walls were painted with hundreds of bright geometric shapes, positioned in a seemingly random fashion.

"You have a lovely home, Puella. We thank you for taking the time to see us."

The wrinkled old mouse pointed to a green door at the far end of the room.

"We should go in there?"

The ancient mouse nodded, her gnarled paw running across a bright red beaded necklace, her eyes on Orville.

The two best friends stepped over to the green door, pushing it open. Orville peered into a long sky blue room, a single brightly flowered sofa sitting in front of a wall of windows. Orville strolled across the floor, flopping down on the soft couch.

"Comfy. This view is amazing. Look how big the city is. How long do you think it will take her to translate the book?"

"She didn't take the book, I still have it. I think we're supposed to wait here for her."

"I hope she doesn't take too long, I'm kind of hungry." An oatmeal cookie blinked into his paw.

Sophia was about to make an extremely humorous comment about Orville's eating habits when she heard a soft clinking sound coming from across the room.

"Orville, look at that mouseling."

Orville grinned when he saw the furry little mouseling sitting on a soft blanket in the far corner of the room, playing with a pile of carved wooden animals.

"She's cute."

Sophia waved to the mouseling. "Hello, little one, are you having fun playing? I like your toy animals, they're lovely."

"Puella the Wise One must be her grandmum, or maybe her great, great, great, great grandmum." Orville snickered.

"Be nice, we're lucky Puella will see us. You

shouldn't make fun of mice just because they're old."

"I wasn't making fun of her, I've just never seen a mouse that old. She must know a lot of languages."

The little mouseling stood up, toddling precariously across the room toward them, a delicately carved wooden bird clutched tightly in one paw.

"Careful, little one, don't fall."

The mouseling came to a wobbly halt in front of Sophia, holding the toy bird up for her to see.

"What a lovely bird, you're lucky to have such a nice toy. How did you ever get to be so cute?"

Sophia steadied the mouseling with one paw. "It's very nice to meet you, my name is Sophia, and this is my very best friend Orville, we're here to see your grandmum Puella."

Whenever Orville would tell the story of their trip to Cathne, he would always say this particular moment was the most startling moment of his life, the moment Sophia's voice came out of the little mouseling's mouth.

"I am Puella the Wise One. You have brought me a book to translate?"

Two furry mouse jaws dropped simultaneously. "Did she just... what?"

A thousand thoughts raced through Sophia's head. How was this possible? How could the mouseling be using her voice, speaking like an adult?

"You have a book for me to translate?"

This was the first time Orville had ever heard Sophia stammer.

"Yes, um... I'm sorry, Puella, you surprised me with... um... well, here's the book, if you wouldn't mind... I didn't..."

Puella's painted bird clattered to the floor as she took the red book from Sophia. With wobbly little steps she tottered back to her blanket and flopped down, waving the book above her.

"Is she playing with it? How can a mouseling translate a book?"

"I don't have the slightest idea what's happening here."

Puella the Wise One closed her eyes, resting the red book on her little round furry tummy. A moment later she was fast asleep.

* * * *

Sophia's eyes were drooping when Puella the Wise One gave a little yawn and sat up.

"Orville, wake up!" Sophia jabbed him sharply in the ribs with her elbow.

Orville's eyes popped open. "Ow! What time is it? Did I oversleep?"

"Puella's awake."

"Did she read the book?"

"No, she took a nap with the book resting on her stomach."

Orville snickered. "That's how I used to study for my science exams."

81

Puella rolled onto her stomach, after two attempts managing to stand up while still holding the red book with both paws. She teetered across the room, coming to a stop in front of Sophia, holding out the book for her.

Sophia took the book, steadying Puella with one paw. "Did you have a nice nap, little... I mean, Puella the Wise One?"

Puella touched Sophia's knee. "Who shall carry the knowledge contained within the book?"

"What?"

"Who shall hold the memory?"

Orville looked at Sophia, then back at Puella. "Are you saying you read the book and you want to tell one of us what was in it?"

"Only one shall carry the memory for the rest of their days."

"Well, Sophia has a much better memory than I do and she understands all that science stuff, so she's probably the one you should tell. How did you read the book while you were sleeping?"

Puella clutched Sophia's paw.

"You will need to rest when we are done. You are ready to receive the knowledge?"

"I think so. You're going to tell me what was in the book?"

A blinding orange light flared in front of Puella.

Orville covered his eyes. "What is that? What are you doing?"

Sparkling yellow strands of shimmering light

streamed out from the orange orb, wriggling their way toward Sophia.

Orville tried to pull Sophia away from Puella.

"Stop. The knowledge will be lost if you interfere."

"It's okay, Orville, I trust her." Orville let go.

The undulating filaments of light attached themselves to Sophia, waves of pulsing white orbs flowing into her arms and shoulders and chest. Her eyes drooped, then closed.

"So strange... I'm floating... conscious, but there is only the book, don't know where I am... but the book is here, there is only the book."

Puella released Sophia's paw and the brilliant orange sphere of light vanished. Sophia gave a small groan, slumping over onto her side. Puella took Orville's paw. His eyes widened when he heard his voice coming from her mouth.

"She will carry the memory for all of her days. She must rest now, then you must find your own way. She shall face her greatest fear in Elysian. You must help her remember."

"Her greatest fear? What's Elysian? What does she have to remember?" Orville turned to Sophia, now sleeping soundly on the soft pillows. When he looked up again, Puella was back on her blanket playing with the wooden animals.

Orville held Sophia's paw while she slept.

The late afternoon sun was dipping toward the horizon when Sophia opened her eyes, Orville's worried face the first thing she saw.

"What's wrong?"

"Are you okay? You've been asleep for almost three hours."

"Three hours? The last thing I remember was Puella–" Sophia stopped in mid sentence, her eyes wide.

"Orville, the book, I know what it is! I know every word of it, I understand everything!"

Chapter 11

Project Haven

"I don't understand how Puella could translate the book if she didn't read it."

Sophia gazed down at the rolling emerald forests passing below, absently listening to the drone of the Dragonfly's powerful duplonium motors.

"I've been thinking about that. Remember how Haukesworth Mouse said he could read books without understanding the language they were written in? He said he could sense the pure formless ideas embedded in the words?"

"He never told us how he did it though."

"I know, but I think that's what Puella the Wise One was doing. She didn't read the words, but somehow she absorbed the ideas while she was napping, then transferred those ideas into me. While I was sleeping, my own mind turned those formless ideas into words I would understand, into the language I'm familiar with."

"So Puella didn't actually translate the book?"

"Exactly, she just absorbed the ideas and transferred them to me. I also have a feeling when she spoke to us, it wasn't the little mouseling we were talking to, it was her inner self borrowing our voices and language."

"How could a little mouseling be so connected to her inner self?"

"I guess that's why they call her Puella the Wise One. I can't begin to imagine what she'll be like when she grows up."

"What was the book about?"

Proto poked his head between the seats. "The very question I was about to ask. Puella the Wise One is quite a conundrum, but the content of the red book is a far more pressing concern."

Sophia leaned back in her seat. "It's so strange, I can see the book in front of me as if I'm holding it, written in words I understand, but I don't need to read it because every word and every idea it contains is imprinted in my memory."

"So the book is about…"

"It's a history book."

"A history book? We went through all this for some moldy old history book?"

"It's not some moldy old history book, it's called *A Brief History of the Calamitous Metaphonium Haven Project.*"

"Um… just to be clear, what exactly does 'calamitous' mean? It's something bad, right?"

"It means it was a disaster, a tragedy, that something went terribly wrong."

"That's what I thought. What's a Metaphonium?"

"It was an invention which was supposed to save millions of lives, a device designed at the beginning of the Anarkkian wars by one of the greatest scientific minds in Mintarian history, Chief Master Scientist Gnuj. When the war was in its infancy, the Mintarians watched as dozens of planets were devastated by the Anarkkians, countless millions of lives lost. When it became clear the Anarkkian invasion forces were moving inexorably toward Mintari, Chief Master Scientist Gnuj turned to a machine he had been working on, realizing the device might be used to save countless Mintarian lives.

"Gnuj had spent years designing an impossibly complex device capable of creating a synthesized world, a world of such substance that a Mintarian could step into it in their physical form. Gnuj called his device a Metaphonium, and he was the first to test it, the first to enter a synthetic world. More importantly, he returned safely, with no apparent ill effects from his time in the new world.

"Each Metaphonium held within it the gateway to a single world capable of housing millions of Mintarians, providing them safe haven from the horrors of the deadly Anarkkian invasion fleet, protected from the silver attack spiders and horrific cloud bombs. Once the war was over, the Mintarian citizens would exit the Metaphoniums and return unscathed to Mintari. Their homes and cities would have to be rebuilt, but they would have survived the war.

"The Metaphonium Haven Project became a top priority for the Mintarian Science Guild. Within weeks, teams of Mintarian engineers and scientists were laboring around the clock in secret facilities, rushing to build the Metaphoniums before the Anarkkian invaders reached Mintari.

"As the Anarkkians drew closer, their massive armada only a few galaxies away, an epidemic of fear swept through Mintari, the population in a state of panic over the impending assault, the power and brutality of the Anarkkians being legendary.

"Three months before the first battle cruiser arrived, the Mintarian Science Guild announced the completion of twenty-nine Metaphoniums, assuring citizens the machines would provide a safe haven from the ravages of war.

"Even as the Mintarians streamed into these synthesized worlds, Gnuj was working furiously on a revolutionary new design. In a flash of insight he had realized his Metaphonium could be modified to create not one, but hundreds of thousands of synthetic worlds. The entire Mintarian population would be safe, but Gnuj had to modify the existing Metaphoniums before the Anarkkians reached Mintari.

"Fortune did not favor Chief Master Scientist Gnuj. He had modified only one Metaphonium with the new multi-world system when time ran out. The Anarkkians arrived, thousands of titanic Interstellar Assault Cruisers blinking into view around the planet. The Mintarian forces which had been sent to counter the armada using massively powerful time throttles had been utterly destroyed. In desperation, many thousands of Mark VI Time Throttles were fired at the battle cruisers from Mintarian ground based defense systems, but it was not enough. The devastation of Mintari had begun.

"A single blast from an Anarkkian battle cruiser's photonic beam projector could obliterate half a city, and one city in their sights was the great metropolis of Thuvia, home to over twelve million Mintarians. It had been evacuated several months earlier, many citizens taking refuge in one of Master Scientist Gnuj's Meta-phoniums, now hidden deep beneath Thuvia in a secure time vault. Unfortunately the Mintarians had drastically underestimated the ferocity and power of the Anarkkian weapons, the time vault's defense system proving woefully inadequate. In one calamitous moment the Metaphonium which lay beneath Thuvia was vaporized, the gateway between its synthetic world and the world of Mintari permanently severed. Eight million Mintarian civilians would survive the war, but they would never return to their home planet, trapped forever in a synthetic world.

"There was a great public outcry, wave after wave of Mintarians making their exodus from the Metaphonium Havens. These refugees brought with them terrifying tales of life within the synthetic worlds, whispers of the dreadful creatures who flickered out of nothingness, the sudden unnerving appearances of long deceased friends and relatives, of great cities which came and went in a single day, oceans where there had once been forests and deserts. It was these stories and countless others which brought a sudden and ignominious end to the great Mintarian Metaphonium Haven Project.

"The Mintarian Science Guild evacuated the synthetic worlds and destroyed the Metaphoniums. Millions of citizens managed to escape through spectral doorways to distant worlds, but most were not so lucky. Chief Master Scientist Gnuj's Metaphonium Haven Project would become a small and painful footnote in the Mintarian history books."

"That's horrible, all those lives lost. I'm glad I didn't live back then. It doesn't make sense, though. Why would I bring back some weird old history book from Okeanos?"

"I don't know the reason for it, but choosing that book was no accident. There's something we're missing, some piece of the puzzle we can't see yet."

"Do you think someone could have just made up that whole story? How could a machine have a whole world inside it? That's like trying to stuff Muridaan Falls into your shoe."

"It's not fiction. Remember your dream about Castle Caligari, when you were in the dungeon facing Mendacium the Dark Wizard?"

"It was terrifying."

"But it was just a dream, all in your head?"

"Of course it was, you were there in the dream with me."

"Here's my question, how did you fit Castle Caligari inside your head? Your head is about the size of a

TOM HOFFMAN

coconut, but you had a huge castle inside it."

Orville gave his best cackling laugh. "You're being loopy, it was a dream, the castle wasn't real, it was just something I was thinking about, imagining in my mind."

"Did the castle seem real when you were walking around in it?"

"Of course it did, it was completely real, and terrifying. Wait, are you saying those synthetic worlds might not really exist? That they were just thoughts inside a machine?"

"I'm saying those worlds might exist when you're in them, but not after you leave them. And anyway, the world wasn't destroyed, only the gateway leading to the world."

Orville groaned. "You're giving me a big giant headache, I need a cookie." He flicked his wrist and a freshly baked oatmeal cookie appeared in his paw.

"Mmm… one thing I know for sure, this yummy cookie is real."

"Is it? Maybe it's just a tasty illusion, maybe it's all in your head just like Castle Caligari was."

"Then it's a tasty illusion that I'm not sharing with you."

Chapter 12

Revelation

Orville rose with the morning sun, threw his clothes on and dashed down the stairs to find Proto in front of the wood stove.

"Morning, Proto, I hope you didn't forget today is painting day. Is that oatmeal?"

"Warm oatmeal with brown sugar, cinnamon, and a smattering of crunchy red snackles and lizard tails."

"Lizard tails is one of your weird Cube vegetables, right?"

"Quite so, they have some resemblance to green beans but I chose to give them that rather whimsical name to make them sound more appealing, enticing you to eat veggies."

"It's a good name, but it doesn't exactly make me want to eat them. You're going to help us paint Ebenezer's house, right? Sophia will be here in a few minutes. She wants to hear Ebenezer's story. She thinks it's important, that it might have something to do with my dream about Okeanos and the red book."

"I would be delighted to help. Are you going to mention to Ebenezer that we saw him disappear when he stepped through his front door?"

"No, I want to hear what he says about Aislin first. There's definitely a lot he hasn't told us, but he's a good mouse. He really misses Aislin, loves her a lot."

Orville was helping Proto with the dishes when he felt the sharp pinch on his leg.

"Giant crab in the kitchen!"

Orville whipped around to see a smirking Sophia doing her best impression of a gigantic angry crab.

"Very funny, let's all tease Orville about the giant crab again. If you remember, I was the first one to see the crab and I'm pretty sure I saved both your lives."

Sophia clasped her paws together, batting her eyes. "Orville Wellington Mouse, my hero!"

Orville flicked his wrist and three large paint brushes appeared in his paw. "I saved your lives on the Isle of the Serpent, but there's no escape from painting Ebenezer's house."

With all three of the adventurers helping, the first coat of paint was on by late afternoon. Orville stepped back to admire their work.

"It looks amazing."

"I love the color. It's such a nice warm yellow, like a sunny day. It really brightens it up, makes it nice and cheery."

Orville turned at the sound of approaching footsteps.

Ebenezer stepped around the corner, his eyes on the freshly painted cottage.

"I'd forgotten how lovely this house was." He stood silently for a moment, a faraway look in his eyes. Orville knew he was thinking about Aislin.

"We'll put the second coat on tomorrow and paint the trim white. It should look really nice. We were thinking about painting your front door a nice bright blue."

"That sounds perfect. I can't thank you enough for doing all this. I've decided to start working on the garden, try to make it look like it did when Aislin was here."

"It must have been lovely."

"It was beautiful, she was a natural gardener, loved her flowers, especially blue moreilias. Let's go inside, it's time you heard the whole story."

Orville stepped into the house, sensing he was one step closer to a confrontation with the horrific black smoking stick figure. He had faced fearful creatures before, but nothing like that.

Ebenezer took a seat in a wooden chair, facing the three adventurers, an uneasy look on his face.

"Not sure where to begin. I told Orville how Aislin got up in the morning, played the Sound Piano, started breakfast, said she was running to the store. When she didn't come back I searched everywhere, talked to everyone. She would have walked past dozens of mice on her way to the store, but I couldn't find a single mouse who saw her that morning.

"It took me almost a year to eliminate every possibility except one. Aislin's disappearance had something to do with the Sound Piano, something to do with the notes she played that morning. When she opened the front door she said, 'Good heavens'. The way she said it made me think she was seeing something beautiful, something she had never seen before. I remember a few of the sounds she played, but I was half asleep at the time, and she'd played a lot of different ones, more than usual.

"Day after day I sat at the Sound Piano, playing a few dozen notes, then running to the front door and opening it, each time hoping to see something different, something that would have surprised Aislin.

"One morning when I played four particular notes something unexpected happened. One of the six yellow lights on the Sound Piano turned violet. I wrote down the four notes I had played and continued, trying endless combinations. Three days later another yellow light turned violet. I finally realized what was happening. The Sound Piano keyboard is divided into six sections, each one holding thirty-six keys. When I played four keys in a row in one section, the yellow light would turn violet. The solution was obvious, all six lights had to be violet.

"I sat down at the piano, played four notes in the first section, watched the light blink violet. Then four notes in the second section. Another violet light. Then the third, the fourth, the fifth, and finally the sixth. All six lights were violet and the Sound Piano was making a deep humming noise I had not heard before.

"Walking across the room to the front door was the hardest thing I've ever done. If I was wrong about the Sound Piano being responsible for Aislin's disappearance, then my last hope of finding her would be gone. I was not wrong. When I swung the door open I stood facing an ancient forest filled with magnificent blue trees, the tallest I'd ever seen. The air was rich, earthy, the fragrance from the forest sweet and intoxicating. A great iridescent aquamarine bird glided past so slowly it looked as though it was floating, long flowing golden tail feathers trailing behind it. This had to have been what Aislin saw.

"I didn't hesitate, I stepped into the forest, calling Aislin's name as loudly as I could. When I turned back to look at my house, I saw only the front door floating six inches above the ground in the midst of a vast primordial forest. When I opened the door I saw the inside of my house. A sharp hissing came from above me and I looked up, spotting an enormous orange and yellow striped snake winding its way down through the massive gnarled tree limbs, its long green tongue flickering in and out. Another movement caught my eye, two more of the gigantic striped snakes were rapidly descending from the adjacent tree, heading toward me. I am terrified of snakes, and this was too much. I ran into my house, slamming the door behind me, my heart pounding, my legs shaking. Once I had calmed down, I cracked the front door open and peered out. The forest was gone, Muridaan Falls had returned."

Orville realized he'd been holding his breath.

"Creekers! That's incredible!"

Sophia's eyes were on the Sound Piano.

Proto added, "Most curious, it sounds as if the Sound Piano opened a spectral gateway to a distant world. Certainly the Anarkkians and the Elders had such advanced technologies, but your Sound Piano is like nothing I've ever seen before."

"You wrote down the key combination you used to reach the blue forest world?"

"I did, and all the key combinations used to reach the other worlds I have visited. The number of possible key combinations is staggering, but I will not stop searching. I have visited over two hundred worlds with no sign of Aislin. Some of the worlds are brutally inhospitable, many filled with terrifying snakes."

"The precise number of possible key combinations is three hundred and fifty-three thousand, four hundred and twenty-seven. If you visited one world a day, it would take you nine hundred and ninety-three years to visit them all. There is always the unlikely possibility the next world you visit will be the one Aislin entered, but the odds of such an event occurring would be quite astronomical."

"None of that matters. I will keep searching until I find her."

"That snow you tracked into the house last summer was from a world you visited?"

"A stark, frozen, inhospitable land. No mouse could survive it, and Aislin would not have entered such a frigid world."

"A few days ago we were flying a Dragonfly over your house and saw you disappear when you stepped out of your front door."

"I stepped into a stark and beautiful desert, quickly proving itself to be a fearsome world filled with ferocious lizard creatures."

Sophia had been silently studying the Sound Piano. "Orville, do you have the red book with you?"

Orville pulled the book out of his coat pocket, giving it to Sophia.

"I should have thought of this sooner. There's a diagram tucked into the back cover." Sophia slid out the yellowed sheet of paper, gingerly unfolding it. "It's a schematic circuit diagram for the Metaphonium. Proto, do you recognize these symbols?"

Proto glanced at the drawing curiously, something catching his eye.

"Good heavens, is this really possible?"

Sophia nodded. "It's more than possible. You saw the number of integrated subcarrier sensors?"

"Two hundred and sixteen. That cannot be coincidental."

"No, it can't be. This is why Orville brought the red book back from Okeanos."

"What are you talking about? Two hundred and sixteen sub what?"

"This is a diagram of the internal circuitry of the Metaphonium. It has two hundred and sixteen integrated subcarrier sensors. The Sound Piano has two hundred and sixteen keys."

Orville stared blankly at the diagram. "Are you saying the Sound Piano is a Metaphonium? That's not possible."

"Why not?"

"It just isn't."

"Think about it, it makes perfect sense. You brought the red book back from Okeanos two days before Ebenezer showed you his Sound Piano. The timing of the events is beyond chance. This is not a Sound Piano, it is the last Metaphonium ever made, the Metaphonium modified by Chief Master Scientist Gnuj with his new multi-world system."

Orville approached the Metaphonium, running his paw across the strangely shaped keys, the smooth brass dials, the yellow lights. A framed photograph hanging above the enigmatic instrument caught his eye. It was a faded wedding picture portraying a handsome young Ebenezer Mouse and his beautiful bride. Orville could scarcely breathe. There was no doubt, none at all. The mysterious white robed mouse Orville had seen at the Okeanos book fair was Aislin Mouse.

Chapter 13

Proto's Discovery

"You're absolutely certain it was Aislin?"

"Yes, I recognized her the instant I saw the photograph. I didn't want to tell Ebenezer because the last time I saw her she was a ghost. We shouldn't say anything until we know why she wanted me to have the red book, what that black smoking stick creature is, and if she's still alive."

"I agree, it would upset him too much. We'll wait until we know more."

"Who do you think hid the Metaphonium in Ebenezer's house?"

"We'll probably never know. The book said the Mintarian Science Guild destroyed the twenty-nine Metaphoniums from the Haven Project, but it didn't mention anything about the last Metaphonium, the one Gnuj modified. It doesn't really matter how it got here, what does matter is finding Aislin."

"Proto's still up in his room with the red book. He's

researching the circuit diagram through that portal connection to his crystal storage records back at the Cube. I had to make my own breakfast this morning."

"A scrumptious bowl of oatmeal cookies and a plate of tasty little cakes?"

"Very funny. For your information, I had a healthy breakfast of warm oatmeal, diced red snackles, and a glass of fresh snapberry juice. I'm trying not to eat so many sweets, get a little more protein in my diet." Orville did his best to sound thoughtful and mature.

Sophia turned at the unmistakable sound of Proto's heavy footsteps descending the stairs.

Proto entered the kitchen, his face wreathed in a victorious grin.

"You found something?"

"Are you referring to my current research project regarding the internal circuitry dynamics of the last Metaphonium?"

"Of course she is, what did you find out?"

"As it turns out, I may quite possibly have single handedly solved the puzzle of the last Metaphonium. It's Proto to the rescue, once again." He raised one eyebrow dramatically, glancing back and forth between Orville and Sophia.

"Proto, did you or did you not find out where Aislin is?"

"A simple question, but one demanding a complex answer. I do not currently know where she is, but I am confident I have discovered the means to determine her location. The answer has been sitting in front of us all along."

Orville and Sophia jumped to their feet, their ongoing discussion of Orville's eating habits forgotten. Ten minutes later the three adventurers were standing in Ebenezer's living room.

"Proto thinks he may be able to recover the key combination Aislin used."

Ebenezer dropped to the sofa, his paws clasped together.

Proto approached the Metaphonium, holding up the red book.

"After some rather extensive research into ancient Mintarian synthetic neurosynaptic data retention, I discovered the last Metaphonium contains within it a tiny ferillium crystal, its sole purpose to track and record the synthetic gateways existing within it. Fortunately for us, Ebenezer kept a detailed record of all the worlds he has visited. Logic would dictate that the world created immediately prior to Ebenezer's snake infested primordial blue forest world is the one we are looking for, the world created by Aislin."

"How does it work? Do we have to look inside the Metaphonium?"

"It's far simpler than that. Chief Master Scientist Gnuj was quite brilliant, providing a most elegant solution. All I have to do is push the circular brass knob directly beneath the first yellow light. When I do, the twenty-four keys used to open the previous world should light up."

Ebenezer rose from the sofa and hurried to his room,

returning moments later with a tattered canvas bound book. "This is my journal, a record of all the worlds I visited and all the key combinations I used."

"Excellent." Proto opened the journal, flipping to the most recent entry. He pointed to Ebenezer's diagram.

"If I am correct in my assessment, these are the keys which should light up." He gave a reassuring smile to Ebenezer, then pressed the brass knob beneath the first yellow light.

Twenty-four Metaphonium keys glowed brightly. Proto studied the diagram closely, then nodded.

"The key combinations match."

Proto pushed the brass tab another two hundred and fourteen times, methodically checking and rechecking to make certain the glowing keys matched the ones listed in Ebenezer's journal.

Orville's head was nodding when Proto called out, "That last combination was for the blue forest world, the first one Ebenezer visited. The next key combination that lights up will be the world created by Aislin."

Ebenezer's eyes were riveted to the keyboard. Sophia gripped Orville's paw tightly.

Proto pressed the tab. Twenty-four Metaphonium keys glowed brightly.

"You found Aislin."

"We have not found her yet, but we have found the synthetic world she entered."

"You'll find her, I know you will."

Sophia rubbed Ebenezer's shoulder, her eyes meeting Orville's. They both knew finding Aislin would be far more difficult than simply stepping into another world and bringing her back. More troubling to Sophia was Aislin's appearance as a ghostly apparition.

Scenes of imagined confrontations with the burning charcoal stick figure filled Orville's mind. He was also remembering the words spoken to him by Puella the Wise One, words he had not shared with Sophia.

"She shall face her greatest fear in Elysian. You must help her remember."

Chapter 14

Brother Solus

"Mum, it's perfectly safe, we know which world Aislin is in and we know how to get back home. Ebenezer has visited hundreds of synthetic worlds."

"You sound just like your papa before he would go on a mission, always telling me how safe it was. It's so nice of you and Sophia to help Ebenezer, but please be careful."

"I promise we will. Ebenezer seemed really cranky at first, but now I like him. He's kind of funny sometimes, and he really loves Aislin. I hope we find her, I hope she's not a ghost."

"I remember when she disappeared, we all helped search for her. Ebenezer was devastated, he was never the same after that. He hardly came out of his house." Mum turned to Sophia with a smile. "You'll take care of my little Orville?"

Orville gave a screech. "I'm not your little Orville! I'm a Metaphysical Adventurer and a member of the

Dragonfly Squadron."

"I know that, I was just being funny. Oh, before I forget, I want to show you that thing we were talking about." She gave a conspiratorial grin, holding out a small piece of folded paper for Orville, her eyes on Proto.

Orville unfolded the paper and read it, a smile crossing his face.

Proto was instantly curious, ambling over to the spice rack in an ultimately futile attempt to see what was written on the paper. Orville turned his back to Proto, crumpling the note and stuffing it into his pocket. It was clear to Proto that Orville did not want him to see it.

Proto's eyes were on Orville's pocket.

"Would anyone like another flapcake? There's still plenty of snapberry syrup left."

"I'm full, thanks, and I should go finish packing."

"You're quite certain you don't want me to bring a heavy particle beam vaporization projector?"

"I'm certain. I'm not worried about Aislin's world. If it was really creepy with giant snakes and centipedes she wouldn't have entered it."

Proto was about to mention the possibility that a horrific creature with razor sharp claws had grabbed Aislin and dragged her out of the house, but thought the better of it, not wanting to upset Mum. He frowned, unable to put the mysterious note Mum had given Orville out of his mind. Why had Orville stuffed the note into his pocket? Proto couldn't think of a single reason why they would be keeping a secret from him, and Proto was not fond of secrets.

After many hugs and an abundance of sound advice from Papa on staying safe in other worlds, the three adventurers headed to Ebenezer's house. The bright blue front door swung open just as Orville raised his paw to knock.

"I hardly slept at all last night. I don't know how to thank you for doing this. You'll be careful won't you? I'm old enough to know the chances of finding Aislin are slim, that she would have come back by now if she could." Tears were welling up in Ebenezer's eyes.

Sophia gave him a warm hug.

"I promise you we'll do everything we can to find her. Everything."

Proto stepped over to the Metaphonium. "Are we ready?"

Orville nodded.

Proto tapped the key combination to Aislin's synthetic world. One by one, six yellow lights blinked violet, a low hum emanating from the Metaphonium.

"That's the sound it makes when the gateway opens. Please be careful, don't take unnecessary chances."

Orville swung open the front door.

"Creekers!"

Sophia peered over his shoulder across a vast rolling meadow of brilliant pink and yellow wildflowers sitting beneath a sparkling azure blue sky. Beyond the meadow lay a magnificent emerald green forest.

"This is incredible. I can see why Aislin wasn't

afraid, it's almost like the world of the Others."

"Nothing compares to that. Nothing."

"I know, but it's still really beautiful. There's a path, we should take it, it's probably what Aislin did."

The three adventurers stepped across the threshold into Aislin's world. With a wave and a smile, Orville closed the door behind them. He eyed the narrow path that wound through the glorious blossomed meadow.

"I know it looks peaceful here, but we should keep our eyes open for danger. There's a reason Aislin didn't come back, and whatever it is, we don't want it to happen to us. I wish I knew why she appeared as a ghost, and how she got from here to Muridaan Falls."

Proto's eyes glowed with a pale green light. "I am scanning the area but have found no life forms other than vegetation and small insects."

Orville grinned as he strolled through the carpet of colorful blossoms. "That's good news, no giant snakes like the ones Ebenezer saw."

"The path goes all the way to the forest. The trees remind me of the ones in Muridaan Falls."

"It is nice, it feels familiar. I like that."

The trio trekked across the meadow, stepping into the forest, warm sunlight flickering down through the branches across the leaf covered forest floor.

"The forest is smaller than I thought it would be, only a half mile or so across. Nothing scary so far. I wonder why Aislin didn't come back? Maybe she got lost."

When they emerged from the forest Orville stopped short, holding up one paw.

"It's Okeanos. I recognize the thatched roofs, the winding dirt lane that goes through the village."

"Perhaps our adventure shall be a short one. Perhaps we shall find Aislin in the round building where the book fair was held. Perhaps we shall not encounter even one scary creature on this adventure." Proto did not sound happy.

"If she was just sitting around at a book fair she would have come back through the doorway."

Sophia studied the cottages as they trekked through the village. "It's a little weird the village is deserted. It's not exactly spooky, just a little weird. The windows on that one house are broken, like something was trying to get inside."

"This could have been one of the worlds used in the Metaphonium Haven Project, abandoned when everyone was evacuated. Maybe they were angry and smashed the windows."

"That's possible, but the Mintarians had advanced technology. It's highly unlikely they'd be living in quaint thatched roof cottages."

"There it is, that's the book fair building where I saw Aislin and the burning stick creature."

"I don't wish to cause any undue alarm, but the front door appears to be open, and there is a pair of boots sitting on the steps."

"There weren't any boots on the steps in my dream."

"I think we should go in. A terrifying smoking charcoal stick creature would not carefully place his boots outside the front door."

"And he'd have a lot more boots than that. I couldn't tell how many legs he had, but there were a lot. The book fair sign is gone. Maybe I just made up the book fair in my dream. Maybe I made up the smoking charcoal creature."

Orville approached the weathered round building.

"It has the same thatched roof as in my dream."

"Did you notice the hanging flower baskets? They look almost like the ones Plautilla had hanging outside her inn on Tectar."

"They're pretty. They weren't in my dream either." Orville stopped ten feet from the door. "What's that?"

He walked over to an old weathered board lying on the ground, partially covered with dried leaves and dirt. He kneeled down, brushing off the leaves. The board was old, the wood rotten, the paint almost gone. Orville hesitated, then flipped it over. He groaned, raising the board so Sophia could see the faintly painted words.

OKEANOS BOOK FAIR
TODAY ONLY
ALL VISITORS WELCOME

"It's okay, it doesn't matter. We're here to find Aislin, not to worry about old book fair signs."

"You're right, it's probably nothing." Orville walked to the half opened door, knocking loudly, part of him expecting a great black smoking creature to spring out of the building.

"I hear footsteps."

The creature who answered Orville's knock wore a dark gray cloak, its face hidden in the nebulous shadows of a floppy hood. Orville's eyes widened when he saw yellow claws dangling down from its long tattered sleeves. The three adventurers stood motionless, waiting for it to speak.

"Why are you here? I seek solitude, not chattering visitors."

Sophia attempted a friendly smile. "I'm so sorry, we're new to the area and we seem to have lost our way. I wonder if you might help us?"

The mysterious cloaked figure flipped its hood back, inspecting his three uninvited guests. The creature was a Mintarian, possessing a snake like head and two rows of long curved teeth.

The old Mintarian eyed them with dark suspicion. He stepped in front of Sophia, looking deeply into her eyes, then reached out with one clawed hand, poking her shoulder.

"You seem real enough. Come in. I'm warning you, I do not tolerate insolent or slovenly behavior of any kind."

Orville glanced nervously at Sophia, uncertain of the Mintarian's intentions. They stepped into the building, a shiver running through Orville when he saw the great round table from his dream. The books were gone, the table now ringed by a half dozen rough hewn wooden chairs. Scattered plates and glasses sat on the table along with several unlit candles.

"I'm Orville Mouse, and these are my good friends

Sophia Mouse and Proto the Rabbiton."

The Mintarian did not even attempt a smile.

"I am Brother Solus, last of the Mintarian Grays. What is your purpose here? Be succinct, do not jabber endlessly about inconsequential details."

"We're looking for a lost friend. Her name is Aislin Mouse and we think she may have arrived here twelve years ago."

Brother Solus was silent, his gaze fixed on Orville.

"Um, this is a really lovely village, did mice used to live here?"

"The village has been abandoned for as long as I can remember. Where did you say you were from?"

"We're from a little town called Muridaan Falls, in the country of Symoca."

"Never heard of it. Your missing friend was from there also?"

"Yes, she lived next door to us."

Brother Solus sat down in one of the wooden chairs.

Orville blurted out, "Do you ever have any book fairs around here? I like books a lot. And book fairs."

"You're an odd one, why would I have a book fair? The village is deserted, there's no one here except me. Would I purchase my own books?"

Orville did not mention the sign he had found outside. He did not want to further antagonize Brother Solus.

"Do you happen to know the name of this village?"

"Of course I do, it's Okeanos."

Orville's eyes widened. "Oh...we're really kind of

lost, can you tell us what country this is?"

"There's no country, it's just Elysian. That's all there is. Elysian."

Orville's stomach twisted, remembering Puella the Wise One's words. *She shall face her greatest fear in Elysian.*

Sophia glanced around the interior of the building. "You're quite certain you haven't seen our friend Aislin Mouse? She's very beautiful, I don't think you would forget her if you'd seen her."

"She's beautiful?"

"Yes, very beautiful. Her husband is Ebenezer Mouse and he misses her terribly. He can think of nothing else, he has never lost hope that one day she will return."

Brother Solus' face softened slightly, but he did not answer Sophia's question.

Proto swung his huge pack down, setting it on the floor with a loud thump. He rummaged around inside it and pulled out a colorful metal tin. Orville grinned, knowing the tin was filled with tasty little cakes. Nobody could make new friends the way Proto could.

Brother Solus watched with suspicion as Proto set the tin on the table and gingerly remove the lid.

"I brought a tin of the most delightful tasty little cakes if you would care to try one. They're my own creation, and quite popular back in Muridaan Falls, some saying they're the best little cakes they've ever had."

Brother Solus took one look and pushed the tin away

with a scowl. "Revolting. Are you trying to poison me?"

"Poison you? Oh my heavens, no, these are freshly baked, made from the finest ingredients."

"Poison. Filled with sugar. I won't allow it. I eat only grains, vegetables, nuts, and occasionally fresh fruit, all in extreme moderation."

Proto regained his composure, smoothly returning the tin of cakes to his pack. "You're quite right, of course. Yours is a carefully considered and well balanced diet. Very sound dietary advice indeed."

"I don't tolerate sweets in my home. Shows weakness, lack of fortitude, no self control, slovenly behavior."

"Quite so. If I might ask, were the Mintarian Grays an order of monks?"

"Of course they were, everyone knows that. They've been around for millennia. I am the last one."

"So you've lived here in Okeanos for quite some time?"

"For as long as I can remember. My life is based in solitude and deep reflection."

"Do you happen to remember a very beautiful mouse passing through Okeanos?"

Brother Solus gave an irritated scowl. "You've asked me that question twice already." He paused. "You said her husband misses her?"

"Dreadfully so, I'm afraid. He is quite distraught. She was the love of his life."

Brother Solus' face could have been carved from

stone. "I saw her. The Shadow King took her. Go home while you are still able."

Chapter 15

Caterpillars

"Who's the Shadow King?"

"Return to Muridaan Falls and count yourselves fortunate to still be drawing breath. Your friend is gone."

Sophia's face hardened. "We're not going home. We're going to find our friend with or without your help."

Brother Solus snapped, "You have not an inkling of the path which lies before you. Whatever you may have experienced in past adventures shall have ill prepared you for such a confrontation. The Shadow King is an abomination, a dark insidious creature whose very being infects your deepest thoughts with nightmarish terrors. By its very nature, it is impossible to destroy."

"Where does it live? How do we find it? You say you're the last of the Mintarian Gray Monks. I thought monks were supposed to help those in need."

"I am helping you by telling you to return to your home, saving your lives by my warning. Do such insidious monstrosities hold no fear for you?"

"Of course they do, but I'm not going to let fear stop

116

me from doing what I know to be right, what I know to be good."

Brother Solace leaned back in his chair, studying Sophia's face.

"It is possible I have misjudged you to some slight degree. Clearly you will not be dissuaded from your ill conceived venture. The realm of the Shadow King lies far to the east. The Great River borders his land, a watery line between the known and the unknown, between the light and the dark. Within this shadowy realm great battles are fought and often lost."

"What does that mean?"

"You shall discover the meaning of my words on your own. I will accede to your wishes, take you to the Great River, but I shall go not one step further."

"Do you happen to know exactly what this Shadow King looks like? Is he a big burning charcoal stick creature?"

"I cannot say."

"You said the Shadow King took Aislin, didn't you see him then?"

"It was a dark and confusing time, I have cast aside such bleak memories, all but the memory of the beautiful mouse. I am Brother Solus, the last of the Mintarian Grays, I live a life of tranquility and reflection."

Orville was getting a curious feeling, but couldn't put his paw on it. Something was not right about Brother Solus.

"That would be great if you could take us there."

"We shall leave at sunrise."

"How far is it to the Great River?"

Brother Solus gave a thin smile.

"It all depends."

He rose from his chair and stepped through a narrow doorway, closing and locking the door behind him with a loud click.

"Creekers. He's not exactly friendly, not at all like the Thirteenth Monk. It all depends? What does that mean?"

Sophia shook her head. "He has a lot of secrets, but I have a strong feeling he will play a vital role in bringing Aislin safely home."

"What do you think he meant by all that stuff about great battles being fought? I don't like the sound of that."

"I have no idea. He said we'd discover it on our own."

Proto rubbed his great silver hands together, making no attempt to hide his glee.

"This sounds dreadful, quite dreadful indeed. I wonder what manner of dark creatures we'll encounter east of the Great River, deep in the realm of that dastardly smoking Shadow King?"

Orville slumped down in a chair. "I'm guessing they'll be big burning glowing charcoal stick creatures who like to eat mouse sandwiches for lunch."

Proto's eyes were bright. "Oh dear, what a dreadful thought."

Sophia clapped her paws together.

"Enough scary talk. Let's have dinner, I'm starving.

Orville, why don't you shape some sleeping bags and pillows while I shape dinner."

"Maybe I'll have a couple of Proto's tasty little poisonous sugar cakes."

* * * *

The early morning light streamed through the narrow windows as Orville dressed himself, the fearsome Shadow King occupying his thoughts.

Sophia woke shortly after, quickly converting her sleeping bag back to a thought cloud.

Proto set two plates on the great round table. "Tasty snapberry flapcakes hot off the griddle, and fresh brimbleberry juice."

"Where did you get a griddle?"

"I had one in my pack. There was plenty of room since I didn't bring the heavy particle beam vaporization projector."

"I'm starting to wish you had brought that thing. This whole adventure is taking a scary turn, all that stuff Brother Solus said about battles and the Shadow King. What do you think we'll find on the other side of the river?"

Before Proto could answer, Brother Solus stepped into the room, a long walking stick in one hand.

"You are still determined to enter the realm of the Shadow King?"

"We are. I promised Ebenezer Mouse we would do everything we could to find Aislin."

119

"As you wish, so it shall be. I will guide you to the Great River. From that point on you shall be on your own."

"How big is the river?"

"I have never seen it."

An hour later the party of adventurers was strolling through a grand forest, the morning sun sparkling off the dew covered ferns.

"These trees are amazing. They'd be really fun to climb. We have trees just like these back in Muridaan Falls, but they're a lot smaller, about half this size."

"Brother Solus, have you done much exploring around Elysian? Are there any other villages?"

"I have done a certain amount of exploration, encountering only one other village. It was deserted, just as Okeanos is. These days, I spend my time in quiet reflection."

"It sounds relaxing. Do you ever get lonely?"

"I do not. I am the last of the Mintarian Grays."

"It is nice and peaceful here, and the wildflowers are beautiful. Where did you live before you came to Elysian?"

"I have lived in Elysian for as long as I can remember."

"Oh, right, I forgot. Sorry." A blue thought cloud flashed out of Orville's ear over to Sophia. She drew it to her, hearing Orville's voice in her mind.

"It's kind of weird he doesn't remember how he got here. He had to come from somewhere, unless he was abandoned when he was a mouseling."

"If he was abandoned, how would he know he was the last of the Mintarian Grays?"

"There's something odd going on, but I can't figure it out."

Proto strolled along behind Orville and Sophia, his eyes scanning the spectacular forest.

"The ferns here are quite lovely. They remind me of my youth, when I lived with the family of Elders. The fields behind their home were filled with ferns just like these. Such fond memories I have of those carefree days."

A glint of white beneath a cluster of ferns caught Proto's eye. He reached down and pushed the leaves aside, picking up a crumpled ball of paper. He glanced ahead at Sophia and Orville, smoothing out the note, reading the scrawled words.

I'm tired of him.

Proto frowned. Was this the note Mum had given to Orville? The note he had stuffed into his pocket? If it was, who was she tired of? Perhaps it was someone at her work, certainly not Papa. He tossed the note back into the ferns. This was Mum's business, not his.

Orville's initial anxiety was diminishing. The forest was mesmerizing in its beauty, and he had spotted some lovely blue butterflies fluttering about in the sunlight, their shadows darting to and fro across the forest floor. He held Sophia's paw as they walked along the grassy path.

"Did you see those blue butterflies? They're really pretty."

"I saw them. I'm not too crazy about butterflies, I like birds a lot more. They can soar and swoop through the sky, high above the trees, up into the clouds. When I formshift into a glowbird it's amazing, flying is so much fun. Don't forget Master Marloh said he would teach you how to formshift."

"I didn't forget, it seems a little scary though. Suppose I get stuck being a bird and can't change back? I'd have to spend the rest of my life eating squooshy bugs."

Sophia laughed, squeezing his paw. "Don't worry, I'll put tasty little cakes out on the window sill for you to snack on. Maybe a plate of yummy earthworms."

Brother Solus stopped, raising one hand, glaring at Sophia and Orville. "Something is happening up ahead."

"What is it?"

"Butterflies."

Orville peered through the trees. "Creekers, you're right. There's thousands of them. Where did they come from?"

"I can only speculate as to their origin."

Sophia felt an inexplicable fear roll through her, but said nothing, doing her best to shake it off. She had not slept well the previous night. She was tired.

They pushed on beneath the spreading branches of the magnificent trees, more and more of the blue butterflies appearing, fluttering and swooping about in the warm sunlight. One of them landed on Sophia's shoulder. She gave a small shriek and brushed it off.

"I'm really not very fond of butterflies."

"At least they don't have big claws and razor sharp gnashing teeth." Orville grinned at Proto.

Fifteen minutes later Brother Solus stopped again. "This would explain the butterflies. The trees ahead are infested with millions of caterpillars."

Orville stepped forward but Sophia did not. She gripped his paw tightly, holding him back.

"Let's go, I don't want to lose sight of Brother Solus."

Panic filled Orville when he looked at Sophia, her face twisted with fear, her breathing fast and shallow.

"What's wrong?" His eyes darted around the forest, searching for some horrific creature.

"What is it? What did you see?"

"Caterpillars."

"What about them?"

"I'm afraid of them."

Orville gave a quick laugh. "No, really, what's wrong? What did you see?"

"I'm afraid of them."

A conversation from long ago popped into Orville's head. He had asked Sophia if anything ever scared her, and she had said furry caterpillars did. He thought she had been joking.

"You're really afraid of caterpillars? What are they going to do, tickle you with their little feet?" He grinned, rubbing her shoulder.

"We have to go back. I can't go through those trees. I can't."

"I don't understand, those horrible creatures in the

Senyph Ocean didn't scare you, and you weren't afraid of the giant centipedes on Periculum. How can you be afraid of a tiny caterpillar?"

Sophia's voice was low. "I am not going through those trees."

"She shall face her greatest fear in Elysian. You must help her remember."

Orville's mind was racing. Puella the Wise One had known this would happen. What was he supposed to help Sophia remember?

"It's okay, we don't have to go through them. I'm kind of tired anyway. Let's sit down on that log and rest for a bit."

Sophia sat down and leaned forward, paws covering her face. "I'm sorry, I know it's silly to be so afraid of caterpillars."

"Being afraid isn't silly. I'm afraid of lots of weird stuff, hundreds of things. You're only afraid of one thing. You've always been afraid of them?"

"Since I was little."

"Do you remember the first time one scared you?"

"I feel kind of sick, I might throw up."

Orville put one arm around Sophia and held her paw. "You're safe. We'll be fine. You don't have to look at them, you don't have to walk past them. We'll figure something out."

"Thanks. I don't really know when it started, I've just always been scared of them. It's not that I'm afraid they'll bite me or anything, it's just the sight of them, it does something awful to me."

"What does it feel like when you see one?"

Sophia shivered, closing her eyes. "It's the most terrible feeling of dread you can imagine, deep inside me. Like they'll do something. Something really, really bad."

"What would they do?"

Sophia was crying.

"I'm sorry, we can talk about something else."

A sudden movement caught Orville's eye. He looked up, expecting to see butterflies, seeing instead a dark roiling cloud from the shadows drifting toward them. This was bad. Sophia was already terrified, he didn't want to scare her even more. He put both arms around her and held her close, saying, "It's okay, I'm right here with you."

"Orville... the caterpillars..."

The black cloud shot forward, enveloping the two best friends, their minds merging, a forgotten memory flooding through them.

Sophia was small, a little mouseling. She was sitting on her bed, Papa next to her.

"Mum is gone. The doctors did everything they could but they couldn't save her. They tried everything. She was so sick that—"

Papa was sobbing, his arms around Sophia. One of his tears fell on her paw. She watched it soak into her fur. She'd never seen Papa cry before.

She stared out the window, her mind numb, her paws cold. The trees outside were covered with caterpillars.

Papa was wrong, Mum would never leave her, she would never do that. Her mum would never do that. It was the caterpillars. They had taken her mum away. Maybe they were going to come back and take Papa away. Maybe they would come back and take her away.

The two best friends held each other for a long time. Finally Sophia wiped her eyes and said, "The caterpillars didn't take her. My mum was really sick and the doctors couldn't save her."

"I saw everything, I saw what happened."

"I know, I'm glad you were with me when I remembered."

"It must have been awful, I can't imagine. You were so young."

"I hid the memory away, it was so painful, but some deeper part of me remembered seeing the caterpillars, that's why I was terrified of them."

"How are you feeling?"

"I'll be okay, I can do this. We have to find Aislin."

Sophia got to her feet, turning toward the trees, ready to face her greatest fear.

"Orville, they're gone! The butterflies are gone, the caterpillars are gone. They're all gone!"

Chapter 16

The Note

When Brother Solus and Proto realized Orville and Sophia were not behind them, they turned around, heading back down the forest trail. Proto spotted the two best friends holding paws, deep in conversation.

Brother Solus eyed the trees. "The caterpillars are gone, as are the blue butterflies."

Proto was intrigued. "Most curious, the butterflies could have flown away, but I can think of no logical reason for the sudden disappearance of the caterpillars."

"Elysian is full of curious happenings. Do not trouble your thoughts with such matters."

"Quite so, but there must be a logical scientific explanation for it. Certainly millions of caterpillars don't just vanish in the blink of an eye."

"What's done is done, there is no need to dwell on the past."

Proto nodded agreeably, realizing when it came to understanding mysterious events he had a far different attitude than Brother Solus. He waved to Orville and Sophia.

"What happened? Where were you?"

"Sophia tripped on a root and twisted her ankle. She's okay now though."

Brother Solus was certain Sophia had not tripped over a root. He knew exactly where the caterpillars had come from, but had no idea where they had gone.

Proto hurried over to the two best friends. "We should camp here for the night so you can rest your ankle. The sun will be going down in a few hours. We'll set up camp and have a nice relaxing dinner." He leaned over to Sophia and whispered, "I'll leave a tin of tasty little cakes in your tent."

Orville shaped a roaring campfire before he remembered Brother Solus was watching. The look he gave Orville was one of profound disapproval.

Brother Solus retired early, after giving Orville and Sophia a stern lecture regarding the physical and spiritual benefits of going to bed at sunset and rising at dawn. Orville did his best to listen attentively, but his thoughts kept drifting back to the puzzle of the vanishing caterpillars.

With Brother Solus retired for the night, the three adventurers sat around the blazing campfire discussing the events of the day.

"Let's think about this. Puella the Wise One told Orville I would face my greatest fear in Elysian and we ran into the caterpillars. Once I remembered why I was so scared of them, they vanished."

"Do you think remembering what happened somehow made them disappear?"

"I don't know. Mice dream about things they love and things they fear, but this isn't a dream, it's a synthetic physical world we entered through the Metaphonium."

"Maybe we should have some tasty little cakes. That might help us think better."

Sophia laughed, thwacking Orville's arm. "I'm going to tell Brother Solus and you'll get in big trouble."

Proto rose to his feet, stretching his great silver arms.

"I believe I shall take a relaxing stroll through the woods. Even in a lovely forest such as this, we must remain ever vigilant. Ebenezer did say a great many of the worlds he visited were filled with the most dreadfully fearsome snakes, most of them quite venomous I should imagine."

Orville grinned as Proto disappeared into the woods, the grin fading rapidly when he realized the possible implications of what Proto had just said. Was it coincidental that Ebenezer was terrified of snakes and the synthetic worlds he visited were filled with them?

As Proto strolled through the shadowy trees searching for dreadful nocturnal predators, his thoughts began to wander.

"It is odd that Puella the Wise One knew Sophia would confront those caterpillars, her greatest fear. Quite curious. I suppose it has something to do with that inner self Sophia is always talking about. Perhaps

Puella's inner self was able to glean information from a vantage point outside of space and time. There is clearly a scientific explanation for events such as this, but it currently eludes me."

He stopped short when he saw the crumpled ball of paper lying on the forest path.

"That's strange, another paper like the one Orville dropped. I'm quite certain Mum only gave him one note." His eyes narrowed. "Only one note that I know about. Maybe there were others."

He frowned, scooping up the ball of paper.

He spread the note open and flicked on his ear lights.

I wish he would leave.

The paper fluttered to the ground, Proto's arm falling to his side. Who was Mum talking about? Was she talking about him? Were they tired of him, did they want him to move out? He slumped down to the forest floor, his back against a gnarled tree trunk. He did not want to move back to the Cube and live with the glow-birds.

"Maybe I did something wrong. I should help more around the house, prepare only their favorite meals, not try new recipes. I shouldn't have teased Orville about the poisonous vegetables, maybe that upset Mum. I should plant a new vegetable garden with familiar vegetables, not ones from the Cube. I'll clean the house more thoroughly, help Mum more with the errands."

Proto spent most of the night composing a comprehensive list of all the things he could do to win back the favor of Orville, Mum and Papa. He had no idea where he would go if they sent him away. They were the only family he had.

Proto did not mention the disturbing note during breakfast the next morning, attempting instead to be as congenial as possible.

Brother Solus had risen with the sun and was ready to go, his face stern and unsmiling.

Orville nudged Sophia, whispering, "I think he wants to leave."

The adventurers were soon striding along the forest path, Orville balancing a plate of flapcakes on one paw while eating with the other.

"Yummy breakfast, Proto. Thanks for making it."

"Nothing is more important to me than making delicious meals and tasty snacks for you and Mum and Papa."

"Thanks, but don't forget, you don't have to do all the cooking. We can take turns if you get tired of it."

"Oh, good heavens no, I wouldn't hear of it, I'm ever so happy to do all the cooking. And the cleaning and laundry."

"If you really want to, I guess." Orville gave Sophia a sideways glance, sending her a thought cloud.

"Why is Proto being so nice?"

"I don't know, I guess he just wants to be helpful. That's how he was programmed, to be really friendly."

Brother Solus stopped in his tracks a hundred feet ahead of them, calling out, "I'm afraid we have encountered a rather formidable obstacle."

Orville darted down the trail, catching up to Brother

131

Solus. In front of him lay a vast blue ocean stretching out to the horizon.

Chapter 17

The Elysian Inn

"You never mentioned anything about crossing an ocean."

"Elysian is a land of unending surprise."

Orville was growing weary of Brother Solus' cryptic remarks, none of which were helping them find Aislin.

"How do we get cross it?"

Brother Solus shrugged. "It all depends."

Orville's jaw tightened. Brother Solus was supposed to be guiding them to the Great River, but he clearly had no idea where he was going.

Proto scanned the shoreline. "There is a small fishing village two miles to the south. Perhaps they will have a ship capable of an ocean crossing."

"This is way bigger than the Vesarak Sea. It would take months and months to cross it in a little fishing boat."

Sophia strode down the sloping ridge leading to the coastline. "Unless Proto has a Dragonfly in his pack we don't have much choice."

It took the adventurers two days to push through the

thick tangled foliage.

"Creekers, this beach grass is really sharp and taller than I am. I can't see anything, and these thorny bushes are even worse."

"I'd be happy to carry you."

"Proto, no one is going to carry me. I'm a Metaphysical Adventurer, not a mouseling."

"Oh dear, I hope I didn't offend you."

"You don't have to do everything for me. You're my friend, not my servant."

"Your friend?"

"What's wrong with you?"

"Nothing at all. We're almost there, I can see the beach."

Proto broke through the last of the dense brush, emerging onto a pristine white sandy beach.

"How lovely, quite stunning."

Orville stumbled out of the thorny thicket, flopping down on the warm sand.

"This is more like it. Look at all these seashells, they're amazing. I'll take some back for Mum, she loves seashells. I hope the ocean isn't full of creepy centipede fish creatures like the Senyph Ocean was."

He picked up a flat stone and walked down to the water's edge, skimming it across the waves. A sparkling silver fish leaped out of the water, disappearing a moment later with a small splash.

"That doesn't look too scary, it's just like the Vesarak Sea. I hope the fishing village has a big sailing ship, one with comfy bunks we can sleep in."

"And a restaurant that serves tasty snacks and gives foot rubs?"

Orville laughed. "I didn't think of that. If I'm going to wish I may as well wish for something really good. How about a crusty old friendly sea captain who smokes a pipe and has a parrot on his shoulder and lets us ride on his ship for free? Oh, and maybe a–"

"Enough chattering, I should like to arrive at the fishing village before nightfall. A good night's sleep washes away the tribulations of the day."

"Sorry."

Orville was wondering if Brother Solus even knew how to laugh. He had a sudden thought, maybe Brother Solus was like Ebenezer Mouse, maybe he was crabby and humorless because something had happened to him in the past. Maybe he had lost someone he loved like Ebenezer had. He sped up until he was strolling along- side Brother Solus.

"It's a beautiful beach isn't it? We have beaches a little like this on the Vesarak Sea that my mum and papa used to take me to when I was little. It was lots of fun swimming in the ocean. We didn't have all these seashells though. Some of them are amazing."

Orville reached down and scooped up a large white spiral seashell with a gleaming pink interior.

"I'm going to take home a few for my mum. She loves seashells."

Brother Solus nodded. "An admirable sentiment, very thoughtful indeed, but over the years I have learned it is best not to tamper with nature. By picking up that one seashell you may inadvertently be forging a chain of events which will lead to the destruction of the known universe."

Orville set the seashell back down on the sand. It was best not to tamper with nature? Where had Brother Solus learned that?

"So you have no memory at all of how you got to Elysian? Do you think you came here from another world? My friend Amanda Mouse said Okeanos is a name from the ancient mythologies, it's supposed to be a place that exists in the Borderlands, between the world of the waking and the world of dreams."

"These matters are not suitable for discussion. I will not speak of them."

"Okay, sorry, it's probably just some old mythology stuff anyway."

Something sparked an idea in Orville. If Amanda was right, and Okeanos existed between the world of the waking and the world of dreams, wouldn't it hold qualities of both? Maybe Sophia was on to something, maybe the caterpillars appeared because they were her greatest fear, just as they would in a dream. If that was true, it would also make sense that when her fear of caterpillars was gone, the caterpillars would disappear. The image of a gigantic black shiny centipede popped into his head. He sincerely hoped his theory about Elysian was wrong.

The sun was setting when the adventurers strolled into the fishing village.

"Whoa, mice live here, and they're wearing old fashioned clothes. The buildings look like they came out of my history book."

A thought cloud flashed over to Orville. "There should be Mintarians living here, not mice. And why would they be living in a fishing village that looks like Muridaan Falls?"

Brother Solus strode down the cobblestone street, stopping in front of a white three story building. He eyed the green sign that hung above the door.

THE ELYSIAN INN
Comfortable lodging at affordable rates.

"This looks quite presentable, clean and tidy. The sign in the window says they provide both evening and noonday meals. This should prove more than adequate."

He swung the door open and stepped inside, the others following.

Orville scanned the inn's interior.

"It's nicer than I thought it would be. "

In the center of the inn's lobby was a long wooden table covered with books, half a dozen mice quietly reading in comfortable stuffed chairs. Sophia stepped over to the table, curious about the books.

"This is interesting, they have some really good science books here. I wonder why a little seaside inn would have books about deep physics? Oh my, this one is a signed first edition. Orville, could you get us rooms while I look through these?"

Brother Solus picked up a heavy green book.

"Marvelous, a comprehensive history of the Mintari-an Gray Monks." He took a seat, opening the book.

Orville stepped over to the front desk and dinged the little silver bell. A plump mouse dressed in a dark tweed suit hurried out of the back room, greeting Orville with a warm smile.

"Good afternoon, young sir. How may I be of assistance to you?"

"Are there any rooms available? We'll need them for one or two nights."

"Of course. I have four rooms available for two nights, and our rates are quite reasonable. One silver for all four rooms, including noonday and evening meals."

"One silver? That's more than reasonable. I'll take all four rooms. Our Rabbiton friend doesn't sleep, but he does like to read at night."

Orville had purposefully mentioned Proto, curious as to how the clerk would react.

"I understand completely. Four rooms for two nights, meals included. I will include breakfast since your Rabbiton does not eat."

"You've seen Rabbitons before?"

"Of course, I am quite familiar with them. Many of our guests have traveled great distances to visit Elysian. All are welcome at the Elysian Inn."

"Thanks. How long has your inn been in business? It's very nice, we were lucky to find it."

"I thank you for your most gracious comment. Providing comfortable lodging at reasonable rates has always been our top priority. Let me think, how long has the inn been in business? Well, it's been here for as long as I can remember, and I've been here for quite some time."

Orville smiled politely, sliding a silver across the counter.

The clerk smoothly picked up the coin and handed Orville four brass keys numbered one through four.

"Your keys, good sir. Just let us know when you would like your meals and our chef will prepare them immediately."

Orville pocketed the keys, thanking the clerk. He walked across the lobby to find Sophia snuggled in a comfy chair, a large open book in her lap.

"What are you reading?"

"This is amazing. It's a rare first edition of *The Seventh Medallion*, the story of Bartholomew the Adventurer's journey to the lost planet of Thaumatar. It's fascinating reading, I'll have to tell Madam Molly about it. She's been to Thaumatar."

Orville wasn't listening. Something was off.

"Sophia, something's not right. They only charged us one silver for four rooms. That's four rooms for two nights with all meals included, all for one silver. Back in Muridaan Falls one meal for one mouse would cost at least a silver. And think about it, why would they have rare signed first edition books lying around in the lobby? And why doesn't the desk clerk know how long the inn has been in business? He said the same thing Brother Solus did, he's been here as long as he can remember. That doesn't tell me anything."

Sophia looked up from her book. "What?"

Orville groaned. "Nothing, go back to your adventure book. I got us four rooms. I'll ask the clerk about booking passage on a ship."

"Thanks." Sophia flipped a page, once again lost in her book.

Orville made his way back to the front desk. He rang the silver bell and the desk clerk popped out of the back room.

"Good afternoon, young sir. How may I be of assistance to you?"

"Are there any ships in port that make ocean crossings? We're trying to book passage on one."

The clerk rubbed his furry chin, scrunching his face.

"My best guess would be old Captain Tobias down at Pier 29. He's quite a character and they say he knows the Great Sea like the back of his paw. He's the one I would talk to."

"Thanks so much for your help, we'll head down to Pier 29 first thing in the morning and talk to Captain Tobias."

Chapter 18

Old Captain Tobias

Sophia stifled a yawn as they walked down the cobblestone lane leading to the harbor. "I'm so tired, I hardly slept at all last night."

"You do seem a little lethargic. Get it? Lethargic?"

"Yes, Orville, I get it, lethargic was one of your words for the day. Are you still learning a new word every day?"

"Not since you told me I didn't need to use big words to impress you."

"I'm glad. I think you're amazing, even with your tiny little vocabulary."

"Excuse me? You're being rather capricious."

"Stop, I'm too tired. I stayed up half the night reading that book about Bartholomew the Adventurer's expedition to Thaumatar. It was really interesting. Maybe one day Madam Molly will take us there."

"That would be fun, but only if she promises not to read my mind. Oh, I told Brother Solus we'd be back in time for lunch."

Proto strode up alongside Orville. "A lovely fishing village, remarkably similar to Muridaan Falls with its quaint cobblestone lanes. We should have an excellent view of the harbor from the top of this hill."

"We're looking for Pier 29. The harbor must be really big to have that many piers. Muridaan Falls only has three."

Sophia was the first to crest the hill. She scanned the harbor, a puzzled expression on her face.

"Orville, you said Pier 29?"

"That's what the desk clerk told me."

"The harbor only has one pier."

"Huh?" Orville darted up the hill next to Sophia. "You're right, one pier. That's weird, it doesn't make sense."

"Maybe it does make sense. What's your address in Muridaan Falls?"

"It's 29 Brimbleberry Lane, you know that."

"You house number is 29 and the only pier they have is Pier 29. Amanda said Okeanos is in the Borderlands, the land between wakefulness and dreams. If Elysian is simultaneously a real world and a dream world, coincidences like this would make perfect sense."

"I was thinking the same thing. Hey, if it's part dream, maybe that means we can't get hurt here. You always say we can't get hurt in a dream. Wouldn't that be great?"

"Should I kick you in the shins so we can find out?"

Sophia burst out laughing.

"Very funny. I'm going to try something." Orville stooped over and picked up a heavy moss covered rock.

"What are you doing?"

"I'm performing a scientific experiment to determine if this is really a dream world."

"This doesn't seem like a very well thought out experiment."

"Even though it seems kind of real, I'm pretty sure Elysian is mostly a dream world and I can't get hurt." Orville held the big stone directly over his foot.

"Orville, this is a very, very bad idea."

Orville released the stone.

"AAAAGGGHHHHH!"

Sophia slapped her paw over her mouth, trying to hide her laughter.

"Are you okay?"

"It didn't hurt that much."

"Maybe you should try it again, this time with a heavier rock. It's best to perform experiments at least a dozen times, adjusting the variables to insure statistically accurate results."

"Go ahead and laugh all you want, but now we know we can get hurt in this world. We'll have to be careful."

Proto had been listening to the conversation with some interest. He turned to Sophia.

"I am baffled by your response to Orville's experiment. If I dropped a large rock on Orville's foot, you most certainly would not laugh, but when he dropped a rock on his own foot, you clearly thought it to be humorous."

"It's funny because Orville was so surprised, it wasn't at all what he was expecting. Most things that make us laugh are things which are surprising, unexpected."

"Are you saying if a gigantic carnivorous centipede sprang out from behind that tree, you would laugh because it was so surprising?"

"Of course not, that would be terrifying. It's only funny when no one gets hurt."

"Ah, it's only funny when no one gets hurt. This is excellent data, clearly explaining why Orville did not think my deadly poisonous vegetable jokes were humorous."

Orville stepped around a ramshackle warehouse to the wharf. A few rough looking mice were sauntering down the boardwalk, hats pulled low.

"There's the pier."

"There's only one ship tied up. Do you think it's Captain Tobias?"

"I'll ask those mice." Orville stepped over to a group of three disheveled mice leaning against the warehouse, one of them smoking a pipe.

"I wonder if you could help me? We're looking for Captain Tobias. The desk clerk at the Elysian Inn said we would find him at Pier 29?"

One of the ruffians leaned over and spat disgustingly onto the wooden walkway.

"Avast ye, matey, sittin' before ye be the *Sophia,* the finest schooner in all Elysian, mastered by that old sea dog known to all as Captain Tobias, scourge of the Great Sea."

"His ship is named the *Sophia?* Really?"

The ruffian gave Orville a dark look, his paw inching down to the hilt of a vicious looking ivory handled dagger.

"Thank you." Orville turned and darted back to Sophia and Proto.

"What did they say?"

"It's Captain Tobias, and his ship is called the *Sophia*. That can't be a coincidence."

Five minutes later Sophia was still grinning.

"I have a sailing ship named after me. That's so amazing. Orville, how many ships do you have named after you?"

Orville rolled his eyes. "I knew I shouldn't have said anything. Let's go meet Captain Tobias."

The three adventurers made their way down the long wooden pier to a graceful two masted schooner rocking lazily in the early morning breeze. A mouse was sitting on the deck in a crudely fashioned wooden chair, his face hidden behind a large newspaper.

"That must be Captain Tobias."

Sophia stepped onto the gangplank.

"Ahoy, Captain Tobias, permission to board?"

The mouse in the chair lowered his paper. Orville's jaw dropped. Captain Tobias was a crusty old sea captain with a curved pipe in his mouth and a bright green parrot on his shoulder.

"Ahoy, mateys, welcome aboard the good ship *So-*

phia. We sail at morning light for the Isle of the Silver Ship, if that be your port of call."

"It's lovely to meet you, Captain Tobias, my name is Sophia, and these are my two friends Orville and Proto. We're trying to cross the Great Sea."

Captain Tobias removed the pipe from his mouth, his eyes on Sophia.

"The ship that sways beneath our feet bears your name, and the name of my truest love, lost to me long years ago. 'Twas a harrowing tale of the capricious sea, of great magical creatures churning up from the murky depths, of heartbreaking despair and glorious wonder, of a love deeper than any mouse shall ever fathom, but 'tis also a tale to be spun another day. My dear Sophia, not a single silver shall I take in payment, it shall be my honor to convey you and your friends to the Isle of the Silver Ship. As for passage across the Great Sea, once landed on that distant emerald isle ye must make your own way to those far distant shores, entering into the murky realm of the Shadow King."

Orville was stunned. He had laughingly told Sophia he hoped they'd meet a friendly old sea captain who smoked a pipe, had a parrot on his shoulder, and would let them sail for free, and here he was. Brother Solus was right, Elysian was a land of endless surprise.

Chapter 19

Over the Bounding Main

The adventurers rose at dawn, had a quick breakfast, then headed down the cobblestone streets to their early morning rendezvous with Captain Tobias.

Brother Solus had shown no surprise at the curious turn of events leading to their encounter with Captain Tobias, the crusty old sea captain Orville had wished for.

"One should not ponder the vagaries of Elysian, their cause lying far beyond our understanding."

"You're probably right, but it's weird that I thought about a friendly sea captain with a pipe and parrot, and then Captain Tobias appeared."

"Elysian is Elysian."

"There's the *Sophia.* Orville, the *Sophia* is the ship that's named after me. I have a ship named after me, it's called the *Sophia.*"

Orville put his paw to his forehead.

Proto studied the graceful lines of the two masted schooner.

"I have read several comprehensive discourses regarding the construction and operation of such archaic sailing vessels, and I believe a two masted schooner such as the *Sophia* would command a crew of five, yet I see only Captain Tobias."

It took Orville a moment to grasp Proto's meaning.

"Are you saying we're the crew? I don't know how to sail one of those things."

Sophia gave an excited laugh. "This is going to be so much fun! We get to sail it!" She waved to Captain Tobias. "Captain, permission to come aboard the good ship *Sophia*?"

"Permission granted. Ahoy, mateys, we set sail for the mystical Isle of the Silver Ship this very morn. Stand by to release the hawsers and cast away!"

Orville looked at Sophia. "Are we supposed to do something? What's a hawser?"

"Come on, Captain Tobias wants us to release the mooring lines."

"The what lines?"

Proto stepped down the gangplank to the dock. "It's quite straightforward, we unwrap the hawsers from the bollards, pull them in and coil them neatly on the foredeck. Then we need to–"

"Eyes in the boat, laddies! Let us make sail in the favoring wind!"

"I don't know what a hawser is. Is it this big rope

wrapped around the post?"

"That's exactly what it is, and that post is called a bollard."

Proto and Sophia released the two mooring hawsers and dashed up the gangplank.

"Orville, pull in the hawsers and coil them on the foredeck."

"Shove off and make sail, laddies! Mainmast, rig the sheet lines smartly!"

Proto used his enormous strength to push the *Sophia* away from the pier.

"Come on, Orville, help us raise the sails!"

Orville followed Sophia and Proto to the tallest mast.

"This is the mainmast, loosen these sheet lines, then pull them in to raise the sail."

The great sail rose, billowing out in the brisk easterly wind. "Pull until it's tight, then tie it off."

The sail snapped taut, the ship surging forward. Captain Tobias stood at the ship's wheel puffing his great curved pipe, guiding the vessel past the pier into the rolling blue sea. The green parrot on his shoulder squawked, "Set sails, Captain Orville! Set sails, Captain Orville!"

"Sophia, did you hear that? The parrot called me Captain Orville, just like you do. How do you think he knew my name?"

"Eyes in the boat, matey, foremast, make sail, rig the sheet lines!"

An hour later an exhausted Orville slumped down

onto the deck, trying to catch his breath. "This is exhausting, I thought sailing was supposed to be relaxing."

"This is so much fun, almost as much fun as flying a Dragonfly."

"It is sort of fun, I guess. I can't believe you climbed that rope ladder to the top of the mast."

"The extra sails boost our speed. Captain Tobias said we're cruising at eight knots, about ten miles an hour."

"That seems really slow, the Dragonfly cruises at over a hundred miles an hour. Did Captain Tobias say how long it will take us to reach the Isle of the Silver Ship? Why do you think they call it that? He said it was a mystical island. Wait, do you think there's a ship made out of silver on the island, a giant treasure ship?"

"Orville, we're sailing across the mysterious Great Sea in the world of Elysian. It's a glorious sunny day with a brisk wind and Captain Tobias is a friendly old pipe smoking sea captain with a squawking parrot on his shoulder who knows your name. What could be more amazing than that?"

Orville took Sophia's paw. "You're right, it is amazing. How do you think the parrot knows my name?"

"Elysian is part real and part dream, odd things like that are bound to happen."

"I don't really understand how it can be half dream and half real."

"Elysian is Elysian."

"You sound like Brother Solus."

Orville leaned back against the mainmast, enjoying

the warmth of the noonday sun on his fur, the smell of the salty sea air, the wind whipping through the ship's rigging, the shrieking of the gulls overhead, the creaking of the ship as it plied its way through the sparkling blue sea. Sophia was right, this was a singularly perfect moment, one he would remember for all of his days.

Chapter 20

The Blue Pirates

Six days passed and Orville was feeling like a sea-soned deck hand, an old salt. They had fallen into a comfortable routine, working the sails and taking shifts at the wheel, guided by the sun during the day and the stars by night. More precisely, they were guided by the star at night, since there was only one. As was the way in Elysian, the star was fortuitously positioned directly above the Isle of the Silver Ship. Captain Tobias instructed the adventurers on the proper use of the ship's wheel, each of them sharing the duty of guiding the *Sophia* toward the Isle of the Silver Ship. Orville had a wide grin on his face whenever he stood at the ship's wheel.

"Arghhh! 'Tis the brave Captain Orville at the helm!"

On the morning of the eighth day, Captain Tobias raised his gleaming brass telescope, peering across the stern of the ship.

"Sails on the horizon, following in our wake! She's a three master and showing her colors! Look lively, mateys, it's the dread Blue Pirates!"

Orville's eyes popped open. "Pirates?"

Sophia jumped to her feet. "What do we do, Captain?"

"The blue demons hold twice our sail, there's no outrunning them. We have no choice but surrender."

"They're blue?" Sophia was remembering the tall ship crewed by four-armed blue creatures she had seen as they were flying across the Vesarak Sea to the Isle of the Serpent. "Do they have four arms?"

"Aye, lassie, they be the scurvy blaggards come up from the darkest depths of the sea to plunder the very likes of us."

"How long until they catch up to us?"

"Four bells and they'll fire a deadly broadside if we don't furl the sheets and yield."

Orville's eyes were wide. "How long is four bells?"

"Two hours. Relax, we can shape a sphere of defense around the ship to protect us from their cannon fire."

Captain Tobias shook his head. "They wield no ordinary cannons, the Blue Pirates dispense the darkest of all magic, a broadside of deadly purple light, turning ships to dust before a mouse can take a second breath."

"Vaporizing beams! This is bad, our sphere of defense won't stand up to an attack like that."

"They're getting closer!"

"I wish we had a cloaking device like the one on the

Dragonfly."

Proto drummed his long silver fingers on the ship's wheel, deep in thought.

"I have analyzed all possible options regarding our impending assault by the Blue Pirates. As you well know, we are Metaphysical Adventurers, sworn never to harm another living creature, but we are also clearly unable to withstand a broadside of heavy particle vaporization beams. As Sophia has noted, we are currently not in possession of a cloaking device. Our singular remaining option is to outrun the pirates. According to my calculations, we must increase our current velocity to thirteen knots."

"How can we do that? We don't have any more sails to put up."

"What about shaping some kind of duplonium motor?"

"Too complicated, there's too much engineering involved to fit the ship with a propeller. We don't have time."

Orville's mind was racing. "More sail! We could shape more sail."

"We have nowhere to put it, the masts are filled already."

Orville gave a shriek. "Wind! More wind! Just like we did when we crossed that subterranean lake on Tectar."

"That's it! You're brilliant, Orville. We can link minds and shape a windstorm."

Captain Tobias was puffing madly on his great pipe,

trying to keep up with their conversation. "Impossible, the sea wind bends for no mouse, great or small."

"We're not just any mice, Captain Tobias, we're Metaphysical Adventurers."

Proto studied the three masted ship cutting smoothly through the sea behind them, now less than a mile away.

"I have magnified my vision by a factor of thirteen. The ship which is trailing behind us is the very same ship we saw when the stormy world of Saevio over-lapped the Vesarak Sea. The markings are identical, as are the blue creatures with four arms."

"Of course it is, we're in Elysian. We have to hurry! Orville, take my paw!"

Orville and Sophia stood paw in paw on the deck of the *Sophia,* their eyes closed. Proto knew they were concentrating deeply, leaving their physical selves behind, merging their minds, multiplying their shaping powers. When their minds linked, each shared com-pletely the other's thoughts, feelings, and memories. It had been a little frightening at first for Orville to reveal his deepest thoughts and memories to another mouse, but he was used to it now. Besides, Sophia was his best friend in the world, and the mouse he trusted more than any other.

Sophia felt her awareness merging with Orville's. It became difficult to tell where her thoughts ended and his began.

"We need to create a windstorm trailing behind the *Sophia*, about twenty-five knots should be enough to outrun the Blue Pirates."

"Hey, I found one of your memories. You went out with a mouse named Percival?"

"I went to one dance with him. Some of the mice used to make fun of me because I was so smart. I thought it would make me seem more normal if I went to a dance instead of studying all the time."

"Did you like him?"

"Search my memories."

"Oh, right. You thought he was kind of shallow."

"He was nothing like you, he wasn't curious about the world, he didn't notice things the way you do, he didn't find puzzles like you do."

"I like sharing our memories."

"It's nice, but we'd better shape this windstorm before the Blue Pirates catch us."

"Okay, let's do it."

A brilliant golden glow appeared around Orville and Sophia, casting long shadows across the deck. Captain Tobias took a step back, his eyes wide. Proto pointed across the stern of the ship.

"Watch the water."

Dark ripples appeared on the rolling sea behind them, the ripples transforming rapidly to ragged wind-blown waves, then to whitecaps, the salty spray blowing toward the ship, the sails snapping out sharply. The wind was howling now, the sails billowing, the masts creaking wildly under the strain, the ship surging forward, leaving a broad white wake behind it.

"Merciful heavens, what have they wrought? What

manner of dark magic is this?" Captain Tobias' paws were clasped together tightly, his eyes on the wind-blown raging sea behind them.

Proto took the ship's wheel, setting them on course for the Isle of the Silver Ship. "That did it, our current speed is fourteen knots, more than enough to outrun the Blue Pirates."

"You didn't have anyone special you really liked either. You went to a few dances but still felt lonely even when everyone thought you were having fun."

"No one wanted to talk about the things I wanted to talk about. No one was interested in the puzzles I found."

"That's the thing I like about you most."

"Thanks. I'm glad you didn't like Percival."

"We should go back. Captain Tobias is probably very confused by what's happening."

The golden glow surrounding Orville and Sophia faded away, their eyes opening.

"Whoa, we did it, check out that wind!"

Orville grinned at Captain Tobias.

"How's that for a windstorm?"

"You are magicians, wielding great and terrible powers?"

"It's not magic, it's science. We're using the combined power of our minds to manipulate energy fields, in this case to create a powerful windstorm."

Brother Solus was silent, his dour face displaying undisguised disapproval.

Orville sent a cloud to Sophia. "A certain Mintarian

Gray Monk doesn't approve of our tampering with nature."

A cloud flashed back to Orville.

"One should never tamper with nature unless blood-thirsty Blue Pirates are closing in, about to turn you and your friends into glowing space dust."

Chapter 21

Orville's New Watch

With the Blue Pirates safely behind them, long lazy days aboard the *Sophia* rolled by, the indigo blue sea extending out to the four horizons. Other than a few errant shrieking gulls there was not another soul in sight.

"I wouldn't mind being a pirate. It seems like it would be kind of fun. I'd call myself the Dread Pirate Orville, but I wouldn't hurt anyone or steal from them."

Sophia snorted. "You can't be a dread pirate if you don't capture ships and steal treasure."

Proto nodded emphatically. "And make your prisoners walk the plank, turning them into tasty snacks for the terrifying scaly monstrosities roaming the depths of this dark and mysterious otherworldly sea."

"First of all, I'm not going to make a mouse walk the plank, and second, this ocean doesn't seem especially dark and mysterious. The only creatures I've seen are a few silver fish jumping out of the water, not exactly terrifying scaly monstrosities."

Proto continued. "From an ethical standpoint, if you refrain from pillaging and plundering, then the act of calling yourself the Dread Pirate Orville would at best be extremely misleading, and at worst an outright false-hood, quite unconscionable. I would suggest a more appropriate name, something like Orville the Friendly Pirate."

"I'm not calling myself Orville the Friendly Pirate! Just in case you hadn't realized it, I have no intention of actually becoming a real pirate, I'm just saying it would be fun to ply the salty seas wearing a three cornered hat and a black eye patch, singing sea shanties with a crew of old sea dogs."

"Again, I'm confused by your choice of an eye patch as an accoutrement. Your vision is fine in both eyes, is it not? It seems illogical to cover up a perfectly good eye. Clearly, good eyesight would be an invaluable asset in the seafaring trade."

Orville looked helplessly at Sophia. "Is it me? Am I going loopy?"

Proto let out a great staccato laugh. "Ha ha ha ha! I have hoodwinked you soundly. I was fully aware you had no intention of becoming a pirate, clearly under-standing your musings to be nothing more than an idle daydream. My questions were purposefully confound-ing, part of my clever scheme to get your goat."

Sophia cackled, "Good one, Proto!"

Orville glared at Sophia, about to give his undiluted opinion of Proto's peculiar sense of humor when a voice rang out from the ship's wheel.

"Land ho, laddies! Look sharp, there lies the emerald beauty herself, the Isle of the Silver Ship!"

Orville ran to the bow of the *Sophia*. "Sophia, Proto, come look! It's a lot bigger than I thought it would be, and it has a huge mountain in the middle."

Proto scanned the distant isle. "It appears to be a jungle habitat, quite similar to the jungles of Periculum. The mountain you mentioned is unfortunately a volcano, much larger than Mt. Ianua."

Orville's smile faded. "It's all jungle? There's a volcano?" He was remembering the huge carnivorous centipedes they had encountered deep in the jungles of Periculum.

Sophia whacked Orville's arm. "Not every jungle has carnivorous centipedes, and the volcano doesn't look active."

Orville gave a weak smile.

"Captain Tobias, why do they call it the Isle of the Silver Ship?"

"Aye, a fine question, lassie, but one I have no answer for. Ye be on your own to unravel the dark mysteries of this lost land."

"Who lives on the island?"

"Nary a soul, laddie."

"Why do you come here if no one lives here?"

"Not once have I set foot on the emerald Isle of the Silver Ship."

Orville stared blankly at Captain Tobias. "You sail here all the time, but you've never set foot on the island?"

"Aye, laddie, this bein' Elysian, there's the reason why."

Orville nodded, baffled by Captain Tobias' cryptic reply.

"Eyes in the boat, mateys! Furl the sheets, loose the halyards. Prepare to drop anchor!"

The adventurers needed no further instruction. Ten minutes later the sails were down, the anchor dropped, the ship safely moored a hundred yards off the sandy white beaches of the mysterious island.

"Good news, I don't see any carnivorous centipedes enjoying a pleasant day at the beach."

"Lower the longboat, she'll carry you to the shore."

Brother Solus and Proto released the lines, the ropes singing through the pulleys as the longboat fell, splashing into a gently rolling sea. They clambered down the rope ladder into the rocking craft. Proto set the oars in the locks, waiting for Orville and Sophia.

"Captain Tobias, thank you so much for taking us here. We truly appreciate your kindness. We're looking for a lost friend. We think she's in the realm of the Shadow King."

"Aye, lassie, 'tis there ye shall find all things lost."

Sophia gave Captain Tobias a warm hug. "Thank you."

Orville shook paws with Captain Tobias. "Thanks for teaching us how to sail a ship. It was really fun, I won't ever forget it."

"Aye, when the sea calls, a mouse shall answer, 'tis

a truth undenied." He reached into the pocket of his great blue captain's coat, pulling out a worn old pocket watch, holding it up for Orville to see.

"That's a nice watch. Proto said you can use a pocket watch kind of like a compass if you line it up with the sun."

"Aye, 'tis so. The watch is yours now, laddie, a gift from an old sea captain, the captain who heard your call across the Great Sea."

"What?"

"The watch is yours, 'tis the greatest treasure a mouse can ever know. Mark my words well, laddie."

"I can't take it, it's too much, it's your gold pocket watch."

Captain Tobias pressed the watch into Orville's paw. "There's no more to be said. Into the longboat with you. On your way, laddie."

"Well, if you're really sure." Orville reluctantly slipped the watch into his pocket as he and Sophia climbed over the ship's rail and down the rope ladder, taking their seats behind Proto.

"Cast off, mateys! Until we meet again on the Great Sea!"

Orville released the lines, setting the long boat free. Proto dipped the oars into the water, pulling away from the *Sophia*.

Orville gripped the gold pocket watch given to him by Captain Tobias. How could an old watch be the greatest treasure a mouse could ever know?

Chapter 22

Isle of the Silver Ship

Orville was the first to set foot on the island.

"This is beautiful. I've never seen beaches like this, so white, and the sand is so soft. Look at all the sea-shells." He stooped over and picked up several, tucking them into his pack, a gift for his mum. Brother Solus frowned, but made no comment.

Proto pulled the longboat onto the beach, tying it securely to a gnarled jungle tree. "That will hold it until Captain Tobias returns."

Orville turned for a last wave to Captain Tobias and the *Sophia,* but stopped before he could raise his arm. He was staring at a vast and empty indigo sea.

"The ship's gone! It can't be gone, he was just here."

Sophia scanned the horizon. A bright blue thought cloud floated out of her ear to Orville.

"I just thought of something, the red book said the Mintarians who returned from the synthetic worlds told stories of creatures flickering out of nothingness, of long deceased friends and relatives appearing, great cities which came and went in a single day, and oceans where there had been none."

"That's why Brother Solus didn't know about the Great Sea! It wasn't there before. It's why he didn't know how long the trip would take, because everything is always changing. Do you think he knows he's in a synthetic world?"

"We don't even know if he's real. Look at Captain Tobias, he was here and then he was gone, the *Sophia* was gone. Was he real?"

Orville reached into his pocket. "I still have the watch, he must have been real."

"He seemed real when he was here. Maybe he's back at Pier 29, sitting on the foredeck reading his newspaper and puffing on his big pipe."

"I hope so, I liked him a lot. There was something about him."

Brother Solus' voice rang out. "Enough! You are worse than a flock of chattering magpies!"

Orville took a deep breath. How could one Mintarian be so annoying?

"That trail goes into the jungle. Let's take that, although I have no idea where we're going. Maybe we'll find a fishing village along the coast, one with boats."

"Captain Tobias said the island was uninhabited, but there could be an abandoned fishing village, something like Okeanos. At least now we know how to sail."

"And we have Orville the Friendly Pirate to guide us."

Orville laughed. "Avast, mateys, walk that scurvy Rabbiton off the plank into the deep blue!"

"Come on, Dread Captain Orville, let's find out why the universe brought us to the Isle of the Silver Ship."

The jungle habitat proved to be a steaming labyrinth of gnarled trees, vines, and dense undergrowth. Barring the swarms of buzzing iridescent yellow insects with long furry antennae, it did not appear especially dangerous.

"Perhaps we shall encounter a nest of enormous electric vine lizards deeper in the jungle. I should imagine in such a sweltering and oppressive environment as this they would attain unprecedented size and ferocity."

"Thanks, now I have something to look forward to."

Sophia stooped down, examining the trail. "Captain Tobias said the island was uninhabited, but this path isn't a natural formation, someone or something must have–."

Brother Solus' voice cut through the air. "Your logic is fundamentally flawed, your understanding of Elysian equally so. Have you learned nothing since you arrived in this confounding world?"

Sophia attempted a pleasant smile, but could feel her neck getting hot. Her understanding of scientific matters was seldom questioned, and Brother Solus' insinuation rankled her badly.

"How exactly is my logic flawed?"

"You truly do not understand why the jungle trail is here?"

"I merely suggested that animals created it when

they–"

"Wrong, wrong, and wrong again! The trail was not created by animals, or by any other form of jungle denizen, nor by creatures from some far distant world. The trail was created by you. This infernal ocean was created by you, the fishing village was created by you, the Elysian Inn, the books, Captain Tobias, the *Sophia*, all created by you. Elysian is a reflection of you and your inner thoughts. That is the deeper nature of Elysian."

"Which is why you didn't know how long it would take us to reach the realm of the Shadow King. The journey is different for every mouse who takes it, each one creating their own set of obstacles, things they love and things they fear."

"You have surprised me. Perhaps there is hope for you yet, you appear to possess a modicum of understanding."

Orville did not like Brother Solus' tone. "Sophia is the smartest mouse I've ever met. She knows more about science than anyone, and she's traveled to a lot of different worlds."

Brother Solus' face softened. "And in you it is readily apparent she has found a true and loyal friend. I spoke harshly, and for that I apologize. My point, simply made, is that the world of Elysian is like no other, it is a–" Brother Solus stopped, his stern demeanor abruptly reappearing. "Enough chattering about such things, let us proceed." He turned sharply and strode down the jungle trail.

The three adventurers walked along behind Brother Solus, Sophia keeping her voice low to avoid being overheard.

"I've been thinking about the science behind Elysian. The physical matter in these synthetic worlds must be less dense than the matter in our world, more easily manipulated by our minds. The Mintarians who took refuge in the Metaphoniums' synthetic worlds became powerful shapers without realizing what was happening. Whatever they feared or loved appeared in their world. It must have been terrifying for them, oceans and creatures and departed loved ones springing out of nothingness."

"That's why Captain Tobias appeared after I wished for a crusty old sea captain."

"And why my caterpillars appeared. It's possible our shaping skills may be far more powerful here than back in Muridaan Falls. Try shaping something really big, something you wouldn't be able to shape back home."

"Okay, something really big."

Orville thought for a minute, then flicked his wrist. He gave a shriek, momentarily blinded by the brilliant flash of light that blasted out from his paw.

Sophia's paws were over her eyes. "What did you do?"

"I tried to shape something really big, but all I got was a giant flash of light."

"What did you try to shape?"

Orville gave Sophia a nervous glance. "Nothing, just something really big."

"Maybe I'm wrong, maybe Elysian doesn't magnify our shaping abilities. Maybe the environment is only affected by our unconscious thoughts."

Brother Solus stopped abruptly, holding up one paw, bellowing out, "Orville Mouse! Is this your doing?"

Orville jumped, looking anxiously at Sophia. "What did I do?"

"I have no idea. Let's go see what he wants."

The three adventurers hurried down the trail to find Brother Solus standing at the edge of a large clearing. In the center sat a long low building with glowing white walls, an elegant gold sign hanging above the entrance.

Elysian's Spectacular
Cake and Pie Emporium

"Orville?"

"Whoa, it worked!"

Brother Solus gave Orville a distinctly sour look.

Orville darted over to the stately door of the Cake and Pie Emporium, eyeing the gleaming brass fittings.

"Fancy. Looks opulent, very opulent."

"Opulent? Really? I thought you said you were done with your word for the day."

"I am done with it, opulent is just one of the many words I use on a daily basis." Orville grinned, swinging the door open and stepping inside, the air heavy with mouth watering aromas of freshly baked cakes and pies. A fifty foot long display case spanned the room, sparkling glass shelves brimming with hundreds of exquisitely baked delicacies.

"Creekers! Look at all those cakes and pies and cinnamon rolls and cobblers and–"

"How hungry were you when you shaped this?"

Proto gave a small sniff. "I suppose such baked goods might appeal to an unsophisticated palate, but I see nothing approaching the caliber of my tasty little cakes."

Sophia whispered, "Your cakes are the best, Proto. Everyone knows that. Nothing else even comes close."

A wide door behind the long glass counter flew open, a buoyant mouse clad in a starched white apron and tall chef's hat striding out.

"Welcome, my dear friends, to Elysian's Spectacular Cake and Pie Emporium, home of the most irresistible pastries in this universe or any other. Please seat yourselves in preparation for a cake and pie extravaganza you will not soon forget. A most generous sampling of our fare will arrive shortly at your table. You are both welcomed and encouraged to try as many cakes, pies, or pastries as you wish, all at no charge."

"Now I know you shaped this place. No charge for all the cakes and pies you can eat?"

Orville rubbed his paws together. "Mmm... it smells so good, I don't know where to start."

Orville's mouth was watering when the cheery chef appeared with an enormous tray of delightfully flaky treats balanced precariously on his shoulder, smoothly setting it down with one practiced fluid motion.

"Bon appetit, my friends. Do let me know if there

are any particular cakes or pies you are especially fond of."

"Do you have snapberry pies?"

The chef waved his paw across the tray. "Snapberry pie happens to be our speciality, young sir. In fact, this entire section of the tray consists of our own snapberry culinary creations. You'll find snapberry frosted cakes, snapberry pies, snapberry cobblers, muffins, turnovers, strudels, and even some exquisitely flaky snapberry eclairs with brimbleberry frosting."

Orville plucked a half dozen samples from the tray, setting them down in front of him. His eyes lost focus with the first bite of snapberry pie.

"Soooo good, sooooo delicious."

Sophia watched as the cakes and pies in front of Orville disappeared one by one.

"Mmm, yum, so good. I wonder what these are?" Orville pulled six more samples from the tray. "Oh, I love brimbleberry pie!"

Sophia noticed the tray was still full, even though Orville had eaten more than a dozen pastries. She removed a plate of warm brimbleberry tarts, watching as another plate took its place. "It's just like the books at the Okeanos Book Fair."

Orville made no reply, his mouth filled with three kinds of pie.

"Orville, you're going to make yourself sick. You should slow down."

Orville gulped down the pies, croaking out his reply.

"Still starving, not full at all. So good, best pastries

ever. Pie is so good." He dropped his fork, grabbing pastries from the tray with both paws, piling them in front of him.

"Use a napkin, you have pie filling stuck all over your fur."

"So good, can't stop eating. Mmm... so tasty." He shoved his face into a plate of snapberry eclairs, dreadful slobbery sounds filling the air.

Proto nudged Sophia. "Perhaps he has had enough?"

"There's no perhaps about it." Sophia yanked the plate of eclairs away from Orville. "You need to stop."

"What are you doing? These are the best eclairs ever, they have brimbleberry frosting!"

"Orville, we have to go now. You're going to get sick. This isn't right, it isn't like you."

"Can't go yet, haven't tried the strudel." Orville grabbed a plate of warm beezleberry strudel. "Looks so delicious!"

"Proto, help me get him out of here!"

Proto picked Orville up like a furry sack of wriggling potatoes and carried him outside, setting him down at the edge of the clearing.

"What are you doing? What's wrong with you? I never got to try the beezleberry–" Orville stopped, wincing in pain. He gave a low moan, grabbing his stomach.

"I don't feel good, I feel sick, really sick, I think I'm going to– "

Sophia jumped back. "Ewww! Not here!"

Orville darted into the jungle. Ten minutes later a

172

wobbly Orville returned. "Sorry, I think I ate too much."

Sophia watched the Cake and Pie Emporium fade to nothingness.

Brother Solus' lip curled at the sight of Orville's pie covered face. "Slovenly behavior."

Proto pulled a colorful round tin from his pack.

"Orville, would you care for some tasty little cakes?"

Chapter 23

Orville's Bed and Breakfast

Sophia held Orville's arm, steadying him as the party of adventurers made their way through the sweltering jungle.

"What exactly did you try to shape?"

"A cake and pie emporium giving away free samples of the most irresistibly delicious baked goods in the universe."

"You probably should have left out the irresistible part."

Brother Solus stopped, looking back at the adventurers.

"The path to the Shadow King is leading us to the volcanic crater. From this point on there must be no shaping. Wish for nothing, shape nothing. Everything is changing. Your lost friend is growing weaker by the hour."

"How do you know that?"

"This is Elysian, that is how I know."

Orville eyed the rocky volcano, its craggy silhouette jutting up into a brilliant blue sky.

"It's really steep, a dangerous climb. Maybe we could just blink to the top."

"Have you not heard a single word I've said? No more shaping, no more wishing, and no blinking! We are approaching the realm of the Shadow King, this is not your safe little world of Muridaan Falls. If you attempt to blink to the top of the volcano, there is no telling where you might find yourself."

"Sorry."

Brother Solus took a long slow breath. "Orville, even though it may not appear so, I assure you I have your best interest at heart. I am uncertain why this is so, but it has become clear to me that we must rescue your lost friend and return her safely to Muridaan Falls."

"Thanks, Brother Solus. I'm sorry I shaped the Cake and Pie Emporium."

"What's done is done. I suppose at one time I was young and impulsive, though such halcyon days are long forgotten."

Orville nodded even though he had no idea what halcyon days were. It was curious that Brother Solus could not remember his life before Elysian.

As they drew closer to the great volcano, the reality of its staggering size was readily apparent.

"Creekers, it's way bigger than Mt. Ianua. How can we climb something that tall?"

"According to my calculations the volcano stands precisely nineteen thousand and twenty-nine feet tall, almost twice as tall as Mt. Ianua."

"Is there any air up that high?"

Brother Solus answered, "This is Elysian, there will be air to breathe. Of far greater concern is what we shall find within the crater."

Orville's anxiety spiked. "What do you mean? What's in there?"

"I have no answer, but I am being drawn to the crater by a powerful and unfamiliar force."

"Um… maybe we should think about this."

"We have no choice, saving your friend is my last hope."

Orville glanced at Sophia. What did Brother Solus mean? His last hope for what?

The adventurers forged on, Sophia studying the formidable slopes of the volcano. "We should arrive at the base by nightfall. We can set up camp, get a good night's rest and start our ascent in the morning. We can't shape climbing gear so we'll have to improvise, maybe use vines for ropes."

Proto slung off his enormous pack, rummaging around inside.

"Here it is, two hundred feet of stout climbing rope and an iron grappling hook."

Orville stopped in his tracks. "You have two hundred feet of climbing rope in your pack? And an iron grappling hook?"

"One must be prepared for all contingencies."

"You don't happen to have sleeping bags and a tent in there, do you? Maybe a picnic table?"

"I am confused, is that intended to be a lighthearted humorous question, or do you believe it to be within the realm of possibility?"

"Orville was making a joke, Proto. He knows you don't really have a picnic table in your pack."

Proto threw his head back and let out a booming staccato laugh. "Ha ha ha ha! Excellent joke, I shall have to remember that one! You don't happen to have sleeping bags and a tent in there, do you? Maybe a picnic table? Ha ha ha ha!"

Sophia punched Orville's shoulder. "Good one, Orville, you make the best jokes. The best."

Orville's eyes narrowed. "Thanks so much, Sophia. You know how I enjoy making you laugh."

Seven grueling hours later the party of exhausted adventurers staggered to a halt at the base of the gargantuan volcano. Orville dropped his pack and slumped down to the ground.

"So tired. What are we going to do without sleeping bags and a tent? There's probably going to be a million bugs flying around. Hey, maybe we'll find a nice little–" Orville stopped in mid sentence, his eyes wide.

"Maybe we'll find a nice little what?"

"You should probably look behind you."

Sophia, Proto, and Brother Solus turned to see a lovely white stucco building with colorful flower baskets hanging from the eaves, a bright red sign above the front door.

Madam Beasley's
Affordable Bed & Breakfast
Free Maps of the Volcano

Brother Solus whipped back around, his eyes riveted sharply on Orville.

"Great merciful heavens, mouse! Was I not clear when I told you not to shape anything? Could you not grasp that one simple instruction?"

Orville stammered, "I… I didn't do it on purpose. I just thought it would be nice if we… umm… found a nice…" His voice trailed off into silence.

"Nothing else! Keep your mind focused, pay close attention to your thoughts, choose them carefully. Your thoughts change the world around you."

"Sorry. I'm just wondering, though, since the bed and breakfast is already here, and it's affordable, and they have free maps of the volcano, maybe we should spend the–"

Brother Solus glared angrily at Orville. Sophia was trying not to laugh.

"We will spend the night in your unfortunate creation and begin our climb at sunrise." Brother Solus yanked the front door open and stepped inside, slamming it shut behind him.

Orville grinned. "Maybe they serve dinner. I hope they have snapberry pie. I'm starving."

Chapter 24

Madam Beasley

"I wonder what Madam Beasley is like? My mum has a friend named Madam Beasley who grows all kinds of different violets. She makes yummy jelly from them."

Orville followed the others into the cozy interior of the structure.

Sophia nodded her approval. "This is nice, much better than a tent. I like all the comfy couches, and those quilts on the wall are beautiful. I still have a quilt my mum made for me when I was really little. I used to bunch it all up and hold it, pretending it was her."

"I'm sorry, I didn't mean to… you know."

"It's okay, things remind me of her, that's all."

Orville grabbed Sophia's arm, his voice a low whisper.

"At the desk, it's her! It's Madam Beasley, my mum's friend. I'm sure it is."

Sophia turned, studying the bespectacled mouse seated at the front desk, currently engrossed in an open book.

"She looks a little familiar, but I only met her once."

"I've seen her a lot, and that's her."

The mouse behind the desk looked up at the sound of voices. She peered over her glasses at the adventurers.

"Orville Mouse? What in the world are you doing here? Is that your lovely friend Sophia?"

"Um… what?"

Sophia gave a friendly wave. "Hello, Madam Beasley, it's so nice to see you again. You have such a lovely bed and breakfast. I love your quilts."

"How sweet of you to say so, dear. What in the world are you two doing here?"

Orville managed to shake off the surprise of encountering Madam Beasley in Elysian, and was now intensely curious.

"Hi, Madam Beasley, it's nice to see you. How long have you had a bed and breakfast here?"

"Oh, dear, let me think, the years do roll by, so hard to keep track. It must be ten years since I first opened it."

Orville was surprised by Madam Beasley's reply. "You remember when you first came to Elysian?"

"Indeed I do, it was the nicest dream I'd ever had, so pleasant, the volcano so fetching in the early morning light."

"The nicest dream you ever had?"

"Yes, ever so nice, that's why I decided to come back. Every night after I fall asleep I think about Elysian, imagining every detail of the bed and breakfast, and poof, here I am. I didn't really make all these lovely quilts, I just dreamed them."

Orville was feeling dizzy. "Wait, you're dreaming this?"

"Of course, but it's still so nice to see you and Sophia, even if it is just a dream. You make a lovely couple, you know. Your mum is so happy you found Sophia, and so proud of the fine young mouse you've become."

"You're dreaming this?"

Sophia rescued a very confused Orville. "It is a lovely dream, and what a wonderful view of the volcano you have, quite spectacular. The sign out front said you have free maps?"

"Oh, yes, you wouldn't want to climb up to the crater without a map, it would be ever so dangerous with all that dreadfully sharp volcanic rock. I've climbed it more than a few times and the view from the top is simply breathtaking, you can see the whole island from up there."

"You've climbed the volcano? Isn't it dangerous?"

"It's not dangerous at all if you use the map. The stairs around the volcano take you all the way to the top."

"There are stairs going up to the crater?"

"I dreamed those the first year I was here. I practice my yoga every day, and I'm quite fit, but I'm not as young as I used to be, and I certainly couldn't climb a volcano like that without stairs. I also have my guests to think about, some of them getting on in years, and the stairs make it so much more enjoyable for them."

"What's yoga?"

"What's inside the crater?"

Madam Beasley furrowed her brow. "How strange, I can't quite remember, isn't that silly? I remember seeing something there, but I can't quite put my paw on it at the moment. It will come to me, I'm sure. Now, how long will you be staying?"

"Just one night, I think. We want to climb the volcano in the morning and take a look at the crater."

Madam Beasley gave a conspiratorial wink to Orville and Sophia. "No charge for dear friends like you, and I'll even fix you a lovely dinner. You must be famished from your long hike through the jungle. I have a freshly baked snapberry pie, if anyone is interested." She winked at Orville.

"Mmm, snapberry pie."

"It's settled then, I'll show you to your rooms and give you time to freshen up before dinner. There's a map of the volcano on each bedside table. So lovely to see you both, and I'm so glad you brought Proto with you, such a charming fellow, and everyone does love his tasty little cakes."

Chapter 25

Reach for the Stairs

"I've packed a wholesome lunch for your hike up the volcano, with a little extra snapberry pie for Orville. You have your maps?"

"Yes, it looks simple enough, take the trail east for three miles, look for the silver stairs, walk up the stairs to the crater."

"It's as easy as pie, you'll have a marvelous time. This has been a lovely dream, so nice to catch up with you and Sophia. Do say hello to your mum if you can remember when you wake up."

"Thanks, Madam Beasley. You have a lovely bed and breakfast."

Brother Solus gave an exasperated groan. "If you're quite done with the pleasantries?"

Sophia paid no attention to Brother Solus, giving Madam Beasley a warm hug.

Less than an hour later they stood at the base of a seemingly endless silver staircase winding around the volcano.

"Creekers, we have to climb a nineteen thousand

foot tall spiral staircase? That's almost four miles high."

"Come on, Dread Pirate Orville, think of the wonderful view we'll have at the top. Madam Beasley said you can see the whole island from up there."

"I wonder what's in the crater? I hope it's not scary, full of molten lava."

"It all depends. Keep a tight rein on your thoughts, I don't wish to encounter another purveyor of pastries and pies."

Sophia poked Orville in the ribs. "Orville puts the 'pie' in pirate."

Orville laughed. "That was actually kind of funny."

"You don't happen to have sleeping bags and a tent in there, do you? Maybe a picnic table? Ha ha ha ha! Ha ha ha ha!"

"Um…that was funny, Proto, but your timing was a bit off. We weren't really talking about a pack or anything you could put sleeping bags in."

"I have calculated the number of steps to the top, arriving at a figure of seventy-two thousand and forty-nine steps. The volcano is nineteen thousand twenty-nine feet tall, and the stairs spiral around the volcano at a rate–"

Orville groaned. "My feet hurt already and we've only gone up a few hundred steps."

"Two hundred and twenty-nine steps."

On step four thousand and twenty-one Sophia sat down with a groan. "My feet are killing me. Orville, how about giving me a nice foot rub?"

"Sorry, the Dread Pirate Orville doesn't give foot rubs."

On step five thousand and thirteen Orville stopped in his tracks. "Get down! I saw something moving behind that big rock up ahead, something red."

"Oh, dear, perhaps it's a deadly mountainous variety of red carnivorous centipede. Not to belabor the point, but the only scary creatures we've seen on this adventure have been the blue pirates, and they were almost a mile away."

"The caterpillars were scary."

Proto blinked several times, attempting to compose a reply which would not hurt Sophia's feelings.

Orville hissed, "Shhh! Nobody move, I'm going to sneak up there and see what it is."

Step by step, Orville crept up the stairs, keeping as low as he could, being careful not to dislodge any small rocks or stones which might give him away. Inching his way forward, he peered around the huge rock.

"Sophia! You'd better see this!"

A minute later all four adventurers were eyeing a colorful sign hanging above a rustic wooden bench. Seated on the bench was Madam Beasley, looking quite lovely in a red and yellow flowered frock.

Madam Beasley's Complimentary Foot Rubs

Madam Beasley gave Sophia a sympathetic smile.

"Have a seat, dear. Put up those poor aching feet and

I'll give you a nice relaxing foot rub. There's a pitcher of cold lemonade on that table, if anyone is thirsty from the long climb."

"Madam Beasley, how did you get up here?"

"This is a dream, dear, I can be anywhere I want."

"That feels so good. Orville wouldn't give me a foot rub."

Brother Solus' expression was dour.

Proto was frowning. Relaxing foot rubs on a perilous adventure seemed entirely inappropriate. "I'm beginning to think we won't see any scary creatures at all, just bide our time while certain mice get relaxing foot rubs."

Brother Solus sidled over to Proto, whispering in his ear.

Proto's eyes opened wide. "Oh, dear, are you quite certain?"

Brother Solus continued.

"How awful!"

Brother Solus stepped away from Proto.

Proto's eyes were bright. "Oh my, how absolutely dreadful, quite terrifying indeed. It will be a miracle if any of us survive." He rubbed his great silver hands together, his face wreathed in a wide grin.

On step nineteen-thousand three hundred and twenty-one Orville plopped himself down on the stairs with a groan.

"Can't go any farther... legs burning... too tired... so thirsty."

"Oh no, I left my favorite blue socks back at the bed

and breakfast. Orville, could you run get them?" Sophia gave a cackling laugh.

"Very funny. We're almost a mile up in the air and you're making jokes. I didn't get a nice relaxing foot rub like some of us did. Hey, Brother Solus, you were right, the air up here is fine, not hard to breathe at all."

"This is Elysian. Perhaps we should rest for a while. That lava tube looks promising, we could set up a rudimentary campsite in there, safe from the elements."

Proto tilted his head, studying the black opening.

"It may not be a lava tube at all, perhaps residing within it is a nest swarming with deadly venomous mountain spiders."

"I feel a lot better now, not so tired." Orville darted up the stairs.

On step thirty-one thousand and fourteen Sophia sat down with a sigh. "That's it for me. I need some dinner and a comfy sleeping bag."

Brother Solus looked as though he might drop. "If you insist. We can sleep beneath that big outcropping."

"Do you think it would be safe to shape sleeping bags?"

Brother Solus closed his eyes, a pained look on his face. "You shape at your own peril. We are approaching the realm of the Shadow King. All the rules are changing."

Orville flicked his wrist. There was a flash of orange light and a leather shoe filled with soft moldy cheese blinked into existence, a dreadful smell filling the air.

"Creekers, that doesn't exactly look like a sleeping

bag. I guess I won't try to shape dinner. We can finish the lunches Madam Beasley made for us."

Sophia, Orville, and Brother Solus were sound asleep before the sun met the horizon. Proto dangled his legs over the edge of an eight thousand foot precipice, his silver body reflecting the golden rays of a setting sun, a gleeful grin on his face. This was going to be fun.

Chapter 26

The Crater's Secret

"I don't know what happened. I tried to shape flap-cakes and got this."

"Eww, it looks like a big pot of clam pudding, if there is such a thing. It smells awful. No more shaping food, this could be poisonous."

"Never fear, it's Proto to the rescue. I have six boxes of flapcake mix and two jars of snapberry jam in my pack. We mustn't dally, the sooner we reach the crater the sooner we'll get to the realm of the Shadow King."

"You're in a good mood today."

"There's nothing like a thrilling otherworldly adventure to boost the flagging spirits."

"Right." Orville's eyes narrowed slightly.

On step fifty-two thousand and eighteen Orville heard Proto humming a catchy little tune.

"Say, Proto, you haven't seen any scary creatures, have you? You know, big claws, really hungry? The kind of creatures you like?"

"Not a single one. My nocturnal vigil was calm and peaceful, quite suited for quiet reflection."

Orville and Sophia looked at each other, eyebrows raised.

On step sixty-eight thousand and twelve Orville stopped, scanning the landscape lying almost three miles below them.

"Whoa, Madam Beasley was right. This is a spectacular view. I can see most of the island. I don't see any villages though, it's all jungle except for the sandy beaches."

"It's beautiful. I wish I'd brought a camera."

"Hey, Proto, you don't have a camera in your pack, do you?"

Proto threw his head back and gave a great staccato laugh. "Ha ha ha ha! That's a good one, I'll have to remember that one. You don't have a camera in your pack, do you? Ha ha ha ha!"

Orville shook his head.

On step seventy-one thousand and six, Orville spotted the rim of the volcano. "We're almost there! Just another few minutes!"

Sophia was the first to reach the top. She stood silently, staring into the vast crater.

Orville scrambled up next to her. "Creekers! What is that? Is it a building? It must be a mile across. Do you think someone lives down there?"

Sophia shook her head. "No one lives down there. It's not a building, it's an Anarkkian interstellar battle cruiser."

"The Isle of the Silver Ship!"

"Exactly."

Brother Solus stepped up behind them, peering into the crater. He took one look and collapsed, Proto grabbing him as he fell.

Orville kneeled down, shaking his shoulder. "Brother Solus! Are you all right?"

Proto scanned Brother Solus' vital signs. "His blood pressure is highly elevated. I believe he fainted at the sight of the Anarkkian battle cruiser."

Brother Solus' eyes flickered open.

"Unhh... where is..."

"You fainted, but you're okay. You saw the big silver ship in the crater and you fainted."

"Nonsense, I did no such thing. I simply had too much sun climbing those dreadful stairs." He rose unsteadily to his feet, brushing bits of crushed volcanic rock off his cloak.

"You're sure you're okay?"

"Enough."

"Let's climb down to the ship."

Proto set his great pack on the ground. "As I previously mentioned, I have two hundred feet of stout climbing rope, more than adequate for our descent."

"Perfect, the hull of the ship is less than a hundred feet down."

"Brother Solus, do you know why we're here, what we're looking for?"

"I have not the faintest idea. Clearly I have never been here before, never set eyes on this monolithic silver creation. You say it is some type of war vessel?"

"It's an Anarkkian interstellar battle cruiser. They

were everywhere during the Anarkkian wars, destroying hundreds of planets, billions of lives."

Brother Solus eyed the titanic ship. "Why would they do that? Why did they take all those lives?"

"Their leaders placed more value on power and wealth than on life."

"Do you think we could fly this thing?"

Sophia shook her head. "It takes a crew of several hundred to operate a ship like this one. It's not like flying a Dragonfly or a blinker ship."

"Hey, maybe they have scout ships on board we could use. We've flown a blinker ship before, it can't be that different."

"That's a good thought. Most battle cruisers had scout ships and escape pods. They weren't as fast as blinker ships, but they were very reliable."

Proto tied the climbing rope around an outcropping of volcanic rock. "Who would like to go first? We shouldn't dilly dally, Aislin is waiting for us."

Orville gave Proto a suspicious look. "You're in an awfully big hurry to get to the realm of the Shadow King. Is there something you're not telling us?"

"I'll go first, just to make certain the rope is strong enough." Proto slipped over the crater's edge and slid down the rope, landing on the ship with a resounding thud.

"He's up to something, I know he is."

Orville went next, followed by Sophia and Brother Solus.

"This is incredible. How could they make a ship this

big? It must be a mile across."

"They built them in dark space Star Yards. This one must have been damaged in battle and crashed into the volcano."

A thought cloud flashed out of Orville's ear to Sophia. "How could an Anarkkian interstellar battle cruiser get into Elysian? There were no battles fought in the synthetic worlds."

"You're right, it's not possible. Someone in Elysian must have shaped this, or dreamed it, just like Madam Beasley's Bed and Breakfast. Do you think she could have done it?"

"She wouldn't know anything about the Anarkkian wars."

"That leaves only one other person."

Orville's eyes were on Brother Solus.

"He said he's never seen a ship like this before."

"I know, but there's something odd about him, and he doesn't remember how he got here or where he came from."

"The red book said millions of Mintarians entered the synthetic worlds. Maybe Brother Solus is a refugee who was left behind."

"Fourteen hundred years ago?"

"Good point, he doesn't look a day over nine hundred."

Sophia snickered. "Don't be mean."

Proto and Brother Solus had gone ahead, strolling down the sloping surface of the battle cruiser.

"Proto stopped at that big dome, maybe he found an

entrance."

Orville and Sophia hurried down to the large gleaming structure.

"It's transparent like the dome on the *MV Bermitar*, and has those yellow transport discs on the floor. How do we get in?"

Brother Solus stepped over to a pale blue translucent grid of discs on the dome, gazing at it in silence. He tapped nine of the discs, then stepped back. The dome became a soft wavering field of light. Brother Solus stepped through, motioning for the others to follow.

"How did you do that? How did you know what code to use?"

"The numbers just appeared in my head."

"From where?"

Brother Solus did not answer.

Proto looked at the three foot wide yellow discs on the floor.

"These are the transport tubes which blink us to the various sections of the ship, but I am unable to decipher the glyphs."

"We're looking for a docking bay that has scout ships or escape pods."

Brother Solus approached one of the yellow discs, watching curiously as the color changed to violet.

Sophia grabbed his arm. "Wait, don't step on it, it might not work properly. This ship wasn't built by the Anarkkians."

Brother Solus pulled away and stepped onto the disc, vanishing in a flash of blue light.

Chapter 27

Squeaky

"What should we do? Suppose he got transported into dark space or some other weird–"

Orville gave a start when Brother Solus reappeared in a flash of blue light.

"The transport tube system is functioning properly. The disc took me to the third level forward cargo hold."

"How do you know what section of ship you were in if you've never seen one before?"

"Enough of your questions. I simply knew what it was. There is nothing more to say."

"Sorry, it just seemed…"

"Did you see any escape pods or scout ships in the cargo hold?"

Proto answered, "Such vehicles would not be located on the cargo deck, they would be on the main battle weapons deck or in the hangar bay just beneath the topside flight deck. Massive elevators carried the scout ships from the hangar bay up to the flight deck. Escape pods are on the weapons deck and launched directly from there, exiting from port and starboard launch tubes at over a thousand miles an hour, a suitable arrangement for dark space, but not for the interior of a volcano. Some battle cruisers launched smaller scout ships vertically through exit tubes on the upper hull. Those are the ones we should be looking for."

"So... we need to find the hangar bay? You said it's below the flight deck?"

"Correct, but a battle cruiser of this size would have numerous flight decks and numerous hangar bays."

"How do we find them?"

"We search the outer hull for highly shielded areas, their presence indicated by low blue domes through which defensive energy field screens were projected. Hangar bays would lie beneath these blue energy domes, and the launch centers beneath the hangar bays."

"I'm getting confused. What are we looking for?"

"A big blue dome on the outside of the ship."

"Okay, looking for blue domes. Let's split up and search for them. I'll check the outer perimeter of the hull."

Orville exited through the wavering energy field, heading across the expansive hull, weaving his way through a field of immense gleaming gold cylinders.

"I wonder what all this stuff is? Must be weapons or something. These round things have little blinking lights on them. That's good, it means the ship still has power. We'll need it to launch a scout ship. I hope

Sophia knows how to fly one. Proto can probably fly them since he knows all about Anarkkian technology from those historical glowbird records at the Cube."

Orville stepped through a maze of spiky structures protruding from the outer hull of the battle cruiser.

"Mirus Mouse would love all this stuff. Maybe I can find a weird device to take back to him. I should find something for Papa. I got those seashells for Mum, but I don't have anything for Papa."

Orville froze when he heard the low growling coming from behind a tall black spinning cylinder. He was about to pop up a sphere of defense when he remembered Brother Solus' stern warning about shaping this close to the realm of the Shadow King.

He silently backed away from whatever was lurking behind the cylinder.

"This can't be good. I have to warn the others, there might be more of these creatures. Okay, I'm a fast runner, even Sophia says so. On three I'm going to turn and run like lightning. Faster than lightning. One, two, THREE!"

Orville spun around and leaped forward. Unfortunately, in doing so he collided with the large silver cube directly behind him, thumping his head quite severely. He staggered backwards, paws on his forehead.

"Ow! My head!"

The growling instantly transformed into a terrifying roar, the sound of claws scraping wildly against the hull ringing in Orville's ears. He gave a piercing yelp and took off running, shrieking, "Sophia! Proto! Crazy monster is after me! Help! Proto!"

Orville dashed across a flight deck embedded with long rows of blinking red lights. The beast's roar was growing louder with each step.

"It's getting closer! Proto! Sophia! Help, monster attacking me!"

He tore around two spinning orange panels, streaking across a sloping forty foot wide glimmering blue dome.

"Hey, it's one of those blue domes! Proto! Sophia! Where are you?"

As luck would have it, just as Proto and Sophia darted around a towering silver dish, Orville tripped on a section of black metal conduit, careening across the deck, sliding to a stop at Proto's feet.

"What is it? What are you hollering about?"

"Monster chasing me! Growling! Big claws!"

Proto's eyes lit up. "A monster with big claws? Oh, dear!" He stepped forward just as the roaring creature slid around the orange panels, skittering into view.

Sophia looked at the growling red-eyed creature, then at Proto, then at Orville.

"This is your monster?"

"Good heavens, it's a RoboPup! I haven't seen one of these since I lived with my family of Elders. We had a RoboPup named Squeaky, such a lovable little fellow."

Sophia snorted. "Whoa, Orville, I can see why you were so scared, that little fellow is terrifying! I'll probably have nightmares for months, look how he's wagging his tail, so scary!"

The gleaming silver RoboPup sat down in front of Proto, his eyes on Orville.

Proto rubbed the puppy's head. "Hello, little fellow, I'm going to call you Squeaky."

Squeaky lay down, resting his head on Proto's foot, his tail still wagging.

"That's not what was chasing me! It was growling and roaring and had huge claws! It's still out there!"

Proto grinned at Sophia. "Squeaky, intruder alert!"

Squeaky let out an ear-splitting roar, jumping to his feet, growling and snarling, his claws raking wildly against the Morsennium deck.

Orville took a step back, his eyes wide. "What is that thing?"

"It's a RoboPup, quite ubiquitous among the Elder households in the days of my youth. RoboPups performed a wide variety of home security functions, but of course would never harm family members. Little Squeaky was a beloved member of our family."

"I was only scared for a minute, and that was because I didn't see him, All that growling and roaring would have scared anyone. Anyone."

Sophia smiled pleasantly.

"Is that a smirk? Are you smirking? You would have been just as scared as I was if you'd heard him."

"I guess so." Sophia was still smiling.

"Anyway, I found a blue dome back that way. Is that RoboPup thing coming with us? It seems like it might be a nuisance, getting underfoot, kind of bothersome.

Does it bite?"

"Oh, good heavens, no. Little Squeaky would never do anything like that." Proto gave a low chuckle.

Orville's eyes narrowed, wary of Proto's peculiar sense of humor.

The party of adventurers made their way back to the blue dome.

"This is where they project the defensive energy shields?"

"Correct, but only when the ship is under imminent threat of attack."

"How do we in? I don't see any hatches."

"Perhaps our new friend Squeaky will be able to help us."

"He's going to sniff around and find a secret trapdoor?"

Proto pointed to the blue dome. "Squeaky, attack!"

A blinding blast of purple light exploded out from Squeaky's eyes, a six foot wide hole appearing in the blue dome.

Orville's jaw dropped. "Creekers! What was that?"

"That was his heavy particle destructor beam. Quite a useful feature."

Sophia sat down next to Squeaky and rubbed his back. "I think he's cute. Hi, Squeaky, my name is Sophia."

Squeaky put his paw on Sophia's knee, then cautiously curled up on her lap.

"I guess he's a little cute. He seems pretty friendly. He won't blast us with that destructor beam will he?"

"Certainly not. He is autonomous, but when I give him a verbal command I am also transmitting a 32 digit security code accessing his defense program and authorizing its use. I have added all of us to his authorized family member list."

"So if I told him to attack he wouldn't do anything?"

"Correct, but he would attack if he thought you were in danger."

"I guess that's not so bad. It's not like he just goes around vaporizing stuff whenever he feels like it."

Brother Solus's voice rang out. "This endless chatter is bringing us no closer to the realm of the Shadow King. Proto, the climbing rope, if you would?"

Proto pulled the rope from his pack and looped it around a black cube, dropping the other end into the ship's interior.

Orville peered into the darkness below. "It doesn't look too scary. At least there won't be weird creatures down there." He slid down the rope into the ship.

Chapter 28

Time for Launch

"What is all this stuff? Proto, aim your ear lights over here."

"It appears to be a command and communications center, either for the flight deck or the energy shields. That door looks promising."

Sophia pressed a glowing violet tab and the silver door slid open. She stepped into a cavernous hangar, dozens of bright overhead lights blinking on.

Orville gave a shriek, skittering backwards, crashing into Proto. The hangar was filled with dozens of silver Anarkkian attack spiders.

Proto scanned the rows of gleaming eight legged automatons.

"Nothing to worry about, they have been deactivated for interstellar travel. The Anarkkians didn't activate them until the ship was in attack mode. Once they were armed, the hangar door dropped and the spiders would rain down on the hapless city, destroying everything in sight with their deadly force beams."

"That was scary. You modified that attack spider on

Varmoran so we could ride him, but I don't think one of these can help us cross the Great Sea. I wonder what happened to all the Anarkkians who were on the ship?"

A blue thought cloud flashed over to Orville. "This ship is a dream creation, remember? It's not a real Anarkkian ship, somebody dreamed it. I'm starting to think you're right about it being Brother Solus."

"There's no one else it could be."

"And he knew the code for the transport tube dome."

"We should definitely keep an eye on him."

Proto pointed to the far end of the hangar. "That big gray cylinder is a launch tube for scout attack ships. The ladders next to it should go to the lower deck."

Brother Solus nodded. "You are correct. There are scout ships there which will be more than–"

Before he could finish, the ship shuddered violently, tipping wildly to one side, the adventurers tumbling to the floor, the great attack spiders careening across the hangar, metal squealing and rending as the monstrous eight legged automatons smashed against the outer bulkhead, a section of the upper deck collapsing with a thundering crash.

It was over as quickly as it had begun.

"What happened?"

Brother Solus groaned. "My leg is pinned by this beam. I can't move."

Proto dashed over and grasped the Morsennium beam with his great silver hands, raising it enough for Orville and Sophia to pull Brother Solus to safety.

Proto kneeled down, a pale green light from his eyes

scanning Brother Solus. "There are no broken bones."

Orville sensed a change in Brother Solus. This was not the stern rigid monk they had come to know, this was a scared old Mintarian.

"Please, we have to go back to Okeanos. This is wrong, the realm of the Shadow King is a dark and vile place, a land to be avoided, a ghastly world of horrors beyond comprehension."

"What kind of horrors?"

Sophia's face hardened.

"Brother Solus, I understand you're afraid, but we're going into the realm of the Shadow King with you or without you. We came here to rescue Aislin Mouse, and that is precisely what we're going to do. You'll be a lot safer if you come with us instead of trying to return to Okeanos on your own. If we have to use our shaping powers to defend ourselves, we will do the best we can, but I think Proto and Squeaky will provide all the protection we need. You saw what Squeaky did to the blue dome."

Proto looked up at Orville. "He told me the Shadow King's realm has the most fearsome creatures imaginable, beasts torn from nightmarish visions, great clawed squirming monstrosities not found in any other universe."

Orville made a croaking sound. "If the realm of the Shadow King is as bad as he says it is, maybe we should think about–"

"Do you want to be the one to tell Ebenezer Mouse we were too scared to look for Aislin, that we gave up without even trying?"

"I wasn't saying we should turn around, just that we might want to think about it."

"Brother Solus, are you with us?"

The old Mintarian rose up, wincing in pain.

"It would appear fate has provided me with limited options. I will travel with you into the realm of the Shadow King. I have no other choice."

"It won't be as bad as you think, we've faced things like this before, even worse than this. I should tell you about Mendacium the Dark Wizard, he was one scary mouse."

Brother Solus put his paw on Orville's shoulder. "I apologize for my unduly harsh and inconsiderate behavior."

"That's okay, we all get crabby sometimes. You said something about scout ships below us?"

"Follow me." Brother Solus limped toward the ladders leading to the lower deck.

A thought cloud flashed out from Sophia to Orville. "Be careful, I think Brother Solus is unconsciously trying to prevent us from reaching the Shadow King."

"You think he made the deck collapse?"

"I'm sure of it. It happened the moment he told us where the scout ships were. He's not purposefully doing it, but part of him is trying to stop us, the part of him that is terrified of what he will find there."

With Proto's help, Brother Solus gingerly climbed down the ladder.

The adventurers found themselves in a long dark

corridor, a set of pale green doors at the far end.

The doors opened as Brother Solus approached them, revealing a cavernous hangar filled with ten foot tall blue spheres.

"Scout ships. These conveyor belts carry them to the launch tubes. In the event of an attack, ships can be launched every two seconds."

"This might work, they look a lot like blinker ships." Sophia peered inside one, studying the control panel. "I can fly this. Brother Solus, do you know how to activate the launch system?"

Brother Solus pointed to a ladder reaching up to an elongated window high above the hangar floor.

"The control center is behind that window. Next to the main panel is an orange emergency button used to initiate the launch sequence."

"Once we push the button, how long until our ship launches?"

"It takes a little over a minute to launch all thirty ships."

"So one of us has to climb the ladder, open the door, push the button, then get back to the ship in less than a minute, while the conveyor belt is moving? That's not possible."

"One of us will have to stay behind."

"Maybe I could blink back, that might work."

Brother Solus glared at Orville. "No blinking."

Proto picked up Squeaky, rubbing the top of his head.

"I believe my old friend Squeaky may provide a

more satisfactory solution to this vexing problem."

Orville looked dubious. "What can he do, bark at it?"

"Our friend Squeaky is full of surprises. First we should locate the last scout ship in line to be launched, maximizing the time Squeaky has to push the button and return to the ship."

"Squeaky can climb a ladder?"

Sophia strode down the row of scout ships.

"This will be the last ship to launch. It looks good, no external damage." She peered through the porthole. "Control panel lights are on, the ship has power. How do we get inside?"

Proto scanned the outer hatch, then pressed his hand against the ship.

"That's it, I have opened a link to the engineered intelligence core. This should do it."

The hatch whirred open, the interior lights blinking on.

"You're sure you can fly this?"

"It's just like a blinker ship."

"Everyone strap in."

"Check."

Proto scratched Squeaky's head. "Okay, little one, I want you to go up to the command center, open the door, push the orange launch button and return to the ship as fast as you can."

Squeaky gave a loud bark.

"Go!"

Orville's jaw dropped when Squeaky lifted off the

ground and flashed through the air toward the command center.

"Squeaky can fly? Seriously? A flying puppy?"

"Ha ha ha ha! I told you Squeaky was full of surprises. He has an integrated micro anti-grav displacer unit with enough power to fly continuously for up to an hour."

Orville watched through the open hatch as Squeaky hovered next to the command center. A blast of purple light shot out and the door vanished. Squeaky disappeared into the command center and seconds later an ear splitting alarm blared. The massive conveyor belt roared, the scout ships lurching toward the launch tube.

"Here he comes!" Orville grinned as Squeaky flew into the ship and landed next to Proto with a loud bark.

Sophia punched a yellow tab and the hatch slammed shut.

"Three more ships, then it's us! Hold on tight!"

Whenever Orville would tell the story of their launch from the mile long Anarkkian interstellar battle cruiser he always used the word 'flapcake'. Even with the inertia deadeners on, the force of being blasted out of the launch tube at almost a thousand miles an hour felt like a colossal paw pressing him down, trying to turn him into an Orville shaped flapcake. He freely admitted that he had shrieked, but claimed he was not the only one, that Sophia had also screamed, something she emphatically denied.

Sophia yanked back on the silver control lever,

bringing the ship to a hover at twenty-three thousand feet.

"I've got it, the ship is functioning perfectly, violet lights on all systems."

Orville was still disoriented from the launch.

"Whoa, I think I left my stomach back in the hangar."

Proto released his safety harness and stood up, peering out the porthole. "I see no sign of the other scout ships. Most curious."

"Let's fly down and buzz Madam Beasley's bed and breakfast."

"We don't have time, and it would probably scare her."

"I didn't think about that. Which way do we go?"

Brother Solus pointed toward the rising sun. "Directly east until you see land. Things will change drastically as we near the realm of the Shadow King. Make no attempt to shape anything, pay close attention to your thoughts."

"What kind of drastic changes?"

Brother Solus did not answer, but the look on his face was not reassuring.

"Heading due east, increasing speed to three hundred miles an hour."

"Whoa, this is way faster than a Dragonfly. Brother Solus, how long will it take us to reach the eastern shore of the Great Sea?"

"It all depends."

"Oh, right, it all depends."

Three hours later there was no land in sight.

"This must be a really big ocean."

"Increasing speed to five hundred miles an hour."

Orville watched the waves flashing by beneath them.

Four hours later there was no land in sight.

Orville eyed Brother Solus. Something was wrong. They had traveled over three thousand miles and there was no land in sight.

"Brother Solus, if someone was trying to prevent us from reaching the realm of the Shadow King, could they create an infinitely wide ocean, one we could never cross no matter how fast or far we flew?"

"You are suggesting I am responsible for this? You think I'm the one creating this infernal ocean? It is most certainly not me who–"

"I see land!" Sophia pointed to the ship's holoscreen.

Orville jumped up and looked out the porthole. "Creekers. the sun is blue. Why would the sun be blue?"

"Slowing to one fifty miles an hour, approaching the coastline."

"What are those flashes of light? It looks like big explosions."

Sophia magnified the holoscreen.

"That's exactly what it is. There's a huge city on the coast and it's under attack."

Brother Solus groaned. "We should not be here."

"Strap in! Three ships approaching!"

A thunderous explosion jarred their craft, knocking

Orville and Brother Solus to the floor.

"Hold on!" Sophia jammed the two sticks forward and the scout ship shot up at over four hundred miles an hour. "Proto, do we have a cloak?"

"Top left panel, green tab."

Sophia slapped the tab and sent the ship into a screaming dive, shooting past the three attacking vessels. Seconds later they were inches above the waves, streaking toward the flaming city.

"That did it, we lost them. Brother Solus, what is this place?"

Brother Solus was hunched over, arms wrapped around himself. "We should not be here."

"I'm heading east, this feels like another obstacle placed in our path, just like the ocean."

Sophia jammed the stick forward and they shot over the coastline, now a thousand feet above the cacophonous explosions and spectacular flashes of red and purple light.

"Spiders! There's thousands of Anarkkian spiders down there and the attack ships are everywhere! There are creatures running through the streets, but I can't tell what they are, maybe mice, maybe Mintarians."

"This is not good, the city goes on as far as I can see, there's no end to it, no end to the devastation, ships and spiders everywhere. The good news is our cloak is working, I'm taking us up to three thousand feet."

Brother Solus shrieked, "We should not be here!" He shook his fist at Sophia. "We do not belong in this place!"

Sophia never saw the attacking ship, only a flash of purple light and the gaping hole that suddenly appeared in their hull. She was knocked out of her seat, slammed against the bulkhead by the two hundred mile an hour wind that exploded through the cabin.

Orville was suddenly weightless, the ship plummeting toward the flaming city below.

"We've lost power! Emergency canopy!"

He pushed himself to the top of the cabin and grabbed the bright red ring, giving it a sharp tug. He heard the muffled explosion as the canopy deployed, felt the ship jerk sideways, swaying wildly back and forth just before he was slammed to the floor and knocked unconscious.

Chapter 29

Downtown Bellumia

Sophia put her paw over Orville's mouth, silencing him.

"Shhh! Don't talk. Spiders are everywhere."

The last thing Orville remembered was pulling the emergency ring. The orange canopy was draped over the ship, fluttering in a gentle breeze. Outside the ship's partially opened hatch he saw great piles of stone rubble, the remains of a once colossal building demolished by invading Anarkkian forces. A thought cloud floated out to Sophia.

"How many spiders are out there?"

"There were lots of them when we landed, but we kept hidden in the ship. Most of them left, but a few are still prowling the area. Proto said you saved our lives by pulling the emergency ring."

Orville grinned. "Any dread pirate would have done the same thing."

Sophia kissed him on the cheek. "You're the bravest dread pirate I know."

Brother Solus hissed, "I told you we didn't belong

213

here. If the attack ships don't destroy us, the spiders will."

"Master Marloh says happiness lies on the other side of every obstacle."

"Clearly he has never faced an attack spider."

Proto peered through the wide hole left by the attacker's vape beam.

"This is a Mintarian city, I recognize the architecture, and I saw three Mintarians being chased by a spider. I'm going to send Squeaky out to survey the area. I have linked his optical transmission system to my holoscreen so we'll be able to see what he is seeing. He should be able to map a safe route past the spiders."

"I'm starting to like that little RoboPup. Sorry I said he was a nuisance."

"We should travel east, get out of the city."

"It's called Bellumia. The city is called Bellumia."

"What?"

Brother Solus looked exhausted. "I don't know why I said that, I've never heard of a city called Bellumia. I just want to go back to Okeanos, I want to be alone. I'm tired, I need sleep." He curled up on the floor and closed his eyes.

Proto whispered, "I'm sending Squeaky out."

Squeaky shot through the open hatch, soaring upward. A holoscreen blinked on in front of Proto.

"It's working. I told him to fly east and keep an eye out for spiders."

"He's about two hundred feet up, but I don't see any spiders. That's odd, they must have moved on."

"The explosions have stopped. Do you think the Anarkkians left? Maybe the invasion is over, maybe it's safe to go out now."

"Why would the invasion suddenly stop? Let's think about this. We know this isn't a real Anarkkian invasion, it's a dream invasion, an obstacle created by one of us, or maybe even the Shadow King."

"Brother Solus is asleep."

"And the invasion stopped."

"It's him, he's the one creating the city and the invasion."

Sophia whispered, "Let him sleep, let's see what happens."

Proto pointed mutely to the holoscreen. Squeaky was flying over an eerie forest filled with tall black trees.

"What is that? Where's the city?"

Sophia looked out through the ship's open hatch.

"Orville, look out there."

The demolished city was gone, replaced by a dark shadowy forest.

"I don't like this. That forest looks really spooky."

Proto's eyes were bright. "Very spooky indeed, more than likely filled with the terrifying beasts Brother Solus said were roaming the realm of the Shadow King."

"Stop, I'm already scared enough. Maybe we should wake Brother Solus. I'd rather face attack spiders than some creepy forest full of weird monsters."

Proto tapped Orville on the shoulder, pointing to the holoscreen. Orville's heart almost stopped when he saw the gigantic shiny black centipede slithering through the forest.

"What's that thing on its back? Something is riding on the centipede's back!"

Proto magnified the image. "It's a blue translucent figure carrying a big axe and wearing an eye patch."

"Seriously? It's wearing an eye patch? A ghost pirate riding a giant centipede in a dark creepy forest? Could anything possibly be scarier than that?"

"Orville, this is good news, not bad. You're creating the centipede and the ghost pirate, the things you're most afraid of. That's why they're appearing."

"Wait, if Brother Solus was creating the Anarkkian invasion, that would mean it was his greatest fear."

"You're right, and if he was one of the Mintarians who took refuge in a Metaphonium synthetic world, he would have seen Anarkkian attacks and have been terrified by them. Maybe he lived in Bellumia, maybe he saw it destroyed by the Anarkkians."

"He never said anything about it."

"He probably doesn't remember. It could be something he forgot because it was too painful. Maybe he lost friends or family in the invasion."

"Like you forgetting about the caterpillars."

"I'm starting to feel kind of sorry for him. He reminds me a little of Ebenezer."

Proto was listening absently, his eyes on a piece of crumpled white paper under Sophia's seat. He pretended to stretch his arms, surreptitiously taking the paper. He turned his back to the others, reading the note.

I wish he'd move out. I wish we'd never met him.

He ripped it into tiny pieces, his eyes on Sophia.

The adventurers let Brother Solus sleep until he woke up.

"How long did I sleep? Not too long, I hope, one should not fritter away the day lost in dreams."

"You were tired, you needed sleep. Everyone needs a nice long rest once in a while."

"Perhaps you are right, I must admit I feel quite refreshed, almost ready to face a ravaged city filled with Anarkkian attack spiders."

"They're gone, they vanished when you fell asleep. Bellumia is gone."

"I see. What is out there now?"

"A dark forest with tall black scraggly looking trees. Squeaky saw a ghost pirate with a big axe riding on a giant carnivorous centipede."

Brother Solus turned to Orville. "I am guessing you are responsible?"

"Yes, I'm afraid of ghosts, pirates, giant centipedes, and creepy forests."

For the first time since they had met him, Brother Solus smiled. "As are we all, my young friend."

Proto stood up, slinging his great pack onto his shoulder. "We should go. The sooner we rescue Aislin, the sooner we can get back to Muridaan Falls. I have some business to attend to back at the Cube."

"Back at the Cube? What kind of business?"

Proto stepped into the forest without answering.

Chapter 30

Fear

Orville's eyes were anxiously scanning the trees as they made their way down the meandering shadowy path.

"You didn't hear that? That rustling sound? It could be the ghost pirate."

"Relax, the pirate only exists because you're afraid of him. It's kind of funny if you think about it, a ghost pirate with a big axe riding on a giant centipede? I'm surprised he wasn't pulling a wagon filled with snap-berry pies."

Orville frowned. Why did everyone think this was funny? Even Brother Solus had laughed. That wasn't so bad though, it was nice to see Brother Solus laugh instead of being stern and crabby. Maybe Sophia was right, it was a little funny. He peered into the forbidding depths of the forest as he strolled along next to Sophia.

"These trees are so close together that a gigantic centipede couldn't fit through them anyway, which means I don't have to worry about–"

Time seemed to stop when Orville saw the beautiful ghostly mouse floating in the shadows, saw the weary face of Aislin Mouse, her gaze meeting his, her voice in his thoughts.

"You came. I knew you would, the Shadow King said you would. Cross the Great River. I long for the moment I can once again hold Ebenezer in my arms."

"Orville, what's wrong? Why did you stop?"

"What?"

"Why did you stop?"

"You didn't see her?"

"See who?"

"Aislin Mouse, I just saw her. She was a ghost. She said the Shadow King knew we would come. She said we have to cross the Great River."

"The Shadow King knew we were coming? How could he know that? How do we rescue Aislin if she's a ghost?"

"She said she longs for the day she can hold Ebenezer in her arms again. She can't be too ghosty if she has arms."

Sophia grinned. "Good point. We have to get to the Great River. When we cross that we leave the real world behind us."

"I'm not sure I'd call Elysian the real world. Things appear when you think of them, like ghost pirates on giant centipedes. That's not exactly Muridaan Falls."

"Whatever you call it, it's the world we're in. We have to find the Great River and we have to rescue

Aislin."

Brother Solus had been listening to their conversation.

"The Great River lies to the east. Once we cross it, for better or worse, we are in the realm of the Shadow King."

Proto sent Squeaky ahead of them, flying high above the dark forest. "Ha ha ha ha! Orville must be hungry. Squeaky just flew over a pastry shop."

"Orville, did you shape a pastry shop?"

"I can't help it, I'm starving, and I keep thinking about those yummy snapberry pies. At least I'm not thinking about a ghost pirate riding a centipede."

Proto stopped short. "Oh dear, you probably shouldn't have said that." Proto pointed down the forest path to a translucent blue ghostly pirate mounted on a monstrous black centipede.

"I think I'm going to throw up."

The great centipede scuttled toward them, its sinuous body undulating, its colossal legs moving in waves with a horrible metallic clicking sound.

"Orville, control your fear, stop thinking about the centipede."

"How can I stop thinking about it? I can't not think about something that's right in front of me!"

"Wait, I'm going to try something I do when I'm having a scary dream."

"What?"

Sophia strode toward the gigantic centipede and its ferocious ghost rider. She held up one paw, motioning for the pirate to stop.

"Excuse me, I wonder if you could help us?"

The pirate gave a cold laugh, raising his blue axe high above his ghostly head.

"Arghh, 'tis a tasty little snack for me trusty mount. Ye shall be feasting on fresh mouse this very day, laddie."

"Excuse me, do you happen to know if there's a flower shop nearby?"

The pirate lowered his axe.

"Arghh, what manner of devilry be this? Prepare to meet ye maker, scurvy mouse."

"First of all, you shouldn't say *arghh* so much, it just confuses everyone because no one really knows what it means. Secondly, I'm looking for a flower shop be-cause Orville's mum's birthday is tomorrow and we want to get her a big bouquet of blue moreilias. They're her favorite flower and she's been feeling sad lately, flowers would really cheer her up. You know how much mums love to get flowers on their birthday."

"Arghh, 'tis so, there's no denyin' the truth in that. My own dear mum fancied the very same blue moreili-as."

The pirate had a faraway look in his eyes, his great blue axe now resting on the centipede.

"We'd be so grateful if you could help us find a flower shop, such a kindness would help lift her spirits. Think of how your own mum would feel if someone brought her a lovely bouquet of flowers."

The pirate's axe vanished. "I be recallin' them days

of my youth, Papa and I carryin' flowers to me own dear mum. 'Tis a fond memory, one not thought of for many a year. Arghh."

"You'll help us? Your mum would be so proud of you, I can almost hear her saying how much she loves you."

The centipede vanished. The ghostly pirate was now standing alone on the forest path.

"Arghh, 'tis true, she herself ha' told me so many times. The love of me dear mum is not to be forgotten."

The pirate transformed into a bright yellow bird and flew off into the trees.

"Creekers! What was that? What just happened?"

"It's what I do in scary dreams. Instead of being afraid, I show kindness, love, and ask them to help me. The scary thing always changes into something beautiful. It worked for everything except the caterpillars."

Brother Solus was staring at Sophia, a curious light in his eyes.

Two days later there was still no sign of the Great River.

"Why do we always wind up in creepy forests?"

"The forests on Tectar weren't creepy, they were beautiful, lots of lovely wildflowers."

"That's true. Hey, Proto, how come you never get scared? You love all those creatures with claws and fangs."

"I suppose it is because I was once afraid to set foot outside of the Cube, terrified I might encounter a dreadful Anarkkian attack spider. I am almost indestructible, and yet they held great fear for me. There is a certain giddy delight in no longer being afraid of the fearsome creatures that once terrified me."

"It must be nice not to be afraid of anything."

Proto spotted a crumpled ball of white paper on the forest path. He kicked it into the scraggly brush. He didn't need to read it, he knew what it would say. It held the words he feared above all others.

"Brother Solus, what about you? What scares you?"

Brother Solus stopped, studying Orville's face for any sign of insincerity, but found none.

"The unknown, that is what scares me above all else, that infinite domain which holds the secret of my past."

"The secret of your past?"

"I am unable to recall even a single moment of my life before Elysian. I yearn to remember those lost days, but there lies within me a deep and terrible dread of the horrors such memories may reveal. It is a dread so profound I cannot find proper words to describe it."

"That sounds really scary. It can't be that bad though, you seem like a nice fellow, not someone with a dark and scary past. You seem true, that's what the Thirteenth Monk calls it. Maybe it was just something really sad, like Sophia and the caterpillars."

"Perhaps there is some truth to what you are saying. Perhaps my fear outweighs the darkness to be found in those lost memories."

"I see the river!"

Orville and Sophia darted ahead, stopping at the edge of a broad raging river.

"This has to be it, it's huge."

Brother Solus strode up next to Orville. "We have done it, we have reached the Great River, no small feat, I assure you. I can also assure you that crossing it will be far more difficult than you might imagine."

Chapter 31

Charon the Ferrymouse

"It's flowing a lot faster than I thought it would be, and it's almost a mile wide. There's no way we can swim across it."

"We could build a boat."

"We can't build a boat if we can't even shape a saw to cut the trees down. Hey, Proto, you don't have a big saw in your pack, do you?"

"Ha ha ha ha! Good one, I'll have to remember that one."

"I believe the solution to our problem lies scant yards away."

Brother Solus pointed to a wooden shack sitting a hundred feet downriver. Tied securely to a rickety dock was a wooden longboat with two oars resting in the locks.

"Where did that come from? That wasn't there before."

"This is Elysian. Let us discover what fresh obstruction has been placed in our path."

"This is good news, not bad. We found a boat."

Brother Solus appeared less than convinced.

Orville and Sophia made their way down the river's edge to the shack. In front of the forlorn ramshackle structure sat a rough hewn rocking chair, currently occupied by a disheveled mouse wearing a tattered brown and red robe secured around his waist with a length of frayed rope.

A crudely painted sign dangled from a nail on the front of the shack.

Charon's Boatworks
Reliable Ferry Crossings
Reasonable Rates

The bedraggled old mouse was sound asleep, his mouth open, raspy snoring sounds wafting across the air.

"Should we wake him?"

"Of course we should, he's our ticket across the river."

"That boat doesn't look very safe, it's cobbled together with old boards and tarpaper and globs of dried goopy stuff."

"It's floating, isn't it?"

"Sort of."

Sophia gently tapped the old mouse on the shoulder. He snorted loudly, his eyes popping open, a dark look appearing on his face.

"What is it? Who are you? What do you want?"

Sophia gave her brightest, friendliest smile. "We're trying to cross the river and we saw your sign. Would you be able to ferry us across in your boat?"

Orville added, "Your sign says reasonable rates."

The old mouse rose to his full height, which was significantly less than Orville's.

"I am Charon the Ferrymouse, I carry souls across the River Styx to the Land of the Dead."

"The River Styx? Is that the name of this river?"

"Why else would I be here? I am Charon the Ferrymouse, I carry souls across the River Styx to the Land of the Dead."

"Right. How much do you charge? Wait, what do you mean you carry souls to the Land of the Dead? Isn't the realm of the Shadow King across the river?"

"It is not. Across the River Styx lies the Land of the Dead. Payment for passage is one danake per soul. That's a total of three danakes for your party. No charge for the metal rabbit or the little mechanical puppy, since they do not possess souls."

Proto blinked. This was something he had not considered. Maybe this was why they wanted him to move out, move back to the Cube. Maybe Charon was right, maybe he didn't have a soul.

Brother Solus lost all patience. "I believe, good sir, you are acutely misinformed regarding your current location. This is the Great River, not the River Styx, and the realm of the Shadow King lies on the far bank, not your mythical Land of the Dead."

"Preposterous, my dear sir. I am Charon the Ferry-mouse and this is the River Styx, of this there is no doubt. I have been ferrying souls of the dead across this river from the beginning of time immemorial."

"It may interest you to note that none of us are dead, all of us quite alive and well."

Charon the Ferrymouse gave a start, giving Orville a sharp poke in the ribs.

"Great Heracles, you are alive, I haven't ferried a living creature across the river since that crafty Sysiphus fellow. I hope you know what you're doing, the Land of the Dead is not for the faint of heart."

Orville nudged Brother Solus. "Are you certain this is the right river? Crossing over to the Land of the Dead doesn't sound like a good idea."

Brother Solus glared at Charon. "What a marvelous boat you have, good sir. Perhaps you could tell me exactly how long you have been ferrying souls from this particular location?"

Charon's pugnacity fell away, replaced with befuddled uncertainty. "It's been a while, of course, let me think... I'd say... I've been here for as long as I can remember."

"You have no recollection of precisely how and when you arrived at this particular location in Elysian?"

Sophia tapped Orville on the shoulder. "I just remembered I left my purse back in the forest. We need to go back and find it."

"You brought your purse with you on an adventure? Seriously?"

"We need to find my purse, Orville, and we need to find it now."

"Oh, right, we need to find your purse. Lead the way."

When Sophia was certain Charon couldn't overhear them, she stopped, a look of chagrin on her face.

"It's quite possible I may have created Charon the Ferrymouse. I was thinking how much this was like the ancient myth of the ferrymouse carrying souls across the River Styx."

Orville grinned. "That's great news, now we know there's no Land of the Dead, and we can use Charon's boat to cross the river. He said he charges one danake per soul. What's a danake?"

"It's an ancient coin, and we don't have any. I don't even know what they look like."

"I'll talk to him, negotiate. I'm good at that sort of thing."

"I don't know if that's the best idea, Orville. He seems a bit cranky, be careful not to antagonize him."

"I'm an excellent negotiator. No need to fret, the Dread Pirate Orville will get us across that river."

Two minutes later Orville stood facing Charon the Ferrymouse.

"Passage across the river is one danake per soul, is that correct?"

"Correct. No charge for the metal rabbit or the puppy."

"I see. The problem is we don't have that particular coin. Could I pay you with silvers? I have nine silvers in my pack, and Sophia has twenty."

"Impossible. We only accept danakes, nothing else will do. Unless you have an interest in taking the Three Question Challenge?"

"The what?"

"The Three Question Challenge. I ask you three questions, if you answer them all correctly your entire party receives complimentary passage across the River Styx."

Orville's confidence evaporated.

"I don't really do very well with three question challenges. I get a little flustered and it's hard to think. What happens if I don't answer all three questions correctly?"

A fearsome light shone in Charon's eyes. "If you miss even one question, you shall be condemned to wander the barren shores of the River Styx in the Land of the Dead for precisely one hundred years, not a minute less."

"Wait, if I miss a question we still cross the river?"

"Correct, but there is the additional hundred year river wandering penalty clause."

"I'll take your Three Question Challenge."

"My questions will not be easy ones, do you wish to reconsider your choice? This is your last chance. Don't forget, one hundred years of wandering and not a minute less."

"I'm good. I'll take your Three Question Challenge."

"As you wish, so it shall be. Question number one, how many souls are currently residing in the Land of the Dead?"

"What kind of question is that? Who could possibly know that?"

"Your answer, please."

"Eleven?"

"Your final answer is eleven? You're quite certain?"

"Yes, eleven souls are currently residing in the Land of the Dead."

"Incorrect, I'm afraid. All of you, into the boat, we're off to the Land of the Dead."

Chapter 32

Lost and Found

"It's some kind of giant beetle and it's rolling a big ball. What do you think it is?"

Sophia peered around the trunk of a gigantic fern. "You don't want to know."

"Why not?"

"It's a dung beetle, and it's rolling a giant ball of dung."

"You mean that ball is made of…"

"Animal dung."

"Eww. What do they do with it?"

"They eat it."

"I think I'm going to barf. That bug must be at least eight feet tall. Look at those big spikes on its legs. Scary."

"That's not the scary part."

"What could be scarier than a giant armored spiky beetle rolling around a big ball of dung?"

"Where did the dung come from?"

Orville's eyes widened. "Something really big."

Proto studied the enormous beetle. "Remarkable exoskeleton, the spikes on its legs look quite deadly. Did you note the size of those white wormy creatures? I couldn't tell precisely what they were eating, but I think it had twelve legs. I suppose it could have been two six legged insects, or three four legged ones, difficult to tell. Quite a grisly scene."

"This is bad. Brother Solus, how do we find the Shadow King? Does he live in a big spooky castle or something?"

Brother Solus' eyes were on the forty foot tall blue ferns swaying in the sweltry breeze, more specifically on the huge red spotted spider spinning a bright yellow web between two of the ferns. "He lives to the east."

"That's a little vague. How do we find Aislin?"

"I cannot say with any certainty. It all depends."

Orville slumped down against the base of a giant blue fern.

"This whole adventure is too confusing. The Shadow King kidnapped Aislin Mouse when she stepped into Elysian, and he's holding her captive in some unknown location, but she keeps appearing as a beautiful ghost mouse and she told me the Shadow King knew we would come to rescue her. How could he know that? Do you think he knows who Ebenezer is?"

"Why do you keep bringing up how beautiful she is? Every time you mention her you say she's beautiful."

"What do you mean? It's just a descriptive word, like tall or funny or well dressed."

"I see, it's just a descriptive word, an adjective. What adjectives do you use to describe me to other mice? Do you call me your beautiful best friend?"

Orville froze, caught in the delicate net of Sophia's words.

"Um...well, it would depend on who I was talking to. Of course you are far more beautiful in your way than Aislin is, but–"

"In my way? What does that mean? Am I beautiful or not? It's a simple question."

Proto stood up, stretching his long silver arms. "Orville has told me many times you are the most beautiful mouse he has ever seen and how lucky he is that you are his best friend. He also said the more you love a mouse the more beautiful they become in your eyes. He cherishes you above all others."

Sophia's jaw dropped.

Orville looked at Proto in stunned surprise. "Why did you say that? I told you it was secret."

"I don't like secrets. Especially ones written on crumpled up pieces of paper."

"What are you talking about?"

Sophia sat down next to Orville with a big smirky grin. "Did you really say all those things about me?"

"Proto promised me he wouldn't say anything. It's kind of embarrassing."

"I don't think it's embarrassing at all, I think it's lovely." She rested her head on Orville's shoulder.

Brother Solus looked ill.

Proto gave a dark look. "I am going to scout the area for predatorial beasts. My old and loyal friend Squeaky will protect you in my absence." He turned sharply and

disappeared into the maze of towering blue ferns.

As he wove his way through the tangled labyrinth, Proto's mind was not on terrifying beasts, but on small crumpled up pieces of white paper with secret notes written on them. He sighed. He shouldn't have revealed Orville's private feelings to Sophia. He had promised he wouldn't, but they had betrayed his friendship with their secret notes, wishing they'd never met him, wishing he would move back to the Cube. That was far worse than what he had done. His body might be indestructible, but his feelings were not.

He leaned against a giant fern, sliding down to the jungle floor, his eyes closing. He would move back to the Cube before they asked him to, avoid any unpleasantness, avoid the awkward painful confrontation. Maybe they could still go on adventures together. Maybe they just didn't want him living in their house.

Proto never saw the little smoking charcoal stick figure creeping up behind him, never saw it transform into a black roiling cloud, never saw it envelope his body.

He had been in the utility room folding laundry when he heard them arguing. Back then the reporters called him 'The Friendly Rabbiton', but the two little bunnies he lived with called him Uncle Rab. He liked being called Uncle Rab, and he liked being part of their family, taking great joy in cooking their meals, baking tasty treats, doing laundry, cleaning, and reading bedtime stories to the little bunnies, always asking how their day had been, if there was anything more he could do to help.

The space pirate birthday party had been his idea. The bunnies loved the Dread Pirate Blackbones stories, so a pirate themed birthday party seemed a logical choice. He had fashioned cute pirate costumes for all twenty-two of the bunnies invited to the party. He had baked a six tier cake, each layer a different flavor, painstakingly decorated with space pirates and inter-stellar battleships shooting deadly force beams. His own costume was spectacular, a tour de force, an artful masterpiece with no detail overlooked, no shortcuts taken. When he wore it he was no longer Uncle Rab, he was the Dread Pirate Blackbones, the bloodthirsty Scourge of Dark Space. He had great expectations for the party, a gala event which he was certain would become a lasting and cherished memory for the little bunnies.

Twenty-two little bunnies burst into tears when Pro-to entered the room wearing his Dread Pirate Black-bones costume, blood red paint splattered across his waistcoat and sword. Twenty-two little bunnies thought the blood drenched Dread Pirate Blackbones had invaded their party with the sole intention of chopping them into little pieces. Two stunned Elders quickly ushered him out of the room, sending him back to the kitchen, telling him they needed ten more batches of cookies.

Proto was oblivious, completely misinterpreting their tears. "They loved it, they were moved to tears! They loved my costume, those dear little bunnies thought I was the real Dread Pirate Blackbones. It is a glorious and memorable day."

Two days passed without incident. It was on the third day that he heard them arguing while he was folding laundry in the utility room.

"He has to go. He scared the wits out of every bunny there. How could he not know all that blood would scare them? They told us he was a Friendly Rabbiton, not a terrifying one."

"He's a Rabbiton, he doesn't know any better. He meant well. He made a nice cake."

"I don't like any of it. The bunnies are starting to think he's one of us. They want him to read their bedtime stories instead of me. I should be the one reading to them, not some talking metal machine. And I will go mad if he offers me another tasty treat or chilled beverage. All those sweets are bad for the bunnies."

A wrenching sob rolled out of Proto as he sat beneath the great blue fern. How could he have forgotten this?

"What are we supposed to do, just send him away?"

"He's a machine, he doesn't have feelings. I don't want him in our house."

"They said he's programmed to have feelings."

"He's programmed to act like he has them. He doesn't have true feelings the way we have them. I want him out of here. However you do it, he needs to go."

"You might be right, I don't really want the bunnies

thinking he's part of the family. Maybe the military could use him. You know, put him to work in a factory or something. He couldn't do any harm there, and he might even do some good. They keep saying the Anarkkians are gearing up for war."

Proto had apologized profusely. He was sorry he'd scared the bunnies. He wouldn't do it again. He'd be careful. He'd ask first if what he was doing was appropriate. His words had fallen on deaf ears.

The Rabbiton representative arrived four days later to give Proto the good news. He had been a rousing success, he had become a beloved member of the family, but it was time to move on, a higher duty was calling. The military had an important job for him, a job which might even prevent an Anarkkian invasion. He was being sent to a surveillance center in distant west Symoca, to a place called the Cube.

Proto staggered to his feet, the pain of his memory almost unbearable. His own family had sent him away, saying he was only a machine, a cold automaton devoid of feelings. And now Orville and Mum and Papa were going to do the same thing, send him back to the Cube.

His thoughts were interrupted by a low growling coming from the tangled foliage. He hoped it was a scary creature, something really dreadful, really horrible, something to make him forget. As he fought his way through the dense vegetation his thoughts were on crumpled notes. Maybe he was wrong about Orville and Sophia, maybe there was some other explanation, maybe the notes were about someone else. Orville and Sophia had never been anything but friendly, always including him in their adventures, even on trips to the grocery store. Just last week Mum had bought him a bottle of silver polish, saying how handsome he looked when he was shiny and bright. Or maybe that had all been an act, maybe they were just being polite, not wanting to hurt his feelings. He did not like Elysian. Orville said there was something off about this world. It was odd that this horrible forgotten memory had come out of nowhere, just like Sophia remembering why she was scared of caterpillars. He wished they were back home again. He wished they'd never come to this world.

He pushed his way through the thorny thicket, branches wriggling wildly, shooting out slippery barbed vines, wrapping themselves around his arms in an attempt to ensnare him. On any other day it would have been thrilling, but for some unknown reason he felt compelled to discover the source of the growling. He pulled the vines off and stepped through the thicket.

The first thing he saw was the cave entrance, the second was a growling RoboPup in the shadows, teeth bared.

"Good heavens, is that Squeaky?" Proto scanned the RoboPup's identification code. It was Squeaky.

"Hello, little fellow, did you follow me here?"

Squeaky gave a loud bark, dashing into the inky blackness of the cave. Proto shivered. This cave was different, it scared him the way Anarkkian attack spiders had once scared him.

"This must be how Orville feels when he sees a cave." What was it Orville had said? Something about the darkest cave holding the brightest light? Maybe there was something in this dreadful cave he needed to see.

Proto flicked on his ear lights and entered the cave. A magnificent six foot tall twelve legged spider scuttled out of a dark tunnel, red glowing feathers fluttering on the end of its antennae. The gloriously horrible creature crept toward him, its long spindly sparking feelers snaking out ahead of it, sensing his presence.

"Yes, very scary indeed, but I'm afraid I don't have time to dawdle, Squeaky wants me to follow him."

Proto sprinted toward the spider, leapfrogging over the hideous beast, hitting the ground with a spectacular tuck and roll landing. The spider hissed its anger, spraying out a cloud of deadly poisonous green gas.

Squeaky had crossed the cave, dashing toward a large tunnel, glancing back at Proto and barking. Proto pounded down the eerie passageway after Squeaky, ghostly shadows from his ear lights leaping and dancing across the walls. He sprang over a swarm of spongy brain beetles, their eye pods tweeting wildly, ten thousand little red legs scurrying after him.

"Very scary, Orville would not like this one bit."

One of the orange and yellow brain beetles tried to attach itself to Proto's leg, but he jumped aside, shaking it off, bolting down the tunnel after Squeaky. Then came the mounds of squirming purple crystal worms and the hordes of walking leaves with their snappy little poisonous teeth clacking madly as they flooded down the tunnel after him.

Proto entered a vast echoing cavern, quickly spotting Squeaky floating up a tall ladder to a broad stone ledge high above the cave floor. He scrambled up the ladder, leaving the furious chattering mass of walking leaves behind him.

Squeaky sat panting in front of an enormous solid gold treasure chest.

"Great heavens, I wish Orville was here to see this, he's always talking about treasure chests. If the chest is made of solid gold, the treasure within it must be of inestimable value."

It took all of Proto's great strength to raise the monumentally heavy gold lid, but he prevailed, and the chest groaned open, revealing an eight inch square glass box within.

"Not the priceless treasure I was expecting."

He picked up the box, studying it closely.

"Great heavens, this has been carved from a single gargantuan Nirriimian white crystal. Its value is inconceivable."

Proto was about to open the box when a sobering thought popped into his head.

"Sophia would say I have been brought here by the universe for a reason, but perhaps the deeper purpose for my presence here is not one I will like, perhaps it's what she calls the fires of life."

He ran his hand across the lid of the crystal box.

"She also says we must face the fires of life head on, that is how we grow."

He set the box gingerly down on the stone floor, carefully removing the lid.

He blinked.

Sitting in the box was a crumpled up piece of white paper. With trembling hands Proto removed the note and read it.

The Greatest Treasure
4/7

"I have not the slightest idea the meaning of this note. Clearly the golden chest and the Nirriimian crystal box are great treasures, but what is the significance of 4/7?"

He clutched the note tightly, sinking to the floor, leaning back against the treasure chest. Try as he might, he could not deduce the meaning of the cryptic message. He closed his eyes. He was tired. Why did they want him to leave? When he opened his eyes again he found himself leaning against the trunk of a sixty foot tall blue fern. There was no cave and no Squeaky, there was only the mysterious crumpled note clutched tightly in his great silver hand.

Chapter 33

Laurus

A scruffy and disheveled Orville Mouse tumbled out of the blue ferns onto a broad rocky precipice. "Creekers, that was terrifying, a hundred times worse than the giant centipedes on Periculum."

As Brother Solus had predicted, the creatures they encountered in the ferns had been nightmarish, great horrible wormy slithering things with hooks and claws and blinking eyes, creatures that made Proto grin like a mouseling on its birthday. When the hordes of chattering iridescent blood beetles had swarmed down from the forest canopy, spitting out poisonous darts, Orville had instinctively tried to blink a sphere of defense, forgetting Brother Solus' dire warning. Instead of being surrounded by an invisible energy shield, the adventurers found themselves trapped inside a towering circular wall of gleaming Morsennium. Proto's climbing rope and heavy grappling hook had saved the day.

"Whoa, look at that!" Orville's eyes were on a mag-

243

nificent sprawling city far below them. "It's bigger than Cathne, and look at all the flying ships, there's hundreds of them. How could there be a city down there? Where did it come from?"

"Where did the ocean come from? Where did Bellumia come from? This is Elysian." Sophia peered over the edge of the precipice. "We're at least two miles above the city. We'll have to make our way down the cliffs using the climbing rope, then find a way through the city. It's going to be a tough climb."

"Go through the city? That doesn't sound very safe. We have no idea who lives there, it could be filled with bloodthirsty pirates."

"Would they be riding carnivorous centipedes and waving big axes?"

"All I'm saying is we don't know if they'll be friendly or not."

"Orville, clearly millions of people live in that city, and I guarantee they won't pay any attention to us. I grew up near a city almost as big as this one, and that's how it is. Everyone is so busy they don't pay any attention to anyone else. It's probably best not to make eye contact though."

"If they have eyes. They probably have feelers and tentacles."

"You're being a nervous ninny. Any creatures who can build a city that beautiful won't be scary."

Squeaky's flying skills proved invaluable during their descent. He soared below them, searching out the safest route down the nearly vertical cliff face, carving secure footholds for them with his destructor beam.

"We should bring Squeaky on all our adventures. Let's take him back to Muridaan Falls."

The prospect of bringing Squeaky home helped to elevate Proto's dismal mood.

"An excellent idea, he would make a fine and trusted companion for me if I am to be spending any amount of time in the Cube."

"What are you doing at the Cube? Is it some kind of experiment?"

Proto was forming his reply when the twelve foot wide sparkling translucent bubble floated up next to them. Seated inside the bubble was a Mintarian, a look of grave concern on his face.

"How did you get up here? Where's your Bubble Rider?"

Orville's jaw dropped. "It's a Mintarian riding inside a bubble. He's riding inside a bubble."

"Climb over to that ledge and I'll give you a lift down. This is far too dangerous a spot to be climbing. What were you thinking?"

"We're sort of lost."

"Okay, climb over to that big ledge so I can pick you up."

The adventurers made their way across the cliff face to the wide ledge, a perilous undertaking involving Squeaky tying the climbing rope around a massive outcropping of rock and them swinging over to the ledge. The Mintarian bubble ship floated up next to them.

"How are we all supposed to fit in that? It's hardly big enough for him."

The Mintarian twisted a brass dial on his belt and the bubble expanded, reaching a diameter of twenty feet.

"Hop in!"

"How do we hop in? There's no doors."

The Mintarian gave Orville a puzzled look, then a light came on in his eyes.

"You're not from Laurus, and you've never seen a Bubble Rider before. Just walk through the soft energy field, the side of the bubble. Nothing to it, the floor of the bubble is solid, you won't fall through."

Sophia stepped into the shimmering sphere with a wide grin. "This is amazing. I've never seen technology like this, not even on Quintari."

"Where's Quintari? I've never heard of it."

"It's a long way from here. Thanks for helping us. We've climbed more dangerous spots than this, but you've saved us a lot of time."

One by one the adventurers entered the Bubble Rider. Brother Solus was fascinated by the technology, asking a stream of questions, most of which the pilot was unable to answer.

"I don't understand all the technical aspects of it, I just clip the Bubble Pod to my belt and when I push the tab the bubble appears around me. It's not like a soap bubble, it's an energy field. By turning the dial I change the size of the field."

"How do you steer it without controls?"

"I control it with my thoughts, they link the Rider to

your thought signature when you buy it. No one except me can fly it. Where did you say you were from?"

"I'm from a little village called Muridaan Falls, Sophia is from Quintari, and Brother Solus is from Okeanos."

The Mintarian shrugged. "Sorry, never heard of any of those places. Where are you headed? Maybe I can take you there."

Sophia and Orville shared a sudden and powerful message from their inner selves. They were not to mention anything about the Shadow King to the Mintarian.

"Oh, we're just kind of exploring the area."

"Are you miners? That's what I was doing here, hunting for gold. Not having much luck though."

"No, just out exploring, poking around."

"I'm Juvo. Welcome to Laurus, the greatest city in all of creation."

Juvo gave the adventurers a grand aerial tour of Laurus, soaring a mile above the sparkling city, proudly pointing out an array of astonishing technological structures and scenic wonders.

"That big silver orb contains a portal to the tenth dimension, siphoning off energy to power the entire city. The long low building next to it is our food synthesizer. It takes energy from the power orb and compresses it into matter, in this case food for the entire city. There are other synthesizers across the city that produce any number of products and supplies."

"That sounds like shaping."

"What's shaping?"

"Um, it's just a way to make stuff. How many Mintarians live in the city?"

"What's a Mintarian?"

Orville froze. Clearly Juvo was a Mintarian, how could he not know that?

Sophia thought quickly. "Brother Solus is a Mintarian and he bears some slight resemblance to you, so Orville mistakenly thought you were a Mintarian."

"A simple mistake. Quite correct, we are not Mintarians, we are Laurae, citizens of Laurus, the greatest city in all of creation."

"It's a stunningly beautiful city, I've never seen anything like it. Your technology is even more advanced than the Anarkkians."

Juvo smiled politely, unfamiliar with the name.

Orville had a sudden thought. "How long has the city been here?" He wondered if Juvo would be able to remember.

"We have uncovered ancient artifacts buried beneath the city dating to seventy thousand years ago, so it is at least that old. There is no telling it's true age." Juvo bowed his head. "Our world was created by the Great Gnuj, that is all we know, that is all we need to know."

A blue thought cloud flashed out from Sophia to Orville. "Did you hear that? He said Gnuj created this world. That's the Mintarian who invented the Metaphonium! Juvo is a Mintarian, he just doesn't know it."

"Do you think we should tell him he's living in a synthetic world?"

"No, definitely not. Look at the city, it's beautiful, filled with lovely parks and rivers, and the technology is amazing."

"How could Laurus be seventy thousand years old when Gnuj only created Elysian fourteen hundred years ago?"

"Elysian is Elysian."

An hour later the Bubble Rider was hovering high above Laurus.

"Where can I take you? Is there anywhere in particular you would like to go?"

"We're heading east. If you could drop us off on the outskirts of the city we'll find our way from there."

Juvo's smile vanished. "East? You want to go east?"

"Yes?"

"To the east there is only desert and the Black Wall. None have ever passed through it, it marks the world's end."

Orville gave a silent groan. Of course there was a big black wall, there was always a big black wall that no one had ever passed through. He sent a thought cloud to Sophia. "A black wall? Really?"

Sophia did not reply, instead giving Juvo a bright smile. "That's what we came to see, the big wall. It sounds amazing. How tall is it exactly?"

Juvo relaxed. "No one really knows. We've tried to reach the top in Bubble Riders, but the higher we go, the taller it gets. Its existence is one of the great mysteries of Laurus, but most think it marks the world's end."

"What a marvelous sight it must be. Could you drop

us off next to it? I can't wait to tell all my friends about it."

"I would be happy to, it's really quite a marvelous sight, well worth visiting."

As their Bubble Rider sped eastward above the magnificent city, Orville leaned forward, his head in his paws. Why was there always a big black wall? Why were there always giant centipedes?

Chapter 34

Orville the Ghost

Juvo brought the Bubble Rider gently down on the sandy outskirts of eastern Laurus.

"There it is, the great Black Wall, the end of the world."

"It's huge, much bigger than the storm wall on Varmoran."

"Juvo, has anyone ever tried to get through it using a vaporizing beam?" Orville was imagining Squeaky blasting a big hole through the wall.

"Laurus engineers have tried everything over the years without success. Our most powerful disruptor beams are absorbed by the wall. Some scientists say the wall isn't really a physical object. I have no idea what that means, but that's what they say."

"Thank you so much for all your kindness. We'll spend a day or so visiting the wall and then head back to Laurus. You have such a lovely city, I can't wait to see it all."

Juvo smiled, nodding his agreement. "It is the greatest city in all of creation."

The party of adventurers stepped onto the desert sand, waving their goodbyes to Juvo, watching his Bubble Rider lift off and soar back toward Laurus.

"Are we really going back to the city?"

"Of course not, we're going east, through the Black Wall."

"But Juvo said even their–"

"We don't even know if Laurus is real, if Juvo is real, if the wall is real. The whole city could disappear in the blink of an eye, just like Bellumia did. What we do know is the Shadow King lives on the other side of the Black Wall, and that's where we'll find Aislin."

"I can't wait to see her, she's so beautiful." Orville gave a cackling laugh.

Sophia did not.

"I was just kidding. Don't forget what Proto said."

"Let's find out what this wall is made of." Sophia strode across the desert sand toward the towering wall.

A two mile trek across the rolling sand dunes brought them to the Black Wall. Orville pressed his paw against it.

"It's smooth, kind of like black obsidian. Proto, can you make Squeaky blast it with his destructor beam? I want to see what happens."

"Squeaky, attack the wall."

Squeaky let out a ferocious roar and a brilliant purple light blasted out from his eyes. A small section of the wall glowed faintly, returning to its original color seconds later.

"That didn't do much. Maybe we can find an old tunnel running under it, like we did on Varmoran."

"I'm not sensing any tunnels. The deeper we dig, the deeper the wall will go."

"Creekers. Why couldn't they just put a door in it?"

Sophia laughed. "Let's camp here for the night and think about this."

"I have four comfy blankets in my pack and all the ingredients to prepare a tasty vegetable stew. Squeaky and I shall patrol the wall perimeter while you sleep, keeping an eye out for the gigantic horned carnivorous sand snakes."

"What?" Orville's eyes popped open.

"Ha ha ha ha! I hoodwinked you again. Logically speaking, just because I say I am keeping an eye out for something does not mean it actually exists."

"Very funny. Don't forget this is Elysian, just think-ing about something can make it appear."

Orville woke up in the middle of the night, his face pressed into the coarse desert sand. "Drat, I wish I could shape a sleeping bag and a tent. Now I have sand in my fur."

He stood up and brushed himself off. The lights from Laurus were glinting off the Black Wall. He strolled over to it, running his paw across the smooth cool surface.

"This is the most confusing world I've ever been in. Why would there be a big giant wall here?"

"The Black Wall separates the known from the unknown."

Orville gave a shriek, whipping around to see the beautiful and ghostly Aislin Mouse floating behind him.

"Creekers! Why do you always sneak up on me like that?"

"I will not be able to visit you again, I am getting weaker, it is difficult for me to cross dimensions. You must find your way through the wall, the final barrier between the known and the unknown. The way is known to you."

"What do you mean? How do we get through it?"

Orville saw Aislin's lips moving as she faded to nothingness, leaving him alone on the desert sand.

He raced back to their camp, shaking Sophia's arm.

"Wake up!"

"What is it? Why are you waking me? I was having the best dream about my Temporal Distortion final exam."

"I saw Aislin Mouse again. Wait, you were having a good dream about a final exam in a science class? Really?"

"It was so much fun, after I answered all the questions on the test I wrote down my own questions and answers, questions the professor should have asked. He said I was brilliant."

"This is why I never jump into your dreams."

"You saw Aislin?"

"She said the wall is the final barrier between the known and the unknown. She said we already know how to get through it."

Sophia sat up, her eyes bright and focused, her astonishing mind spinning wildly. "We already know how to get through it?"

"What do you think she meant by–"

"Quiet, I'm thinking."

Ten minutes later Orville yawned and flopped down on the sand. "Let me know when you're–"

"Shhh, still thinking."

Orville was sound asleep when Sophia shook his arm. "Orville, wake up, think about it, the barrier between the known and the unknown. Doesn't that sound familiar?"

"Not really."

"Think about your inner self, your secret voice within."

"My inner self exists in the world of the unknown, it knows all the things I don't know. When I go to sleep at night I'm going from our world into the world of dreams, into the world of the unknown, the world of my inner self."

"Exactly. We need to sit in front of the wall and let go of our thoughts, let go of our physical bodies, connect to our inner selves, enter the world of the unknown. It's nothing new, we do it when we link our minds."

"How is linking minds going to help us? We could shape a hurricane and the wall wouldn't budge an inch."

"We don't need to shape anything. Follow me, I know what to do."

Minutes later they stood facing the Black Wall. Sophia sat in the sand, motioning for Orville to sit next to her.

"Take my paw and we'll link minds."

Orville closed his eyes, relaxing, letting go of his thoughts and his physical body. He could feel Sophia's mind joining his, her thoughts and memories merging with his own.

"We don't have to shape anything?"

"No, we just need to relax, get comfortable in this state of being. We'll just chat for a while. I just found your memory of the first time we met. You were really surprised that I liked to talk about the same things you did, you'd never met anyone like me and you couldn't stop looking at me. It wasn't because I was beautiful, you were looking at me with your intuitive mind, trying to understand me."

"I was afraid you were just being nice to me, that you weren't really interested in the puzzles I'd found. The more I got to know you and like you, the more beautiful you got. Now you're the most beautiful mouse I know, the mouse I cherish above all others."

"I knew I had been looking for you the moment we met."

"What do you think will happen when we meet the Shadow King? We don't know what he is, or what he wants."

"We know he's holding Aislin captive, and that's all we need to know. What I don't know is how Brother Solus fits into all of this. He's terrified of the Shadow

King, but he's also strangely drawn to him."

"I guess we'll find out. I'm scared of what's on the other side of the wall. That blue fern forest was the most terrifying place I've ever seen. I can't believe we survived all those horrible creatures. At least Proto had fun. We wouldn't have made it without him and Squeaky, especially when they rescued us from those creepy things that looked like lemon pudding with legs."

"Does Proto seem to be acting strangely?"

"Very strangely. He's giving me a lot of odd looks, like he's trying to figure out what I'm thinking. Sometimes he's way too nice and sometimes he seems almost angry. Maybe he's worried about something."

"He says he's fine, but clearly he isn't. I wish he would talk to us about it."

"I like it when our minds are merged. I like knowing everything you've been through, all the good things and all the bad things."

"I like it too. I like us not having any secrets. Are you relaxed now?"

"Nice and relaxed. All I need is a big plate of snapberry pie. Can I eat pie while our minds are linked?"

"Focus. I need you to listen, we're going to do something we've never done before and it might be a little scary at first. You're going to be a ghost."

"What? Why would I want to be a ghost?"

"Calm down, you have to stay relaxed. Not a real ghost, just something like a ghost. Are you ready?"

"I guess so. Are you going to be a ghost too?"

"Yes, we're both going to be ghosts. Okay, we keep our minds merged just as they are, but when I tell you to, I want you to slowly open your eyes. Remember, keep your mind merged with mine even when your eyes are open."

"Okay."

"One, two, three, and slowly open your eyes."

Orville opened his eyes, his mind still merged with Sophia. He gave a shriek. His body was translucent and he was floating above the sand. "What's happening?"

"Listen to my thoughts, Orville. Just relax, everything is fine. We're in a different dimension now, the same dimension Aislin Mouse is in. That's why she appears as a ghost. Look at the Black Wall."

Orville floated around and looked at the wall. It was no longer a massive solid black impenetrable wall, it was shimmering and vaporous, like his body.

"Creekers, it's a ghost wall!"

"Exactly. The wall is solid in our dimension, but not solid in this one. We can easily pass through it now."

"What about Proto and Brother Solus?"

"We'll have to help them through. I think if we all hold paws we'll be able to pass through. Let's go find them."

"I like floating around like this. Easy on my feet, relaxing, no sand in my fur."

"You're really something, you were so scared of being a ghost and now you like it."

"I'm scared of new stuff, that's all. Most mice are."

"Some mice like new stuff."

"Hey, there's Proto. Watch this, it's going to be really funny."

Orville floated up behind Proto and gave a low moan. Proto whirled around, his eyes popping open when he saw Orville.

"Great heavens!"

Orville made his voice deep and ominous.

"I AM THE GHOST OF ORVILLE MOUSE, HERE TO HAUNT YOU FOR THAT SCARY POISONOUS VEGETABLE JOKE YOU–"

Proto let out a shriek, covering his eyes.

Sophia hollered, "Orville, stop that! Proto, he's not a ghost. We're in a different dimension, so we only look like ghosts. We're in the same dimension that Aislin Mouse is in, the same one as the Shadow King. Wake Brother Solus and come to the wall."

Proto peeked out at Orville, then poked his finger through Orville's shimmering translucent shoulder.

"You're not a ghost? You look like a ghost. Are you dead?"

"I'm not a ghost and I'm not dead, I'm just in a different dimension so I look like one. We found a way through the Black Wall."

"I thought you were a ghost. I thought you were dead."

"Sorry, I wasn't thinking, I didn't mean to scare you so badly. It wasn't funny."

"Sophia said surprising events are only humorous when no one gets hurt. It's not funny if you think someone is dead."

Orville looked at Sophia. Even in her ghostly form he could tell she was glaring at him.

"I'm sorry, Proto."

The party of adventurers made their way to the Black Wall, Brother Solus strangely unaffected by Orville and Sophia's ghostly form.

"Everyone hold paws, form a line. Proto, Squeaky can sit on your shoulder."

Proto and Brother Solus stood between Orville and Sophia. "We're ready. Now what?"

"It's working, you're both starting to shimmer. Now we just walk through the Black Wall and into the final realm of the Shadow King. Once we pass through the wall we'll be solid again."

Orville gulped. This was going to be bad. Really, really bad.

Chapter 35

By Chance

Orville was awestruck by the vista that lay before them.

"Creekers, this is beautiful, almost as beautiful as the world of the Others. I don't understand, I thought the final realm of the Shadow King would be the scariest place of all."

Brother Solus gazed across the rolling meadows and forests, the bright patches of glorious blue wildflowers, the flickering golden butterflies.

"This is most unexpected. It would appear our greatest trial was simply finding the Black Wall."

Sophia nodded. "Each of us facing our greatest fear along the way."

"Like that crazy ghost pirate riding the centipede."

"Which way do we go?"

Sophia studied a small patch of wildflowers. "These are blue moreilias, I don't think that's an accident."

"There's a trail of them leading up that hill. Let's

follow it."

The adventurers trekked through the idyllic meadow, Squeaky soaring and swooping overhead. He landed on top of the hill, yipping and barking at butterflies, then curled into a ball and careened wildly back down the hill.

"Why is Squeaky rolling down the hill?"

"He's playing, that's what puppies do. It looks kind of fun, you should try it." Sophia snickered.

When they crested the hill Orville scanned the distant landscape.

"Hey, look at that tree."

"Is that what I think it is?"

"It's just like the blue tree outside the Blue Monks' monastery on Periculum. It's the same tree, I'm certain of it, it's at least a thousand feet tall."

Proto magnified his vision. "The leaves are perfectly round, just as they were on Periculum."

"The Fourth Monk said their monastery exists simultaneously in many worlds. Elysian must be one of them. That's where we need to go."

"Hey, Brother Solus, maybe you'll get to meet the Thirteenth Monk. You'll probably like him, you can talk about monk stuff with him. He's really friendly but really mysterious, and no one knows how old he is. I'm pretty sure he knows more about the universe than anyone."

Brother Solus did not appear overly enthused about a potential meeting with the Thirteenth Monk.

During their two day march to the blue tree Orville

inadvertently discovered his shaping skills had returned, when he surreptitiously tried to shape a cookie.

"Hey, I shaped a perfect oatmeal cookie! This is great, we get comfy sleeping bags and tents and yummy dinners with snapberry pie for dessert."

"We don't even need sleeping bags here, the meadow grass is really soft and the temperature is perfect."

"There's the orange grove, we're getting close."

"Mmm, those orange blossoms smell heavenly, but it means there won't be any yummy oranges."

"Let's go look at the giant blue tree. Remember when we climbed it in our dream? That was fun."

"I remember you lost the race to the top."

"Not that it matters, but I let you win. That's just the kind of thoughtful mouse I am, always concerned about your feelings."

"Nice try, monkey butt, I beat you to the top by almost a full minute, and I wasn't even out of breath, you were puffing like an old duplonium powered steam engine."

The adventurers wove their way through the orange orchard to the titanic towering blue tree.

"That trunk must be a hundred feet across. We never did solve the puzzle of the round blue leaves. The Thirteenth Monk said if we touched the leaf he gave us and thought of him, he'd transport us to the monastery on Periculum. I wonder how that works? The leaf must have some weird connection to him."

Orville forgot his leaf puzzle the moment he saw the blue robed mouse step around the massive tree trunk.

Sophia recognized him immediately. "It's the Fourth Monk! He's the one who said so many nice things about Papa." She waved and smiled as he approached.

The blue monk studied the group of adventurers. "It is a great pleasure to see you again, Sophia, Orville, and Proto. I see you have brought a friend with you, from all appearances a Mintarian Gray Monk."

"Yes, this is Brother Solus, we met him in Okeanos. We passed through the Black Wall east of Laurus and stumbled on your monastery. It was such a surprise to see the big blue tree."

This seemed to amuse the Fourth Monk. "Yes, such a surprise. The Thirteenth Monk would like to speak with you. He has been following your exploits on Elysian with great interest. Your meeting with Captain Tobias was especially interesting. Quite a marvelous watch he gave you, Orville."

"Huh? How do you know about that?"

"Elysian is a world unlike any other. Shall we go? The Thirteenth Monk is waiting for you in the monastery."

As they made their way around the gigantic blue tree, the towering outer wall of the monastery came into view, its enormous timber doors lined with stout iron bands. In the center of each door was a single gleaming golden eye, the ancient symbol first used by the Thaumatarians, and later adopted by the Shapers Guild and the Blue Monks. The Fourth Monk approached the gates and raised a heavy iron ring, a sonorous gong sounding when it fell.

The gargantuan doors groaned open just enough for them to enter, then rumbled shut behind them.

"I'd forgotten how beautiful your garden is. I've never seen so many flowers, so many colors. It's really lovely."

Orville strolled down the serpentine garden path, artfully created from thousands of smooth colored river stones. The Red Monks were still tending the garden, weeding, watering, planting, snipping spent blossoms.

"It's so peaceful here. No giant centipedes."

The Fourth Monk laughed. "And no ghost pirates."

Sophia said, "I remember when you said the flowers come and go, but the garden is eternal."

"I am pleased you remembered my words."

"Why does the Thirteenth Monk want to see us?"

"Your kindness toward Ebenezer Mouse, your selfless search for his beloved Aislin has opened certain doors to great change. There is far more at stake than you know."

"What kind of things?"

"The Thirteenth Monk will do what he can to aid you in this endeavor."

In the center of the magnificent garden stood a stark gray stone building, twenty feet tall, one hundred feet square. There were no windows, only a single arched blue door bearing the symbol of the golden eye.

The Fourth Monk sang three exquisite notes that lingered on longer than they should have. The blue door silently opened.

Orville whispered to Brother Solus, "The Blue

Monks manipulate energy fields by singing."

"You may enter, the Thirteenth Monk will see you now."

Orville, Sophia, Proto, and Brother Solus stepped into the shadowy interior of the mysterious monastery.

Chapter 36

The Thirteenth Monk

Orville and Sophia knew what to expect, having met the Thirteenth Monk before. The floor of the monastery was made from river stones worn smooth by the footsteps of countless Blue Monks over the millennia. Orville whispered, "Keep your eyes on the far end of the room."

Brother Solus squinted through the nebulous shadows, first glimpsing a flickering blue light, then a floating blue robe, then a mouse wearing a blue robe, then thirteen mice wearing blue robes. One of them stepped forward, slowly making his way across the ancient monastery floor. The remaining twelve monks faded into the darkness.

The Thirteenth Monk came to a halt in front of the adventurers, pausing to study their faces as they waited for him to speak. He turned to Orville.

"Arghh, 'tis the scourge of the Great Sea, the Dread Pirate Orville."

Sophia burst out laughing, slapping her paw across her mouth. "Sorry."

The Thirteenth Monk smiled. "Laughter is the purest expression of joy, there is no need to apologize. It is always a great pleasure to see you. I do hope you are all well?"

"Yes, very well, thank you. This is our friend Brother Solus, the last of the Mintarian Gray Monks. We met him in Okeanos."

"A pleasure to meet you, Brother Solus. How kind of you to offer your assistance in the search for Aislin Mouse."

Brother Solus avoided the Thirteenth Monk's penetrating gaze. "I will confess it was somewhat of an accidental collaboration, not so much a selfless act on my part."

"I see. Nevertheless, here you are, a member of the search party, looking for that which has been lost."

The Thirteenth Monk sang a short but infinitely melodious tune and a group of comfy green chairs appeared. He sat down with a sigh.

"Marvelous, nothing like a soft comfy chair. Everyone take a seat please."

When the others were resting comfortably he continued.

"I am a very old mouse, far older than my dashing youthful appearance might lead you to believe."

Sophia grinned.

"During my lifetime I have acquired many cherished memories, but also many memories most mice would sooner forget. These painful events we all experience are the fires of life. Orville experienced his papa's disappearance, Sophia suffered the loss of her mum at a very young age, and the murder of her papa by Draken Mouse. Both Orville and Sophia persevered through these difficult times, learning from them, growing stronger, kinder, wiser, and more empathetic toward others. Proto, you have had similar events in your life? Events you would rather forget?"

Proto gave a start, glancing nervously over to Orville and Sophia.

"I recently remembered a rather dreadful event which occurred during my time with the family of Elders."

"Come, you may whisper it to me."

Proto rose up, stepping over to the Thirteenth Monk, leaning over and murmuring inaudibly for almost a full minute.

"And that is your greatest fear?"

Proto nodded.

"I can assure you this is a fear shared by all living creatures. You must face it head on, no matter the outcome."

Proto returned to his seat, avoiding eye contact with Orville and Sophia. The Thirteenth Monk stood up, padding across the smooth stone floor to Brother Solus.

"Brother Solus, I am aware of your struggle. It will be difficult, but your memories are the fire that has shaped you, made you what you are. You are far nobler than you think, far stronger than you think, far braver than you think. And you are in the company of three friends who will watch over you, comfort you in difficult times."

Brother Solus had a lump in his throat, something he had not felt in many years.

"Continue your travels to the east. You will know when you have arrived at your final destination."

The Thirteenth Monk turned away, then stopped, his eyes on Brother Solus. He sang three short and powerful notes.

"You will remember."

A shiver ran through Brother Solus.

The Thirteenth Monk faded to nothingness.

"Creekers, what was that all about? Why was he talking about bad memories?"

"I believe it was for my benefit. He is preparing me for events to come, for my impending encounter with the Shadow King and what shall follow."

"I still don't understand who the Shadow King is and why he took Aislin."

"It is not Aislin he wants, it is me. She was a means to an end, a way to lure me to his realm. It was no accident that I witnessed her abduction. He knew when her rescuers arrived I would inexorably be drawn into the drama, drawn into his dark realm."

"Why didn't he take you instead of Aislin?"

"He cannot. Only I can make the choice to confront him, to face him head on."

Brother Solus pushed the blue door open, brilliant sunlight flooding into the monastery.

The Fourth Monk was seated on a wooden bench outside the blue door, Squeaky lying next to him, a garland of bright yellow flowers around his neck. He gave a loud bark when he saw Proto.

"Hello, little pup, that's a lovely collar, although it might diminish your ability to frighten away unwanted intruders."

Squeaky hopped off the bench and stood next to Proto, wagging his tail.

"You will be heading east, to the final realm of the Shadow King?"

"Yes, he is holding Aislin Mouse captive and we are here to rescue her, to bring her back to our friend Ebenezer Mouse."

"Most admirable. The effects of your selfless endeavor will extend far beyond the safe return of Aislin Mouse, but I suspect you already know that. I will tell you something that the Thirteenth Monk did not. Dark times lie ahead, there is a dire swamp you must pass through before you find the Shadow King. Do not lose hope, you must persevere no matter how disheartened you become."

Orville did not like the sound of that. "A dire swamp? Are there weird creatures in it?"

"I must leave you now, I am needed on Periculum. Remember, above all, do not lose hope."

With a quick wave the Fourth Monk disappeared into the monastery.

Orville let out an unusually loud groan.

"Seriously? Now we have to go through a dire swamp? It's probably filled with creepy poisonous wiggly things that bite your legs."

Proto nodded emphatically.

"Undoubtedly there will be hideous monstrosities squirming about in the putrid burbling muck, waiting to snare a hapless victim. How exciting!"

Chapter 37

The Swamp of Despair

"Eww, what's that smell?"

Orville eyed the thick oozing mud at the edge of the swamp, foul smelling bubbles belching and popping up from beneath the stagnant muck.

"It's methane gas bubbling up from decayed vegetation. Quite a dreadful smell, also highly explosive, so no campfires."

"How are we supposed to get through this?"

Sophia stepped into the swamp, sinking up to her ankles in the slimy goop, the brown murky water up to her knees. She pulled out one foot with a horrible glurping noise and took a step forward.

"Not so bad, it just takes a little more effort to walk."

"I just bought these boots, and they weren't cheap. This mud is going to ruin them."

"We can camp on those little islands farther out in the swamp."

"I can't see the other side, how big do you think the swamp is? Maybe we could shape a boat or something."

"The water's not deep enough for a boat. Come on, let's get moving."

Orville grimaced as he stepped into the putrescent gurgling muck. "This is really going to ruin my boots."

Proto strode ahead, his long silver legs seemingly unaffected by the gloopy mud, Squeaky perched comfortably on his shoulder.

Brother Solus followed behind them, a sour look on his face.

Six hours later nothing had changed, they were still slogging through foul smelling muck, the oppressive swamp appearing to have no end.

"There's one of those little islands. We should take a break, I want to clean my boots and dry them over a fire."

"No campfires, it's not safe with all the methane gas."

"Creekers, why did we even come here? These flies are awful, and I won't even mention the mosquitos."

"We came here to rescue Aislin, in case you forgot."

"I didn't forget, it was a rhetorical question. Rhetorical, that means I wasn't expecting an answer. And rhetorical was not one of my words for the day, in case you were wondering."

"I know what rhetorical means, Orville."

Proto pointed to a thicket of gnarled trees growing on the island. "There's a sign hanging from that branch."

Orville pushed his way through the gloppy viscous muck until he was close enough to read the sign.

WELCOME TO
THE SWAMP OF DESPAIR

"The Swamp of Despair? Why didn't the Fourth Monk tell us it was called the Swamp of Despair? That seems like a really important fact to leave out. And why would they put a welcome sign so far inside the swamp? They wait until we're halfway across the swamp and then tell us it's called the Swamp of Despair?"

Proto studied the sign. "According to my calculations we have traveled approximately thirteen miles into the swamp. If the swamp proves to be very large, say five or six hundred miles across, then thirteen miles is relatively close to the outer edge of the swamp, the perfect spot for a welcome sign. Has anyone seen any creatures? Felt anything bite their leg?"

Orville gave Proto a dark look.

Sophia stepped up onto the island. "Everyone is tired, it's been a long day. Let's camp here for the night. We can't have a fire, but we can shape light orbs, tents, sleeping bags, and a nice dinner."

Brother Solus slumped down and leaned back against a tree, attempting to scrape the muck off his boots with a stick. He did not look happy.

Orville slept fitfully that night, waking up numerous times, certain he heard something sloshing its way through the murky swamp. Twice he saw little flickering blue lights in the distance.

"I don't like this place. So creepy, I feel like something is watching us."

Two days later the only thing which had changed was their ever darkening mood. The swamp was endless, the gurgling goop filling the air with horrendous putrid odors, clouds of stinging flies and mosquitos buzzing relentlessly around them.

"Aghh! Another fly just bit my ear!"

"I told you to blink up a sphere of defense, it will protect you from the insects and most of the bad smells."

"It makes it really hot, hard to breathe. I'd rather have flies eat my ears than suffocate in this awful place. Why didn't the Thirteenth Monk tell us how bad this was going to be? It seems like he should have said something."

"Orville, this isn't fun for any of us. We have to stay positive."

"Great idea. Let's see, I'm positive I hate this swamp. I'm positive I wish I wasn't here."

Sophia's jaw tightened. "That's not funny and it doesn't help anything, it makes it harder for the rest of us."

Proto was humming softly to himself. "Any bites yet? I think I may have seen a poisonous snake but I'm not certain. It could have just been a big hungry worm. Hard to tell."

Four days later they took refuge on one of the numerous islands that dotted the swamp.

Sophia and Orville had stopped talking to each other.

Proto was rambling on about scary creatures he may or may not have seen and hideous creatures they might possibly encounter.

Brother Solus sat silently, a perpetual scowl on his face.

"Proto, would you please tell Sophia this cold vegetable stew is absolutely divine. I especially like the tasty dead flies I found in it. Scrumptious, the best part was the crunchy little wings. So tasty."

Sophia glared angrily at Orville. "Proto, would you please tell Orville if he doesn't like my vegetable stew, he can shape his own dinner, maybe a yummy dead fly pudding covered with swamp mud and worm guts."

Orville tossed his bowl to the ground. "We have to go back. We're never going to find Aislin. This swamp goes on forever, there's no end to it. I do not like this place and I especially don't like that we're fighting with each other, fighting with our best friends."

Sophia's face softened. She set down her bowl and scooted over next to Orville, putting her arm around him. "You're right, we shouldn't be fighting with the people we love."

Brother Solus spoke for the first time in days. "Now we know why it's called the Swamp of Despair."

Two nights later a ghostly Aislin Mouse appeared during dinner. Orville gave a shriek, pointing to the wavering apparition. Four sets of wide eyes were watching her.

"Please, please help me." She faded away and was

gone.

Sophia squeezed Orville's paw. "We have to find her. We have to. Did you see the look in her eyes?"

"You're right, just because we're in the Swamp of Despair doesn't mean we have to lose hope. Every step we take is one step closer to finding her, and one step closer to Brother Solus remembering whatever it is he's supposed to remember."

Aislin's appearance rekindled the adventurers' determination, and it was with renewed vigor that they set off into the swamp the following morning.

Orville was the first to see the blue door, a door which happened to be floating six inches above the water.

"Is that…"

"It's Ebenezer's front door. What is it doing here?"

"If it's really his door, we could open it and be home."

Sophia gave him a look he would not forget.

"I didn't say we should open it, I said *if* we opened it. Of course we're not going home without Aislin. It's probably some kind of trap anyway, luring us into a creepy dungeon or something."

Five days later the muddy and exhausted adventurers simultaneously gave a rousing cheer. In the distance was an emerald green forest. They had reached the other side of the swamp. At midday they entered the glorious forest, patches of brilliant pink and yellow wildflowers scattered across the dappled sunlit ground.

"This is heavenly, no more biting flies and mosquitos. There's a big meadow right through there, we can stop and have lunch."

The four adventurers made their way through the towering trees into a delightfully bucolic meadow, a sparkling blue pond in the center of the jade green pasture.

"Whoo hoo!" Orville dashed ahead of the others, jumping into the pond. "Good bye, swamp mud!"

"Cannonball!" Sophia leaped in after him with a huge splash.

Brother Solus was less exuberant in his entry, wading cautiously into the clear fresh water, but the grin on his face was just as wide.

After a rousing and boisterous frolic in the pond which included lots of splashing and several spectacular somersault dives by Orville off Proto's shoulders, the adventurers relaxed in the soft grass, letting their clothes dry in the warm sun.

"This is lovely. What a beautiful spot."

Orville studied the trees at the edge of the meadow.

"It is beautiful, but it also looks kind of familiar. Why do I feel like I've seen it before?"

"I've never seen this pond before."

"Not the pond, the forest on the far side of the meadow. There's something about it. Let's go look. I'm getting a really weird feeling."

Sophia and Orville strolled across the meadow to the edge of the forest.

"It does seem familiar, but I think it's just that the trees are like the ones in Muridaan Falls."

"Look at the path running through the forest."

"Oh, no."

Orville ran down the path, stopping short when he emerged from the forest, pointing mutely to the rustic thatched homes which lay before him.

"It can't be. It's not possible."

They had come full circle, back to the beginning, back to the village of Okeanos.

Chapter 38

Okeanos Revisited

Orville sank to the ground. "It was all for nothing, we're back where we started."

Sophia was silent, her eyes on the thatched huts.

Brother Solus stared blankly at the village. "How did we get here?"

Sophia held up her paw. "Stop, let me think. The answer is here, I just have to find it."

Orville lay on his back, his eyes on the azure blue sky above him, on the puffy white clouds floating overhead. "We're never going to find Aislin, the Shadow King tricked us. We did all this for nothing."

"He didn't trick us. I know why we're here. Everyone follow me."

Sophia strode forward through the village, the others trailing behind her.

"Orville, keep your eyes open, you're going to like this."

"We've already seen Okeanos, we've already been

here."

"You've already been here, but nobody else has."

"What are you talking about?"

As they rounded the final curve in the narrow village lane, Sophia pointed to the round weathered gray building at the end of the path, a freshly painted sign resting on a wooden easel.

Orville's eyes grew wide.

OKEANOS BOOK FAIR
TODAY ONLY
ALL VISITORS WELCOME

"Who put the sign up? I don't understand."

Sophia turned to face the others.

"The journey we made was to another dimension, not to another place. We never left Okeanos, but we did travel to another dimension occupying the same space. This is where Orville found the red book, where he encountered the Shadow King and saw Aislin Mouse."

"Are you saying the Shadow King is in that building?"

"He has always been there, we just couldn't see him. Now we can see him, now we can rescue Aislin."

Proto's eyes were blinking rapidly. "Most confounding, but I cannot find fault with your impeccable logic. At long last we shall meet Orville's terrifying Shadow King." He rubbed his silver hands together.

"What are we going to do? We can't just go barging in and face that crazy burning charcoal stick creature.

You didn't see him, you don't know what he's like. He was terrifying, the scariest thing I've ever seen."

Brother Solus stepped forward, placing his clawed hand gently on Orville's shoulder.

"I will go first. It is time I did what is right, what I know I must do. Whatever fate may have in store for me, I will know I did the right thing." He glanced curiously at the book fair sign, then swung the front door open and entered the building.

"Come on, he's going to need our help."

Orville gulped.

When they entered the building Orville's insides turned to ice. The great round table was there, piled high with mounds of books. Standing next the table was a haggard but very solid Aislin Mouse. She looked weak, as though she was having trouble standing, leaning on the table for support.

She stared at Orville, trying to focus on him. "Are you real? Are you really Orville?"

"Yes, I'm Orville, we're here to take you home, back to Ebenezer, back to Muridaan Falls."

Before Aislin could reply a dreadful scratching sound filled the room. Orville gave a yelp.

"It's coming! The Shadow King is coming!"

The far wall shimmered and blurred. The scratching noise was almost unbearable, Sophia pressing her paws over her ears.

The horrendous noise stopped abruptly when the burning and smoldering charcoal stick creature scuttled into the room, leaving a trail of orange and yellow sparking embers behind it.

Orville's legs grew weak. It was far worse than he had remembered.

Sophia called out to the creature. "What are you? What do you want?"

The great smoking beast glowed brightly, flames licking out from the dreadful confusion of smoldering charcoal sticks.

"He wants me." Brother Solus stepped toward the monstrous creation.

The charcoal stick figure stopped at the sound of Brother Solus' voice. Orville couldn't tell if the creature was speaking or if he was hearing its thoughts.

"Brother Solus, you are here of your own accord?"

"I am here by my own free will."

"You cast me out, rejected me."

"You were too painful, I would not have survived with you in my thoughts."

"And now?"

"I have lived for centuries not knowing the truth of who and what I truly am. I have played the part of a reflective and virtuous Mintarian Gray Monk, but Brother Solus was my own creation, my escape from impossibly painful memories. My goal was to forget, not to remember, my deepest desire to remain ignorant, not to increase the depth and breadth of my understanding."

"And now?"

"I have learned a great deal in the last few weeks from my new friends. It is time for you to release Aislin

Mouse. Let her go home. I am ready."

"As you wish, so it shall be. Aislin Mouse, you are free to go. You may return to Muridaan Falls with your friends, or you may travel back in time to the moment before you opened the door and stepped into Elysian, all memory of this place forgotten. You will open your front door, walk to the general store, purchase a bag of flour, and return home to find Ebenezer still asleep in his bed. No time will have passed. What is your choice?"

It took Aislin only a moment to make her decision. "I want to remember this. I will go back with Orville and his friends. I have learned a great deal from you, from this shadow world of the unknown, seen many things I do not wish to forget."

"As you wish, so it shall be."

Brother Solus moved closer, standing directly in front of the Shadow King.

"You terrify me. You are the dark shadow of myself?"

"I am the unknown, both the light and the dark. I am everything you have forgotten, everything you shall learn, everything you may have been or will be. I am the hidden darkness within you, I am the hidden light within you."

"And yet I hold power over you?"

"You hold the power to cast me out, and likewise the power to close your eyes and listen to my voice."

"I will listen to you. That is my choice."

The sparking embers stopped falling from the Shadow King, the flickering flames dying away, the edges of the great charcoal sticks softening, becoming blurry and diffuse.

Orville stepped back. "What's it doing?"

"Do you wish to remember the reason you cast me out?"

"Of my own free will, I choose to remember."

The Shadow King transformed into a great roiling black cloud, swirling and crackling. Brother Solus held out both paws, the dark roaring miasma that was the Shadow King streaming into him.

"Oh no. No, no, no!" Brother Solus sank to his knees, great wracking sobs pouring out of him. The Shadow King was gone.

Orville, Sophia, and Proto could not move, stunned by what they had just seen, stunned by the overwhelming waves of grief coming from Brother Solus.

Sophia stepped over to Brother Solus and put her paw on his shoulder. Orville did the same.

Brother Solus looked up at them, a look of horror on his face. He falteringly rose to his feet. "I'm sorry, I'm so sorry. It was all my fault."

"There's nothing to be sorry about."

"Where did the Shadow King go?"

"He is back inside me, my lost memories, my secret voice within, my inner self. When I arrived in Elysian I cast him out, rejected him, forgot everything, forgot who I was, what I had been. I created a new self, a new personality, a safe one. I became Brother Solus, the last of the Mintarian Gray Monks."

"Who are you?"

"I am Mintarian Chief Master Scientist Gnuj, creator of the Metaphonium Haven Project, and I am responsible for the death of eight million innocent Mintarians."

Chapter 39

A Knock on the Door

"You came to Elysian after the Metaphonium in Thuvia had been destroyed, trapping the eight million Mintarians in the synthetic world?"

"Yes, the Metaphonium Haven Project was over, all twenty-nine Metaphoniums destroyed, but I still had the modified multi-world Metaphonium in my laboratory. I could not live on Mintari after what I had done, so I used the last Metaphonium to enter Elysian. Soon after I arrived I cast out all memory of my life before Elysian. I became Brother Solus."

"That's how we got here, using your multi-world Metaphonium. Aislin and Ebenezer found it hidden inside a wall in their house in Muridaan Falls."

Master Scientist Gnuj took a step back. "It was not destroyed?"

"No one knows how it got there, but it still works. Aislin, I was just thinking, how did you know what keys to push to get to Elysian?"

"It was just by chance that I pushed one of the dials and twenty-four keys lit up. I pushed them all, but nothing happened until I opened the door and saw Elysian."

Gnuj let out a yelp. "That's it! I am such a fool, why didn't I think of this before? The first generation Metaphoniums were capable of creating only one synthetic world, but the modified version can create hundreds of thousands of worlds!"

"What does that mean? Why is that good?"

"It means I can use the last Metaphonium to access the synthetic world created by the Thuvian Metaphonium. It means I can bring everyone home."

"It's been a long time, over fourteen hundred years. Are you sure you should do that?"

"I have to try. I recorded the data for all twenty-nine Metaphonium worlds in my journal. It's somewhere in this mound of books, I hid it before I cast out my memories."

"Do you remember what it looks like?"

"It's yellow, square, and well worn."

An image popped into Orville's head. He'd seen a yellow tattered book just before he found the red book.

"When I was here the first time, the books changed as I walked around the table. I remember seeing a beautiful green book the color of budding spring leaves, because I mentioned to Aislin how pretty the color was. When I walked around the table again the green book had vanished, replaced by a tattered square yellow book."

Proto scanned the enormous mound of books, then strode over to the table and pushed a small pile of dusty volumes aside, revealing a bright green book the color of budding spring leaves.

"That's it, that's the one! Don't move." Orville took one turn around the table, then began his second turn. "See how the books are changing on my second time around the table?"

"They're not changing, Orville."

"Yes, they are, look at them."

"They may be changing for you, but they're not changing for us."

When Orville completed his second trip around the table, the green book was gone, in its place a tattered yellow book. He plucked the book from the table, triumphantly holding it up. "Got it!"

Gnuj ran over to Orville, grabbing the book.

"This is it, it's my journal! Everything I need is in it. You have to take me back with you, back to the last Metaphonium."

"We can return through Ebenezer's blue door."

"Orville, wait, I have an idea! Help me move all these books off the table."

* * * *

Orville's mum stopped and listened, her ears perking up.

"Did you hear that?"

Eldon looked up from his morning newspaper. "Hear what?"

"That odd sound coming from upstairs."

Eldon disappeared in a flash of blue light, blinking to the upstairs hallway. He could hear thumping and thudding sounds coming from Orville's room. He blinked up a powerful sphere of defense, then flicked his wrist. The bedroom door flew open.

Eldon stood motionless, trying to comprehend what he was seeing. Hundreds of books were falling down from the ceiling, Orville's bed covered with heaping mounds of dusty old tomes, volumes spilling out across the bedroom floor. Eldon blinked off his sphere of defense, gently closing the door. He grinned to himself as he walked down the stairs and back to the kitchen.

"It's nothing serious, just books raining down from Orville's ceiling."

Orville's mum gave a sigh. "You'd think after all these years I'd be used to such things."

"At least we know they're safe. I'm guessing Sophia had something to do with it. You know how much she loves books."

Ebenezer's paw was resting on the Metaphonium, his eyes on Aislin's photo, his thoughts a lifetime away. He straightened the picture, running a feather duster across it, giving a start when he heard a knock on his door.

"Why do they keep pestering me? I told that sales-mouse I don't need an Excelsior Electro-Vacuumator, I have a perfectly good broom that suits me just fine."

He padded across the room and yanked the door open.

In a single blinding moment Ebenezer's world was turned upside down. Aislin was standing in the doorway. His duster fell to the floor. Before he knew what was happening her arms were around him, tears streaming down her face. "Ebbie, I'm home."

When he finally looked up he saw Orville, Sophia, Proto, and a gray robed creature with long yellow claws standing on the front porch. He wiped his eyes, his arms still around Aislin, barely able to speak. "You found her, you found her."

The adventurers stepped inside. Orville had a lump in his throat, Sophia's eyes were welling up.

"She'll need lots of rest, she's been through a lot."

"I'll be fine, I'm home, that's all that matters. Ebbie, I have so much to tell you."

Ebenezer nodded, unable to take his eyes off his beloved Aislin.

Gnuj was staring at the last Metaphonium. He took a step forward, stopping when Sophia grabbed his arm.

"Tomorrow. You can see it tomorrow. Today is for Ebenezer and Aislin."

Sophia looked through the open door to the glorious blossomed meadows of Elysian. "I don't know about anyone else, but I'm glad to be back in a world where oceans and cities don't appear out of nowhere."

She closed the front door, then opened it, grinning when she saw the familiar tall trees of Muridaan Falls.

They were home.

Chapter 40

Papa's Old Trunk

"What are you going to do with all the books you brought back from Okeanos?"

"They're going to the Metaphysical Adventurers library. Master Marloh said a lot of them can be translated. Most are ancient technical volumes, lots of early Anarkkian tech. I'm going to give the history books to Amanda."

Orville grinned. "I can't wait to see her face when you give her a big box of books from Okeanos. That was a good idea to drop them through the silver book into my room."

"Would anyone like more snapberry flapcakes?" Proto stood at the great iron stove sporting mum's brightly flowered apron.

Gnuj raised his clawed hand. "Yes, please, they are extraordinarily delicious. Perhaps I could also have one more of those tasty little cakes?"

Eldon smiled. "Orville tells me Mirus Mouse has a

shop where you can work on the Metaphonium?"

"He does. It will take me several days, but once I am able to open the lost Thuvian synthetic world, I will return to Mintari with the Metaphonium and open the door to all who wish to come home."

"It has been a long time since the war. I don't mean to dishearten you, but it's possible there won't be anyone to bring home. Many generations may have come and gone, and time may pass at a far different rate in that world."

"Nevertheless I must try, I could not live with myself if I did not try."

"I understand. I hope you don't still blame yourself for what happened. Your intentions were good, you were doing the best you could to save as many lives as you could."

"I have come to accept that even our best efforts are sometimes not enough, and that is part of life. Sophia put it quite nicely when she said even if we fail in our attempt to make the world a better place, we succeed in changing ourselves, and that is what truly matters. I no longer need to hide from my memories, hide behind the mask of Brother Solus."

With the help of a steam powered duplonium cart borrowed from Mirus Mouse, Orville and Sophia moved the last Metaphonium from Ebenezer's house to Gnuj's new workshop.

Watching from the front porch as the Metaphonium was loaded onto the cart were Ebenezer and Aislin Mouse.

"I, for one, am happy to see it go."

Aislin nodded. "As am I. My time in Elysian was both terrifying and astonishing. The Shadow King was sometimes frightening, but never cruel, he simply wanted to be reunited with Master Scientist Gnuj. There were many times when he was kind to me, teaching me skills like the Traveling Eye."

"That's how you appeared as a ghostly apparition?"

"He taught me how to leave my physical body, how to send my consciousness across worlds, how to create a ghostly form which could be seen by Orville. It was exhausting, but I had to do it. It was the only way to bring Orville and Sophia into the world of Elysian, the only way to help Gnuj regain his memory, and the only way for me to come home again to you. I didn't appear to you because I didn't want you to think I was a ghost, think that I had died."

"You haven't aged, you look the same as the day you left."

"Time is different in Elysian. Gnuj was there for fourteen hundred years."

"Can you still love an old gray mouse like me?"

Aislin gave a soft smile. She gently touched Ebenezer's forehead, her paw glowing with a shimmering golden light, watching as his mottled gray fur turned a rich warm brown, watching as the years were washed away, watching as Ebenezer was transformed into the handsome young mouse she remembered.

Ebenezer stared at his soft brown fur. "How did you do that? My leg doesn't hurt anymore, I feel strong again."

"It's not magic, if that's what you're thinking. It's just shaping, the Shadow King taught me. I can teach you, it will come in handy on our travels."

"Our travels?"

"It's time we saw the world, time we left Muridaan Falls for new horizons. There is so much to see and I want to see it with you."

Ebenezer put his arms around Aislin, holding her close.

"I'm ready for a new adventure, especially one with you. I hear southern Grymmore is lovely this time of year. I also heard from Sophia there's a marvelous new shaping school in Penrith."

Orville and Sophia wheeled the hissing duplonium cart into a small red building in Mirus' complex.

Gnuj hovered about, his gray cloak replaced with a starched white coat, the uniform of a Mintarian master scientist.

"Gently, please, we don't want to damage it. Against that wall will do nicely. " He rubbed his clawed hands together, his eyes on the Metaphonium.

"You're all set then? You have the journal, everything you need?"

"What? Oh, yes, everything I need. Mirus has given me access to his extraordinary collection of old Mintarian technology, including all the tools I need to work on the Metaphonium. It should only take a few days to modify it with the Thuvian world data."

"How will you get the Metaphonium back to Mintari?"

"Mirus has an old Anarkkian Spectral Field Actualizer we can use."

Orville nodded, but had no idea what a Spectral Field Actualizer was.

Sophia nudged him. "It creates a spectral doorway to Mintari. Anarkkian Troopers used them on secret missions."

The two adventurers said their good byes, leaving Gnuj to work on his Metaphonium.

"I'm not sure Gnuj is doing the right thing. Even if the Mintarians are still in that world, I don't know that they'll want to come back. Besides, where are they going to put eight million Mintarians? What will they do? They won't be familiar with any of the new technology."

"I don't think I'd want to come back. After fourteen hundred years they might not even remember where they came from."

"How is Proto doing? Is he still acting strange?"

"He is. I asked him if everything was okay but his answer was vague, I could tell he was hiding something. He said he might be moving back to the Cube for a while."

"Why would he do that?"

"He wouldn't say. It could be some weird experiment he's working on, something to do with those scary creatures he likes so much."

"If it was just that he'd probably tell us."

"Here we are."

Orville stepped up onto the porch and opened the front door.

"We're home!"

Orville's mum popped her head around the corner. "Papa wants to see you, he's in the kitchen."

Orville and Sophia found Eldon seated at the kitchen table reading a letter. He glanced up, a grin on his face.

"I have the final documents from the Fortress of Elders. We're all set for tomorrow."

"What time?"

"About two in the afternoon."

Orville suddenly remembered the gold watch Captain Tobias had given him. He pulled it out of his pocket and set it on the kitchen table. "Do you think this is valuable?"

Eldon smiled, a smile that vanished when he saw the watch.

"You found this in the trunk?"

"What trunk?"

"I had this locked away in the old trunk in the basement."

"No, I got this in Elysian. Captain Tobias gave it to me, he said it was the greatest treasure a mouse could ever know. I thought it might be valuable."

"Captain Tobias?"

"He's a sea captain we met in Elysian. He taught us how to sail a two masted schooner on the way to the Isle of the Silver Ship."

Orville's papa picked up the watch, slowly turning it

in his paw. "You're certain this is the watch Captain Tobias gave you?"

Orville looked over to Sophia, then back to his papa.

"Yes, he gave it to me in Elysian. Is something wrong with it? Is it really valuable?"

"Come with me, both of you."

Orville and Sophia followed Eldon down the rickety wooden stairs to the basement. Eldon blinked up an orb of light.

"It's over there."

He stepped across the dirt floor to an old weathered wooden trunk with tarnished brass fittings, pulling a large iron key off a nail on the wall. The trunk opened with a soft click.

"I keep it in here."

Eldon reached under a heavy blue woolen coat and removed a small carved box. The light orb floated above them, casting wavering shadows on the hard packed basement floor.

"What is it?"

Eldon flipped the box open.

Orville blinked. "Creekers, it looks like this one."

"It's more than that. It doesn't just look like that one, it *is* that one. These watches are absolutely identical in every way, every scratch, every ding, every wear mark. They are the same watch."

Orville was baffled. "I don't understand, how could Captain Tobias give me a watch you already had?"

Eldon studied Orville's face.

"This old trunk and all its contents belonged to Captain Orville Tobias Mouse, your great great grandpapa. He was a sea captain for most of his life. My grandpapa used to tell me stories about him, and grandpapa left me this watch, Captain Tobias' watch."

"Are you saying I met my own great great grandpapa? I went sailing with him in Elysian?"

"That's exactly what I'm saying. Did he have a parrot? A parrot who called him Captain Orville?"

Sophia gave a yelp. "Yes! Orville, remember when you thought the parrot was talking to you? He was talking to Captain Tobias, not you."

"I don't understand. How could I meet my great great grandpapa? How could there be two of the same watch?"

"Did you look inside the watch?"

"No, it just looked like an old watch."

"There's an inscription inside. It will say *With eternal love, S.A.M. to O.T.M.*"

Eldon unscrewed the back of the watch, carefully removing the cover. He held it up to the light for Orville and Sophia to see.

"Creekers, you were right. What does it mean?"

"This was a gift to Captain Orville Tobias Mouse from his true love, Sophia Alexis Mouse."

"That's who he named his ship after! Remember he said Sophia was his truest love, lost to him years ago?"

"So my great great grandpapa and I are both named Orville and we both have... um..."

Sophia snickered. "Best friends named Sophia?"

"Right, best friends named Sophia, that's what I

meant."

Eldon smiled, slipping the watch back into the box.

"I've seen many strange things during my adventures, but nothing like this. I have no explanation for what happened, or how it happened, but here we are with two identical watches, both from Captain Orville Tobias Mouse, your great great grandpapa."

Orville shook his head. "This is one puzzle I won't ever solve, and I don't want to. I love mysteries, and this is the best one ever."

Chapter 41

The Secret

Proto gave a shriek, pulling the smoking snapberry muffins from the oven. Squeaky was barking loudly.

"Drat! I've burned them!" He flung open the kitchen window, fanning wildly with his apron in an attempt to clear the room of smoke.

"Oh dear, this is dreadful. This will be the last straw, they'll surely send me back to the Cube. I saw Orville whispering with Mum and Papa this morning. This is very bad."

"Hey, Proto, what's all the smoke?"

Proto jumped in front of the tray of burned muffins, hiding them from Orville. Squeaky jumped in front of Proto, barking at Orville.

"A malfunctioning stove, I'm afraid, a great deal of smoke but no harm done."

"It smells like snapberry muffins, did you make some?"

"No muffins today, I think we should try a healthier diet, perhaps some nice fresh veggies from the garden."

"I guess. Say, could you do me a big favor? Sophia said Mirus Mouse needs this book right away. I think it has something to do with the Metaphonium, but I can't take it to him because I have some other stuff to do. Could you run it over to him?"

"What kind of other stuff? Another adventure?"

"No, not an adventure, just, um, some stuff. Oh, Papa wants me to clean the basement, that was it."

"I see, clean the basement. Of course, Squeaky and I would be more than happy to deliver it to Mirus. Just set it on the table and we'll take it right over."

Orville's eyes narrowed imperceptibly. Proto was behaving very strangely.

"Okay, thanks, you're the best."

Orville set the book down and disappeared into the next room.

Proto's ears perked up. He could hear whispering coming from the living room. He gave a sigh. It was clear Orville's story about cleaning the basement was a ruse to get him out of the house because they didn't want him here. He dumped the scorched muffins into the trash bin, wiped the counters clean and picked up the book for Mirus. When he walked into the living room there was no one there. The house was silent.

"Let's go, Squeaky, I don't think we're wanted here."

The screen door banged shut behind Proto. He pushed open the front gate and didn't look back, quite certain he would see Orville or Sophia peering out the window. He strode briskly down the winding country lane, Squeaky running beside him, barking at a pair of squawking glowbirds.

Proto was lost in a cloud of dark thoughts. He knew he was going back to the Cube, back to the glowbirds. He'd seen the crumpled notes Orville and Sophia had dropped on Elysian. Maybe they didn't like him because he was a Rabbiton, because he was different from them. Serus had talked about a colony of Rabbitons living on Tectar, south of the mountain range. He'd be happier living with other Rabbitons. He sighed. They might look like him, but he knew they wouldn't be like him. They wouldn't be friendly, they wouldn't have feelings the way he did. The more he thought about it, the less appealing it sounded. He might not be a mouse, but he had real feelings, and Orville and Mum and Papa and Sophia were his family.

He looked at the book Orville had given him. It was written in ancient Quintarian script and it wasn't even a science book, it was a romantic novel about lost love. Orville was clearly not a master of deception. Proto's jaw tightened. He would deliver the book to Mirus, then go straight to the Cube, avoid the embarrassment of being asked to move out.

The words of the Thirteenth Monk popped into his head. *"You must face your greatest fear head on, regardless of the outcome."*

Proto sighed. He would talk to Mum and find out exactly why they wanted him to leave. Maybe it was just a small thing he could change, something he could do differently.

Two hours later Proto was back on the front porch, the book still in his hands. Mirus had known nothing about it, emphatically stating he had no interest in reading a novel about lost love. Proto tried to calm himself before he went inside.

"I shall face my greatest fear head on, just as the Thirteenth Monk said I should. Whatever happens will happen. Squeaky and I will be fine. We can have our own adventures if we need to."

He swung the front door open, stepping into a dark and silent house. Maybe they were in the kitchen.

It took him only a moment to notice the piece of folded white paper on the kitchen table.

"They don't even want to talk to me, they just left me a note." He picked up the paper, carefully smoothing it out, preparing himself for the worst.

The Greatest Treasure
4/7

Proto stared blankly at the cryptic message printed on the stark white paper. It was the same note he had found in the crystal box on Elysian, but he had no idea what it meant. That was when he heard the whispering and giggling.

Orville popped through the doorway, a handful of papers in his paw, followed by Sophia, Mum, and Papa.

"You read the note? Get it?"

Proto shook his head. He had not gotten anything.

"4/7? The Greatest Treasure? Get it? Clever."

"Orville, he has no idea what you're talking about. Proto, we have something for you, something important."

Papa took the papers from Orville.

"I did some research, contacted Edmund the Rabbiton at the Fortress of Elders in Grymmore. He's the Master of Rabbitons, appointed by King Fendaron. I asked him to find something for me, and he did."

Proto was confused. They didn't sound angry, they hadn't even mentioned the burned muffins.

"Master of Rabbitons?"

"Yes, he's in charge of all the Rabbitons at the Fortress. He's also in charge of the Central Information Repository, where they keep the ancient records."

"Ancient records?"

"We found out when you left the Rabbiton factory. It was on the fourth day of the seventh moon, 4/7. Today is your birthday, Proto."

Proto stared blankly at Orville.

"My birthday?"

Orville grabbed Proto's arm.

"It's your birthday, that's what the note meant. Mum always says friendship is the greatest treasure, that's why it says *The Greatest Treasure 4/7*."

"I don't have to go back to the Cube?"

"Go back to the Cube? What are you talking about?"

Orville's mum nudged Sophia. The two of them disappeared into the other room.

Orville put his arms around Proto, giving him a hug.

"Happy Birthday, Proto. You're my best friend after Sophia."

Sophia and Mum stepped out of the back room carrying a lovely, though somewhat lopsided cake with a single flickering candle on top.

"We put one candle on the cake because this is the first birthday party you've ever had. It won't be the last one though."

"And it would have cost too much to buy fourteen hundred and eighty-nine candles."

"Orville, that's not true and you know it. Okay, let's sing the Song of Birthdays. I'm starving, and that cake looks delicious."

"It's a bit crooked, but that's my fault."

"You'd make a much better pirate than a chef, that's for sure. We should call you the Dread Chef Orville."

Proto stood motionless, caught in the golden light of a single birthday candle. This was the secret they had been keeping from him. His birthday. All those dreadful notes weren't written by Orville or Sophia or Mum or Papa. They were like Sophia's caterpillars, he had created the very thing he was most afraid of, being sent away again by his family. His hands were shaking. He didn't have to leave, he didn't have to go back to the Cube.

After a slightly off key rendition of the Song of Birthdays, Sophia and Mum set the cake down on the kitchen table.

"Okay, Proto, make a wish and blow out the candle.

Don't tell us the wish or it won't come true. Then we have presents for you. Orville even spent his own money, so you know he must really like you." Sophia gave her finest cackling laugh.

Proto made his wish, that this moment would last forever.

Chapter 42

Gnuj's Infinite Wonder

Chief Master Scientist Gnuj stood at the open door, disbelief etched on his face.

"It's not possible, but I cannot deny what lies before me."

He took one last look, just to be certain, then closed the door. It had proven far more difficult than he had anticipated, but after six arduous days of unceasing effort he had modified the last Metaphonium with the correct parameters to access the lost Thuvian synthetic world.

He gazed at the six violet lights and twenty-four glowing white keys on the Metaphonium, then stepped over and flicked the machine off. He needed time to think. Gnuj slumped into a stuffed armchair, leaning back, closing his eyes.

"What shall I do? Whatever shall I do?"

The sun had sunk below the horizon by the time Gnuj made his decision. He crossed the room and took a seat at his desk. Pulling out a sheet of paper and a pen, Mintarian Chief Master Scientist Gnuj, creator of the calamitous Metaphonium Haven Project, began to write.

My dearest friends Orville and Sophia,

In your selfless quest to rescue Aislin Mouse, you also succeeded in rescuing me, something for which I shall be forever grateful. I was lost in Elysian, my memories of the Anarkkian war and my failed Metaphonium Haven Project cast aside, hidden deep within the heart of the Shadow King, secreted away from my consciousness, the terrible burden of my guilt too much to bear. I was certain I had ended the lives of eight million innocent Mintarians. It was your kindness and understanding which gave me the strength to confront the Shadow King, face the truth of those lost memories which had haunted me for so many years. Even as Brother Solus, I knew something was dreadfully amiss, as if some vaporous terror was constantly hovering above me, a sense of perpetual dread in the air.

I am whole again, my memories restored, and I have forgiven myself for my unsuccessful attempt to save the lives of my beloved fellow Mintarians. All living creatures have limitations, and at times our best efforts are simply not enough. That is the nature of the world we live in, and there is no shame in that. All we can do is the best we can do.

I have succeeded in opening the door to the lost

310

Thuvian world. What I saw has shaken me to the core. I would describe it to you in great detail, but there is no need. You have already seen it, you have already been there. The lost Thuvian world is Laurus, the city where we met Juvo in his Bubble Rider, Laurus, the greatest city in all of creation. I have no understanding of how we were able to visit Laurus, but you know as well as I what an infinitely mysterious world Elysian is.

It is only after much introspection that I have decided not to bring back the descendants of those eight million lost Mintarians, descendants who now call themselves Laurae. Where only fourteen hundred years have passed in our world, eons have passed in Laurus. Theirs is a world we all might envy, and I shall not interfere with what they have created. From the ashes of my deepest despair a great civilization has risen, the world of Laurus, a world which will soon become my home.

I am not returning to Mintari, instead I shall step through the doorway into Laurus, and there spend the remainder of my days. I am leaving the last Metaphonium to you, dear friends, but I have removed from its memory the key combination used to open the doorway to Laurus. Do with the Metaphonium as you will. I am also leaving you my journal, within it you will find the key codes for hundreds of unexplored worlds.

I thank you deeply for all you have done.
In everlasting friendship I remain,
Gnuj

P.S. Please give my fondest regards to Proto. I do hope he had a wonderful birthday party!

Gnuj carefully folded the letter, placing it in an envelope addressed to Orville and Sophia, setting it on the Metaphonium. He opened the shed door, taking one last look at the starry night sky above Muridaan Falls, one last look at the world he was leaving behind.

"So many stars, so many worlds, it is truly a thing of infinite wonder and eternal mystery."

He stepped back into the shed, closed the door and strode over to the Metaphonium, quickly tapping the twenty-four keys which would open the world of Laurus. Six yellow lights blinked violet, twenty-four keys glowed brightly.

Mintarian Chief Master Scientist Gnuj, creator of the calamitous Metaphonium Haven Project, stepped out of Muridaan Falls and into Laurus, the greatest city in all of creation.

Chapter 43

The Visitors

Orville answered the door, the identity of their visitor hidden behind a large pot of lovely violet flowers.

"Hello?"

A smiling Madam Beasley peered around the blossoms at Orville.

"A marvelous good day to you, Orville. I've brought a pot of flowers for your mum, and two jars of tasty violet jam, her favorite."

"Hi, Madam Beasley, Mum is out right now, but she'll be back soon. Proto just made some yummy snapberry muffins, if you'd like to have one while you wait."

"Oh dear, it sounds very tempting, but I'm late for my yoga class."

"What's yoga?"

A curious look crossed Madam Beasley's face.

"How unmistakably odd, I just had the most surprising thought. I think I had a dream about you and Sophia. There was a bed and breakfast, and... a mountain... and I think there were quilts, lovely quilts. I wish I could remember it, but dreams do have a way of slipping through your paws."

Orville nodded sympathetically. "Maybe you'll remember it later, sometimes that happens."

"Perhaps so. At any rate, give my very best regards to your mum and papa, and to lovely Sophia, and that charming Proto. Such a nice fellow he his, and a marvelous chef indeed."

"I will. Thanks for the flowers. I hope you remember you dream."

Orville closed the door with a grin. Even if he told her, Madam Beasley would not believe the story of her nightly visits to Elysian. He rubbed his paws together, the smell of freshly baked snapberry muffins wafting through the air. He was halfway to the kitchen when another knock sounded on the door.

"Maybe she remembered her dream."

Orville flung the door open, greeted not by Madam Beasley, but by Aislin and Ebenezer Mouse.

"Whoa, what happened to you?" Orville was gaping at Ebenezer's smooth brown fur.

"As it happens, my dear Aislin has become quite a proficient shaper, courtesy of the Shadow King."

"You look young again. Aislin, you should join the Shapers Guild. I can talk to Master Marloh if you'd like. They'd love to have a new member."

Aislin took Ebenezer's paw in hers. "That's why

314

we're here, we have something to tell you."

Orville's anxiety spiked. He was not especially fond of surprises.

"It's nothing bad, nothing to worry about. May we come in?"

"Sure, sorry, come on in."

When they were seated in the living room, Ebenezer pulled a large brown envelope from his inner coat pocket.

"This is for you and Sophia. The day you brought Aislin home was the day you gave me my life back. There is no way we can ever thank you enough, but I hope this will help."

Ebenezer handed the envelope to Orville.

"You don't have to give me anything. Sophia and I were glad to help, that's what Metaphysical Adventurers do, that's what friends do."

"We both want you to have this."

Orville opened the envelope and peered inside. There was a sheet of yellowed parchment and two brass keys. He took out the paper, scanning it quickly.

"This is the deed to your house."

"It's your house now, yours and Sophia's. We are moving to Penrith, in Grymmore. Bartholomew and Clara Rabbit have opened a wonderful new shaping school in Penrith, and we've both signed on as first year students. It's time for a new adventure, time for us to move on."

"It's too much, I can't take it."

"The papers are signed and we leave tomorrow for

Penrith. The house is yours."

A grin slowly appeared on Orville's face.

"I have a house? My own house?"

"It needs a little work, especially the garden, but I have a feeling it won't be long until it's the loveliest house in Muridaan Falls."

"Proto could help with the garden. He's really good at growing stuff. I can't believe I have a house."

"You and Sophia have a house. I'm sure you will have many happy years together, just as we did."

"Oh, thanks, we don't exactly have plans to marry just yet, but... um... when she finishes school..."

"I understand, you're both still young."

Orville heard a cough from the kitchen doorway. He looked up as Proto stepped into the living room.

"We have our own house? This is marvelous, I can plant my experimental poisonous vegetable garden. I'll need a small laboratory, of course, and a storage shed for my equipment. Nothing too fancy. I still have thousands of unidentified seed packets back at the Cube I'll have to get, and all those frozen eggs, some kind of dreadful talking lizard creature, I think. Mirus can take me there in a Dragonfly, maybe a blinker ship. I won't be back until late tomorrow, so you'll have to make your own dinner. And breakfast. There's a bowl of red snackles on the kitchen counter if you need a snack."

Proto darted out the front door, slamming it behind him.

Orville put a paw to his forehead.

"Creekers."

The front door swung open. It was Sophia.

"Where is Proto going in such a hurry?"

Chapter 44

Aislin's Gift

"I can't believe we own a house."

"I like having the Metaphonium here, it makes it look kind of mysterious."

"Most mice will just think it's a strange looking piano. We should get new furniture, this is nice but it's kind of dated, a bit old. Aislin was telling me Miraculum's has lots of beautiful antique furniture."

"Wouldn't antique furniture be a lot older than the furniture that's already here?"

"Are you trying to be funny?"

"Not exactly. It seems like we should get brand new furniture, because it's our brand new house. Maybe Myrus Mouse could build us some furniture, he's really good at building stuff."

"Orville, I don't want a duplonium powered flying couch with a cloaking device, I want a comfy antique couch I can relax on. Look how beautiful Ebenezer's

318

antique desk is, that's what all our furniture could look like."

"It is nice, it kind of glows. Maybe you're right."

Orville strolled over to the desk and flipped it open.

"Lots of storage space with all these little drawers, plenty of room for pens and ink and paper. I could write in my adventurers journal here. Plenty of light from the window."

Orville absently slid open one of the drawers.

"Hey, they left something behind, a little wooden box. It's nice, inlaid with silver stars and moons. Pretty."

"I hope they didn't forget something valuable."

Orville flipped the box open.

"That's weird. It's a note addressed to you, and something wrapped in tissue paper."

"What does it say?"

Orville unfolded the note and read it.

Dear Sophia, in this box you will find a small token of my appreciation for everything you and Orville have done. It's from Elysian, something the Shadow King gave me. He said he found it in a cave, but he wouldn't say where. I was going to take it with us, but had the strangest feeling last night that I should give it to you. The Shadow King taught me to listen to those feelings, so the ring is yours.

With best wishes and eternal gratitude,
Aislin

"Whoa, this is a nice ring, it looks really old, like some of the rings they have at the museum. It looks kind of familiar, like I've seen it before somewhere."

"The stone is beautiful, look how it sparkles and reflects the light."

Orville studied the orange stone, turning it slowly.

"I don't think it's reflecting the light."

He cupped the ring in his paws, holding it up for Sophia to see.

"You're right, the light is coming from inside the ring. That's odd."

"Let's look at it in the coat closet."

Orville and Sophia squeezed into the hall closet, their eyes on the glowing orange ring.

"Whoa, what is this thing?"

The ring was shining brightly, pinpoints of light moving across the walls and ceiling.

"I've never seen anything like it."

"I don't think you should wear it until someone looks at it. It's from Elysian, we have no idea what it might do."

"You're right, we should have Master Marloh look at it, maybe show it to Mirus Mouse. He knows a lot about old technology. I'm getting a strange feeling about it."

"Let's not show it to them just yet, I'm not ready for another adventure. I need to relax, have some quiet time, enjoy our new house. I've had enough excitement for a while. Proto said there's a new pastry shop near the Book Emporium. He said they make snapberry pie.

We should stop by there tomorrow for lunch."

"You're right, we should wait. It'll be fun, give us time to paint all the rooms in our new house, maybe put in new wood floors, and the kitchen definitely needs some work, a new stove for sure. I was thinking a warm yellow color for the living room, maybe wide alternating stripes, nice and cheery during the long winters. Pale green for the bedroom would be nice, that's a calming color. I noticed the window in the back room is cracked, so we'll need to replace the glass. What color do you want to paint the kitchen?"

"Um... on second thought, this ring could be really important, maybe we shouldn't wait. Let's take it over to Mirus and see what he says."

Sophia grinned in the dark, trying not to laugh. She put her arms around Orville and kissed him.

"I like the way you think, Orville Mouse."

Chapter 45

Treasure

"I still can't believe Aislin and Ebenezer gave us their house."

"The only house in Muridaan Falls with a Metaphonium. Think of all the worlds we can visit."

"Not the ones with giant centipedes."

Sophia smiled, her eyes on the rolling blue sea, the sound of screeching gulls filling the air, thirteen sails snapping in the brisk ocean breeze, the three masted ship plowing through the azure blue waters.

"You named your ship 'The Sophia'?"

"After my truest love, just like Captain Tobias did."

"I like this dream."

"So do I. Do you think this eye patch makes me look too scary?"

"Not scary exactly, but sort of like a pirate."

"It's kind of hard to tell how far away things are when I'm wearing it. I think I'll take it off."

"You'll still look like a pirate with that three cornered hat."

Sophia gazed up at the crisp white billowing sails, squinting her eyes in the bright sunlight.

"Did I tell you about the watch Captain Tobias gave me?"

"What about it?"

"It turns out it's not identical to the one Papa has."

"What do you mean?"

"When I took off the front cover I found something etched inside it."

"What does it say?"

"It doesn't say anything. It's a map."

"What kind of map?"

"I think it's a treasure map, it has an X on it. Maybe that's what Captain Tobias meant when he said it was the greatest treasure a mouse could ever have."

"Maybe."

"What do you think Gnuj will do in Laurus? Do you think he'll tell them who he is, tell them the whole story of how Laurus was created?"

"I don't think so, but I do think he'll find the peace he's been looking for."

"And he'll get to fly in one of those Bubble Riders. How fun would that be? It's funny how something he thought was so tragic turned into something so amazing."

"Life is like that sometimes. If Papa hadn't been killed I never would have met you."

"I don't know, we still probably would have met,

just in a different way."

"You sound like Papa. He says if you love someone, you just roll through life toward each other until you meet again."

"I wonder how long we've been friends?"

"Probably forever, maybe longer."

Orville looked up at the sound of approaching footsteps.

"Arghh, pardon my intrusion, Captain Dread Pirate Orville, 'tis white sails plyin' the seas to the east. Shall we give merry chase, run down the scurvy blaggards and rid them of their gold and gems?"

"Maybe later, I'm kind of hungry right now. Is there any snapberry pie left?"

"Arghh, 'tis three whole pies still at the ready."

"Yum, sounds good. Sophia, do you want some pie?"

"No thanks, but a glass of lemonade would be nice."

"Arghh, as ye wish, so it shall be."

"Orville, I know it's your dream, but do you think the pirates need to say 'arghh' so much?"

"That's what pirates say, everyone knows that. Arghhh."

"You're kind of cute for a dread pirate."

"You think I'm cute? Not scary looking?"

"Cute and scary looking."

"I guess that's okay."

"I saw some islands to the west, maybe we should explore them."

"We might find treasure."

Sophia leaned her head on Orville's shoulder, taking his paw in hers.

"We already have, Dread Pirate Orville."

If you enjoyed reading
Orville Mouse and the Puzzle
of the Last Metaphonium
please leave a short review or rating
on Amazon.com
Reviews are the lifeblood of indie publishers –
we can't survive without them!

If you have any comments or suggestions
or would like to be notified of upcoming book
releases and Free Kindle book day promotions,
please email me at
OrvilleMouse@gmail.com

Follow me at:
www.facebook.com/TomHoffmanAuthor/

Best wishes until we meet again,

Tom Hoffman

ABOUT THE AUTHOR

Tom Hoffman received a B.S. in psychology from Georgetown University in 1972 and a B.A. in 1980 from the now-defunct Oregon College of Art. He has lived in Alaska with his wife Alexis since 1973. They have two adult children and two adorable grandchildren. Tom has been a graphic designer and artist for over 35 years. Redirecting his imagination from art to writing, he wrote his first novel, *The Eleventh Ring*, at age 63.